SHE
RUINED
OUR
LIVES

SHE RUINED OUR LIVES

A FUNDERBURKE AND KAIMING MYSTERY

CHRIS CHAN

LEVEL
BEST BOOKS

Author Photo Credit: Troye Fox, UWM Photo Services

First edition

ISBN: 978-1-68512-560-8

Cover art by Level Best Designs

This book was professionally typeset on Reedsy.
Find out more at reedsy.com

As always, to my parents, Drs. Carlyle and Patricia Chan.
And to my sister, Diana. Feel free to repay me by writing your own novel and
dedicating it to me.

Contents

Introduction

Over the years, Funderburke and I have investigated a lot of cases together, but for various reasons, such as time constraints, legal issues, and wishing to protect the privacy of innocent people, we haven't written up many accounts of our work. Last year, Funderburke finally published his account of one of his most personal cases, titled *Ghosting My Friend*, and as much as I love him, my competitive streak won't allow me to just sit back and let him one-up me. So, even though I really don't have the time to devote to writing an entire book about our crime-solving, I've wanted to record my account of the Dolak family tragedy for quite some time. For several months, right before bed, I've been hammering out a couple of hundred words on my laptop before crashing for the night. It's been an uphill battle, but I finally finished this account. A lot has changed in our lives since the events of this book, but it's a case that deeply affected me, and I'm glad that more people will finally get the opportunity to know the truth about what happened that autumn.

For those who have not previously read about our adventures, I'm a teacher at Cuthbertson Hall, a K-12 school in Milwaukee, Wisconsin. Funderburke and I are both Cuthbertson alums, so that's how we met. We were friends for a long time, but several years after graduating, when I was working on my doctorate in United States History and Funderburke had finished law school, ticked off a lot of influential people by exposing corruption in family court, and been driven into private investigation for a career, we grew closer and started dating. Soon afterwards, I started joining Funderburke on his cases, and we became professional partners as well after I earned my P.I. license.

In addition to my teaching duties, I oversee the Bialowsky Fund, which assists teen mothers in their pursuit of an education. It's a cause that's very near and dear to my heart, as I was in a comparable situation at that age. I've said it many times before, and I'll say it again: this happened long before I met Funderburke. In an attempt to get my life on track, I moved to Milwaukee, enrolled at Cuthbertson, and eventually got adopted into the Kaiming family. I owe pretty much everything to my loved ones, and I'll never stop expressing my thanks for this.

Therefore, I'm dedicating this book to my family, especially my adoptive parents, Drs. Keith and Midge Kaiming. The only reason why I've ever been able to help anybody else over the course of my career is because of you.

There's one last point that I want to address, based on the comments of my terrific editor, who had some questions about the dialogue of young Juniper in this book. One of Funderburke's and my greatest frustrations is that since disinterested adults often fail to listen to children, and young kids frequently have trouble giving voice to their deepest emotions, we admit that sometimes we polish what children say a bit in these accounts of our cases, making the kids a bit more eloquent while still maintaining the emotional truth of what they're saying, all to make their points more powerful to the reader. Funderburke says that his major inspirations are *Peanuts* and *Calvin and Hobbes*, where young children often speak with a level of maturity that is not typical of the standard kid, but this stylistic choice has a marvelous way of conveying emotions and arguments that otherwise wouldn't get made, and it's a thumb in the eye to adults who underestimate children. I hope that my words do justice to our young clients.

–*Nerissa Kaiming Funderburke*

Prologue—The Unkindest Cut of All

Layla Dolak stopped loving her younger sister Erika three months earlier, on a humid summer day. Perhaps that was not entirely accurate. It was possible that underneath all of the burning anger and searing resentment some remnants of filial affection still remained. If this was the case, however, Layla was unaware of it. As far as Layla knew, all warm emotions she once felt towards Erika had been severed that sticky August afternoon, when she had taken a nap between shifts at Grobel's Tavern.

Looking back, Layla realized that she should have been warier when her sister had offered her a cookie. Erika wasn't much of one for cooking at all, let alone baking, so Layla ought to have been suspicious. But she was both tired and hungry, so she'd gratefully devoured the cookie without thinking about the incongruity of it. It was not a particularly tasty cookie. The batter was clearly that of a prepackaged plastic-wrapped tube from a supermarket cooler, and there was a slightly medicinal taste that she didn't detect until a few moments after swallowing the last morsel. Normally, she might have asked questions, but she was dead on her feet, so she washed away the crumbs with a few sips of milk and collapsed on her left side upon the living room couch. She rapidly fell into a much deeper slumber than usual and stayed in dreamland for over two hours. Her usual naps lasted forty minutes on average, depending on how well she'd rested the previous night.

While Layla slept, Erika had silently tiptoed behind the sofa, gently grasped Layla's silky tresses with her left hand, and, gripping a large pair of scissors in her right hand, chopped off nearly twenty-six inches in a series of careful snips. Had she simply gathered up her sister's locks into a ponytail and severed them, leaving Layla with a ragged bob, Layla would have been enraged, but not filled with searing hate. But Erika sought to profit as much as possible from her sister's hair, and every fraction of an inch left attached to Layla's scalp was money Erika was denying her own pockets, so she ruthlessly brought the scissor blades as close to Layla's skull as possible, tying up every flowing length of hair with a rubber band and carefully bagging them. In about fifteen minutes' time, she had clipped away every lock of Layla's thick mane, leaving the barest possible covering of peach fuzz over her head.

Erika had then rushed from the house without waking Layla, hurried downtown to a shop that purchased human hair, and after a little negotiating and flirting with the clerk to drive up the price, accepted six hundred ten dollars for her sister's tresses. The proprietor had originally presented a lowball offer of four hundred dollars, but Layla had done her research, and she knew the going rates for a particularly thick skein of glossy dark brown hair that had never been dyed, permed, or styled with heated instruments. The buyer, who had been willing to go as high as six fifty, paid in cash. Erika immediately rushed to the dealer she had known since high school and spent her entire windfall on pills.

Layla was unaware of her new, unwanted hairstyle until a car alarm across the street awakened her, and she stumbled into the bathroom to freshen up before returning to Grobel's. She was surprised to see how long she'd slept, and she had less than an hour left before her shift began. She was groggier than usual, and she realized that her head felt different, but the fog in her mind distracted her to the point where she couldn't pinpoint the cause. She picked up her favorite green scrunchie from a wooden bowl and reached towards the back of her head to draw her tresses back into a ponytail. After a few seconds of fumbling around and being unable to grasp so much as a single hair, Layla turned to the mirror in a state of mild panic. When she gaped at her reflection and viewed her nearly bald head for the first time, her screams were sufficiently loud and piercing to frighten the birds perched on the backyard fence, sending them flying two hundred yards down the street.

Layla's grandmother Celeste had been walking back from her job at a bookstore when she'd heard the screams a block away from the house. She was still a couple of years away from seventy, and though she wasn't quite as fleet-footed as she used to be, she still broke out into a run, recognizing her granddaughter's voice and believing that a burglar had gotten into her home. By the time she reached her back door, her left hip was burning, but she fought through the pain, pulled her pepper spray out of her purse, and rushed into the house, grabbing a kitchen knife as she hobbled towards Layla's screams.

When Celeste saw the sobbing Layla, her first instinct was to shout, "What the heck did you do to yourself?" At the last possible moment, she restrained her tongue, and realized that whatever had caused her granddaughter's newly close-cropped dome, it had not been voluntary. She hugged Layla, and as she gently wiped her granddaughter's eyes with a tissue, she realized who the most likely barber was, and thought about the profit that could be obtained through an unwanted haircut.

Bitterness rushed through Celeste's mind as she realized that Layla's hair was the one object of potential value that hadn't yet been removed from the house one way or another. Layla had started living with her when she was barely ten years old, and Erika had left her mother and moved in with her grandparents when she was in her early teens. Erika was fifteen when Celeste first caught her experimenting with drugs. Three trips to rehab and regular therapy sessions had drained Celeste's savings over the subsequent years, but Erika had seemed to be overcoming her addiction, at least until about eighteen months earlier, when her condition started growing substantially worse.

One day Celeste had come home from her shift at the bookstore and found most of her most valuable possessions missing. A couple of paintings, a few antiques, the large living room television, and several other items of value had been taken from the house. Celeste congratulated herself for having the foresight to keep her jewelry in a safe in her bedroom. After careful consideration, she informed the police of what had happened, making it clear that her primary priority was the return of her property. Despite an officer's coaxing, she remained adamant that she did not want her granddaughter in prison. The paintings, a silver tea set, and most of the other items were discovered at couple of Milwaukee's seedier pawnshops, where they had been sold for a tiny fraction of their value. The television, unfortunately, had been purchased with cash before the police arrived, and there was no way to trace the buyer. The security camera that might have recorded his face had been broken for the better part of a week.

Celeste accepted the loss with as much grace as possible, and five days later, Erika had been found filthy, high, and broke in a dilapidated house on the other side of town, along with a few of her acquaintances who suffered from similar addictions. Celeste welcomed Erika home, extracting no meaningless promises of improved behavior. "No matter what, you always have a place in my house," she told her granddaughter right before shoving her into the shower, "but I will not allow you to strip me bare and penniless."

That day, Celeste rented a storage space, and alongside Layla, they spent the next two days boxing up every item of value in the house that they could do without in their daily lives. Everything from artwork to electronics was boxed and carted to its new home. Erika was still too out of it to realize what was going on, but by the time she returned to her standard level of functionality, the house had been stripped of many of its furnishings. Over the course of the moving project, Celeste noticed that some battered cardboard boxes in the basement containing appliances and knickknacks were nearly emptied. Erika had been helping herself to household goods for quite some time. Celeste took the key to the storage facility, signed up for a safety deposit box at a bank she'd never previously patronized, and placed the storage facility key, all of her important deeds and documents, and all of her jewelry except for her wedding and engagement rings inside the box. She was not worried about the fate of the rings, which, over the course of forty-plus years, had become so securely positioned on her arthritic hands that it would be impossible to remove them without severing her fingers. Three weeks later, she had awakened in the middle of the night to discover that Erika was tugging at her rings in a fruitless attempt to loosen them. When Erika saw her grandmother's eyes open, she immediately adopted a high-pitched tone and said, with exaggerated delight, "Oh, Grandma, I was so worried about you. You weren't moving, and I couldn't hear you breathing, and I was so frightened that I decided I needed to check you for a pulse. It's such a relief that you're all right!"

Celeste made it indisputably clear with a glare more expressive than any amount of words that she wasn't fooled.

As for the key to the safety deposit box, Celeste had worn it around her neck for a few hours before deciding that wouldn't do. After a lot of thinking, she rummaged through the garage until she found an old spare key storage receptacle with a magnetic strip on the back. She then placed the safety deposit box key inside the receptacle and stuck it to the top of the inside of the safe close to the safe's door. It was impossible to see it there, as the safe rested on the floor of her bedroom closet. All that was left in the safe was a few hundred dollars for emergencies and some small treasured possessions either of purely sentimental value or of too much intrinsic value to be left in the storage facility, like a jade carving too long for the safety deposit box and a silver candelabra. Additionally, Celeste kept the keys to her Oldsmobile in the safe when she wasn't driving it. Though she walked to her job at the bookstore in good weather, she needed the car for church and grocery runs. She rarely went anywhere else save for the occasional doctor's appointment. Most of her friends had either passed away or moved to warmer climates.

Life in their home grew increasingly tense. During her spare time, Celeste preferred to read, and her books were one of the few items left in the house. Mostly well-loved paperbacks, the majority of her collection was decades old and unlikely to be purchased by secondhand sellers, most of whom only offered store credit, anyway, which was no good to Erika. Celeste had considered sending a photograph of Erika to every pawnbroker and preowned goods buyer in Milwaukee, along with an admonition never to purchase anything from her, but she decided against it, not wishing to publicize her family's tribulations any more than absolutely necessary.

As for Layla, she only had a few items of value left in the house. The television in their living room was now a twenty-year-old box set that had been rescued from the basement. Erika had brought it to five different pawnbrokers, but none of them was interested in it, so she'd returned it to the safety of a large plastic tub. The screen was only twelve inches along the diagonal, and it was so old that it could not receive modern digital signals. The only way to watch anything live was through the use of a digital converter box, purchased with a coupon provided by the government in 2009 in order to help the public make the switch from analog to digital. Streaming was impossible on that television. Should anyone wish to watch anything that was not currently airing live, the only option was the VHS player that was built into the set. Celeste still had an extensive collection of videotapes, having never purchased a single DVD, believing them to be a temporary fad. Layla's DVD player and movie collection were boxed up and sent off to the storage facility.

In any case, Layla watched most of her entertainment on her laptop. Her computer had escaped Erika's sticky fingers because when it was not in use, Layla invariably wrapped it up in an old sweatshirt and tucked it under some other clothes at the bottom of her closet, locking the door when she left the room. Two and a half weeks before Layla lost all her hair, Erika had managed to pick the old-fashioned locks to both Layla's room and her closet with a wire coat hanger while Layla was showering, and she'd found and taken not only Layla's laptop, but also the smartphone hidden in a bathrobe pocket, and one of Layla's favorite articles of clothing, a cognac-colored leather jacket that had been a gift from her late grandfather. She had kept it even though she hadn't been able to zipper it up for over four years, since the later months of her pregnancy with her daughter Juniper. All had been taken and sold in order to satiate Erika's insatiable need for painkillers.

The loss of the laptop and smartphone took away Layla's access to the Internet, severely hampering her ability to look for a better-paying job more suited to her skills. Not having enough money to replace either of them, she was reduced to purchasing a cheap flip phone for calls, and visiting the local library when she needed the use of a computer. Layla had been only moderately angry by these losses, as she'd been prepared for the possibility that one day Erika would steal her remaining treasures. Now that she believed that she had nothing left worth stealing, she felt oddly free of worrying when Erika would strike again. Layla'd never dreamed that her hair was at risk.

It took a little while, but Celeste finally managed to calm Layla. Once she stopped yelling and crying, Layla returned to the bathroom mirror and began massaging her scalp with her fingertips, as if she rubbed hard enough, she could squeeze more hair out of her follicles like toothpaste from a tube. When she finally admitted defeat, Layla turned to her grandmother with fire in her eyes. "I want her gone. She's not welcome here anymore."

"I know she's crossed a line, Layla. She committed an egregious betrayal; she deserves to be punished. But you know the core principle here. We never abandon family when they need help. If I kick her out, she'll end up on the streets, and who knows what she'll do to stay both alive and high. I know she's gone too far, and believe me, I'm at my wits' end, too. I don't know what to do or how to fix the situation. I've spent the better part of a decade praying as hard as I can and paying as much as I can afford in order to cure her, and nothing has made any difference. It's only gotten worse. We have to do something, I know. Stealing my television is one thing, shaving your head is another. But please, do not ask me to send your sister into the gutter to die."

Layla absorbed her grandmother's words for a few moments. "Move her into the garage apartment." There was a tiny living quarters on the side of the garage that they leased to college and graduate students.

"We need the rent money."

"The new tenant won't move in until the end of the month. When—if—she comes back, keep her there until it's time for that girl to live in our garage."

Celeste considered for a bit and then decided, "All right. If you help me clean out that little room in the corner of the basement, that'll be Erika's new place once the new tenant comes. And there will have to be some sort of other consequences as well, but we won't make any more final decisions now. Some steps have to be made once one's blood temperature cools down."

Glancing at the bathroom clock, Layla said, "I have to be back at the tavern in ten minutes. I can't go out looking like this."

After rummaging through a few of the drawers in her room, Celeste returned with a little pale blue winter hat that she'd crocheted herself before her arthritis had made such crafting difficult. Layla jammed it over her head and stomped off to work.

Had it been two months earlier or two months later, it would have been cool enough for Layla to wear a wool yarn hat without problems. But it was August, and the air conditioner at Grobel's was not particularly efficient. Perspiration poured down her face and droplets contaminated the already watered-down drinks she poured. Eventually, she ripped it off out of self-preservation, and the comments started.

"What were you thinking?"

"You had such pretty hair! Why did you do it?"

"Do you have cancer or something?"

Only Via, the only other female bartender, had spoken positively about the makeover, as she considered Layla's new hairstyle a socio-political statement and wholeheartedly approved. The tiny bit of hair upon the center of Via's head was flamingo pink, and she had seventeen piercings from her neck tattoo upwards.

Layla continued to put up with remarks and questions from co-workers and customers, and the only response she could ever muster was, "I just needed a change." No one at work knew of her sister's issues. Layla had kept them a secret for seven years, and she wanted to keep it that way. She forced herself to block out the comments as best she could, focusing on the confrontation she intended to have with Erika when she returned.

At least once a month, Erika disappeared on a bender that lasted two or three days. But a week passed without a word from her, and Celeste started growing increasingly worried. Layla found herself contemplating the possibilities of the worst happening and feeling discomfited by how satisfied she'd be with that outcome. Finally, around three A.M. on the ninth night following the hair theft, a far from sober Erika let herself into the house as if nothing had happened. Layla had just returned from her shift at the bar, and she had wasted no time in berating her sister. After five full minutes of shouting, Layla screamed, "Why? What did you do it?"

Erika shrugged and unrepentantly replied. "I needed the money. And there's nothing else in the house I can sell anymore."

If Celeste hadn't awakened and come downstairs, there almost certainly would have been a physical confrontation between the sisters.

"Well, it's not like I could sell *my* hair," a defensive Erika shouted. Her addiction had not been kind to her body, and though she had once had hair comparable to Layla's, it was now so thin and brittle that it often broke when it was brushed. No strand of her dull, fragile hair was more than two inches long, and at six points on her temples and crown, little bald spots the size of pennies shone through the remaining coverage.

Celeste informed Erika that she'd be sleeping in the garage apartment for the next two weeks before moving to the basement, leading to an explosion of profanity from Erika about the unfairness and injustice of it all. Before she left the house to her banishment, Erika turned back to Layla with an appraising look at her scalp. "How long do you think it will be until your hair grows back?"

Layla detected no concern in her sister's tone, only dollar signs in her eyes.

"Did you hear her?" Layla snapped after she'd slammed the door shut. "She's going to steal one of my kidneys next."

From that point forward, the sisters spoke as little as possible to each other, even after Erika moved back into the house and into the basement. For a while, a scene from an episode of *Arrested Development* kept running through Layla's head, and she worried that all of the stress in her life would prevent her hair from ever growing back. Thankfully, it soon became apparent that her locks were steadily returning, and after just a few weeks, enough little curls covered her scalp for bar customers to stop asking if she was in the military or if she'd recently had lice.

Once a new tenant moved into the garage, Erika spent nearly all of her time in the basement, disappearing for a one to four-day bender every other week. Shortly before the end of September, Layla and Celeste found Erika sprawled out on a deck chair on the back patio, unwashed, her clothes stained with her own filth and still quite high. When they'd tried to help her into the house, Erika was sick all over Layla's shoes, ruining them and creating another expense Layla could ill afford. By that point, Layla no longer believed that there was any chance of Erika recovering, despite Celeste's continual exhortations to never give up hope. Celeste kept urging Layla to pray, a request that Layla did not believe would do any good. As she tossed her sneakers into the garbage can, Layla made a vow to herself that she would never forgive Erika, speak to her, or even look at her sister again if she could help it.

Erika never apologized for her most recent actions, nor did she even acknowledge them. The summer slipped away, and two and a half months after the unwanted haircut, the mid-October chill greeted Milwaukee with the promise of months of blustery frigidness. A week of mostly blue skies had given way to the overcast grey cloud cover that is a hallmark of late Milwaukee autumns. The foliage was still fairly thick and coloring nicely, and the neighborhood trees probably would hit peak in a week. A downpour earlier that afternoon had knocked a lot of leaves off the trees, and the strengthening wind was blowing them down the street. Every few steps, a damp, brown leaf would smack Layla across the face before sailing down the street in another gust of wind. As Layla trudged home from her lunchtime shift at Grobel's, she wrapped her sweatshirt closer around herself with the mournful realization that it was far less baggy than when she had bought it that past spring. It was not until her fifteenth try that she was actually able to fasten her jeans that morning. She made a pair of mental notes to herself, the first being to dig her heavier hoodie out of her bedroom closet before returning to work four hours later. The second mental note was a promise to herself to run at least a mile every morning immediately upon awakening. Even as she recited that vow in her head, she knew in her heart that she would never keep it. She had made that resolution twenty times in the past three years, and each time, she had managed at most half a mile a day for a week before abandoning her fitness plan altogether.

Though her weight was far from where she wanted it to be, at least her hair was steadily returning. All her life, Layla's hair had grown at twice the rate of the average person, who sees half a foot of length added each year. Now, it was a bit over two inches long. Layla didn't have the funds to visit her hairstylist anymore, and she didn't have the skills to cut it herself, so the new hair sat on her head in a messy, asymmetrical shag.

Turning her thoughts away from herself, Layla thought about her daughter. The previous afternoon, when she stopped by Nolan and Paige's house to spend a little time with Juniper, the little girl had metaphorically stabbed Layla in the heart by referring to Paige as "Mommy."

She hadn't meant to start yelling, but Layla had responded as if she was wracked with pain, as indeed she was. An uncontrollable torrent of fury and hurt feelings erupted, and Layla insisted that Juniper should refer to her, and only her, by that title. Juniper's little four-year-old lungs were more than equal to the task of matching her mother's decibel for decibel, and the nanny had rushed into the room, flustered by the screaming. Layla had sent the nanny away, telling her that everything was fine, even though anybody with ears could have realized immediately that it wasn't. She gulped a few breaths and spoke to Juniper in a quieter and calmer tone.

"You only have one Mommy, Juniper."

"I see my other Mommy every morning and every evening. You only come by a couple of afternoons a week."

"I have to work. That's what grown-ups have to do to survive. Now, why don't you call Paige "Stepmom?" I thought we agreed on that."

"We didn't agree on anything. You just told me to call Mommy Paige that. I never agreed to it. Mommy Paige doesn't care for that name, which is why she said to call her "Mom Paige" or "Mommy Paige," and she's happier when I don't say "Paige." Daddy doesn't like "Stepmom" either."

"I know. They both wish I wasn't around."

"Why do you act like they hate you? They like you, and that's nice of them, especially Mommy Paige, because she ought to be mad at you for what you did to their marriage."

"I fixed their marriage. I can't explain it to you, you're too young, but I brought them back together. Forget about that. The point is–"

"The point is that Mommy Paige loves being around me, and you can't be bothered with me. You won't even let me sleep over with you at Grandma's house anymore."

"That's not my fault. It's because the courts won't let you stay with me at Grandma's because of your Aunt Erika."

"Why? What has she done? I keep asking you, but you never say."

Layla had been left at a loss for words, and despite her best efforts, she hadn't managed to put together a coherent sentence. Eventually, she'd given up, ignored Juniper's continued questions, wiped her eyes on the sleeve of her sweatshirt, and hurried out into the darkening street, refusing to acknowledge the nanny calling out to her. When she'd reached the bus stop four blocks away, Layla had pounded the glass of the enclosure around the bench so hard she'd come close to cracking it, and the tears flowed uncontrollably as she cursed Erika for putting her into a position where the authorities had sympathetically but sternly told her that a house shared with a drug addict with a reputation for theft and reckless behavior was not a fit place for a young child.

Layla knew this was true, but she also knew it wasn't fair.

"But it's not my fault. I can't afford to live anywhere else except my grandmother's," she thought. This was no exaggeration. She had to pay off the student loans from the two and a half years of college she'd completed before the ignominious end of her undergraduate career. As much as Layla wanted to lay the entirety of the blame on Erika, she knew that she had to shoulder a great deal of the responsibility for her own expulsion. She'd poured her heart out to the judge, explaining the tribulations she'd endured over and over, until the family court magistrate had finally silenced her with a condemnatory monologue, criticizing Layla for endangering her daughter and mocking her for her supposed arrogance in thinking she could represent herself. A lawyer was an expense that Layla could not afford, but this fact cut no ice with the judge, who believed that people who served as their own attorney were picking the pockets of properly credentialed lawyers. Layla could visit Juniper at her father and stepmother's home, but for the time being, they had full custody, and any time with Juniper would be at Nolan and Paige's discretion. A final decision on custody would be reached in another month.

The judge's words gutted Layla, but she had no recourse. Not as long as she was sharing her grandmother's house with her sister.

Layla increased her pace in order to escape the chill, but she lost her balance on the slippery wet leaves covering the sidewalk, and she stumbled forward, striking the pavement. She hadn't cut herself, but she knew she would be badly bruised. As she stood and surveyed the damage, she noticed a slight tear on the toe of her left sneaker, the cheapest pair of shoes she'd been able to find. Her jeans, which were similarly bargain-priced, were not made for long-lasting durability. The knees developed holes after only a month of wear, and the seams were starting to fray. Her collision with the ground caused the jeans to rip even further, and on the left knee, a hole that used to be the size of an egg had expanded to the size of a saucer. Realizing that the jeans had suddenly become much more comfortable around her waist, Layla examined them and discovered that the fastening button had broken off and it had vanished under the fallen leaves. A particularly chilly gust of wind made her fear the worst, and a quick examination with her hands informed her that the back of her jeans had split down the middle. *Never mind*, she thought to herself. *I'm a block and a half from home, and no one's around. I'll just have to wear my sweatpants for my night shift.* Pulling off her sweatshirt, she tied it around her waist and immediately regretted it as the increasingly bitter air brought goosebumps to her arms. She made her way back to the house as quickly as she could, being careful so as not to fall again. Two doors away from home, she stumbled in a puddle of thick mud, and she looked down and discovered to her disgust that a large quantity of sludge had oozed through the new hole in her sneakers, soaking her sock and the inside of the shoe. Another two items of clothing, ruined. She had a few pairs of old dress shoes, but she needed footwear that she could stand in for hours without putting undue strain on her feet. The cheap sneakers from the dollar store were no great loss—they pinched the back of her heels and caused small blisters to form—but it was the expense that was the problem. Grandma let her live in the house rent-free and provided plenty of nice food, but the money she earned at the bar just barely covered her monthly payments on her student loans and credit card bills and the other debts she'd managed to rack up through unexpected expenses and poor financial management. It left her with precious little discretionary income, especially as she was saving up for a new smartphone, and her pride would not allow her to ask for more cash from her grandmother.

With mud in one shoe, bruises stinging, her jeans disintegrating with every step, and the wind piercing the skin of her bare arms and finding its way into the marrow of her bones, Layla was fuming. In the past, her thick mane had done a remarkable job of keeping her warm, especially since so much heat leaves the body through the head. But the relatively small amount of remaining hair did little to keep out the chill, and the memory of the afternoon of the haircut, coupled with the fact that two patrons had mistaken her for a boy that day, had soured her mood completely.

Resentment flooded through her mind, as Layla blamed her sister for her poverty, her lack of a bachelor's degree, losing custody of her daughter, and the fact that she couldn't have nice things, including long hair. She fumed, hoping that she'd find Erika at the house. Layla was in the mood for an argument. She wanted to scream at her in the hopes that she could finally break through her sister's opioid-fueled haze and make Erika feel just a little bit of the pain that she'd endured for the last several years.

Halfway up the driveway, the knot in her sweatshirt sleeves untied itself, and the garment slid down her hips onto the ground. As Layla knelt to snatch it up again, she heard her jeans tear even further and whirled in a circle, hoping that no one could see her disheveled state. Nobody was around, and she hurried to the back door and let herself in, leaving her muddy sneakers on the mat and tossing the sweatshirt on a hook. A gurgle in her stomach made Layla wonder if she should take an antacid to counteract the effects of her greasy lunch, but she decided that, at the moment, she wanted an argument more than medicine.

Erika's fleece jacket was on the hook next to Layla's sweatshirt, and as the basement door was unlocked, Layla figured that her sister was down in the cellar, probably watching television on a little analog set with a seven-inch screen. Layla stomped down the basement stairs. They creaked and groaned noisily as her feet pounded upon them, and the noise reverberated painfully against her eardrums. When she reached Erika's new room, the door was open a crack, and Layla pushed it open without bothering to knock.

Erika was lying on the floor with an empty pill bottle a few inches from her right hand. Her lips were an unpleasant shade of indigo, and Layla could detect no signs of breathing. She bent down and pressed her fingers to her sister's neck. No trace of a pulse was detectable.

"Erika! Erika!" There was no response to the shouts. Shaking produced no results, either.

This was far from the first time that Erika had overdosed. Four times previously in that calendar year, Celeste had administered Narcan, bringing Erika back from the brink of death. Layla rushed out of the room and hurried up the stairs. In her haste, she tripped on the hem of the leg of her jeans, and the already large hole tore all the way up to the waistband as she stumbled. After a quick curse, Layla rose and hurried to the kitchen, where a box of spray bottles of Narcan was stored in a cabinet. Pulling one from the box, Layla grabbed a pair of scissors and cut away the foil and plastic. She nearly tripped again on the shredded remains of her pants, and after swearing at the top of her lungs, she pulled off the ragged garment and kicked it underneath the table in the breakfast nook. She rushed downstairs as fast as she could, maneuvered Erika's cold and clammy body into the proper position, and then inserted the ampule into her right nostril.

But she didn't squeeze the bottle.

Layla crouched on the basement floor for the better part of a minute, running the instructions through her mind. *Put her on her back, check her mouth, gently push her head back before administering the spray. No matter what happens, call 911 after providing the patient with a dose.* A couple of times, she tightened her grip on the bottle, but she stopped herself before delivering the dose.

She felt oddly separated from her body. The eerie sensation that she was actually watching what was going on from afar made her feel like she was in a dream. As she held the ampule in Erika's nose, a series of images flashed through her mind. The diploma for the bachelor's degree she'd never earned. Her savings account with just over two hundred dollars in it. The courtroom where the supercilious judge had told her that her living conditions made her an unfit mother. Her possessions that had vanished over the years. All the times she'd tried to hide from her former high school classmates when she'd bumped into them by chance, because she didn't want them to see her working at a bar in cheap clothing and weighing over eighty pounds more than she did on graduation day. Not only that, there were all the questions about what she'd been doing over the past seven years that she didn't want to answer. The constant sense of anxiety that she'd felt every waking hour of every day. Scores of other memories flashed through her mind in rapid succession. The memory of looking in the mirror and discovering her hair loss popped into her mind a bit more frequently than the other thoughts. If her hair had been made into a wig or extensions, she wondered who was wearing it. And Juniper, calling another woman "Mommy."

And if she wakes up, this will all continue for who knows how many more years, Layla thought. A sudden image of her grandmother collapsing from a heart attack induced by stress and anxiety flashed through her mind. If that happened, that'd leave her as Erika's sole caretaker.

Until the theft of her hair, Layla had tended to focus on the happiest possible ending for Erika. Recovery, followed by a full life of sobriety. After the shearing, Layla had, for the first time, actually mentally nursed the possibility of an overdose, or possibly an accident occurring when Erika was high, such as her stepping in front of a speeding car.

In all of her fantasies, it had been her grandmother who had found Erika dead and cold from an overdose. Layla had never considered what she would do in a situation like the one she was currently in, and she felt oddly detached. If her conscience was giving her instructions, she couldn't hear anything. Issues of morality and filial loyalty were absent from her mind. An unsettling yet comfortable daydream flowed through her thoughts. A life with a steady white-collar job, money in the bank, her own apartment, and shared—perhaps full—custody of Juniper. No more worrying about whether or not the items she bought one day would be there the next. She could grow her hair as long as she liked without wondering if she'd wake up with a buzz cut. Twelve times in the last month, Erika had been caught attempting to break into a nearby home or shoplifting from local stores, and Layla and Celeste had been forced to rush to the scene of the crime, collect Erika, and beg their neighbors and the managers to not press charges, please. Celeste was well-known and respected in the neighborhood, and no one wanted to embarrass her. The police were never called, though on a few occasions, a tearful Celeste agreed to pay for broken car or house windows, more expenses that tapped her dwindling retirement savings.

How long after an overdose was the antidote effective? An hour to ninety minutes, she vaguely remembered reading. When had Erika taken the pills? During the late morning, when she was first alone in the house, or more recently? It was three-fifteen now. If she had fallen unconscious before noon, then it was probably already too late. But perhaps a spray of Narcan could still revive Erika. Health professionals were always saying that it worked miracles. With every passing minute, though, the odds of recovery faded.

Layla stared at her sister's face for a little while longer, and then pulled the bottle from her nostril and slowly walked out of the room and up the stairs. She wandered through the house and then climbed up to her own bedroom. The Narcan bottle was still in her hand, so she set it down on her nightstand. She pulled off both socks, crossed over to the bathroom, and rinsed the muddy one in the bathtub before relieving herself. She thought she might be violently ill, but the unpleasant urge passed. Rifling through her bureau, she grabbed a fresh T-shirt, a pair of grey sweatpants, and a blue sweatshirt she'd bought at the secondhand store, then struggled into them with haste.

I came home from work for my three-hour break before going back to the bar, she thought to herself. *I was dead tired because I hadn't gotten much sleep last night. So I went straight upstairs and used the bathroom... And then I lay down for a little nap. Normally, I would have gone downstairs to check on Erika, but I was just so tired, I needed to get some sleep.* Layla flopped upon her bed without pulling back the covers. She closed her eyes, but she knew that she would remain awake.

She lay still for a little over ninety minutes, and then she heard the sound of the back door opening. "Layla? Erika? Are you home?" It was Grandma.

Layla hesitated and decided to do nothing. Her grandmother couldn't prove that she'd heard her. She could always say that she was asleep.

The creak of the basement door was followed by the sound of Celeste's footsteps heading downstairs. There was silence for a quarter of a minute, and then Celeste's voice rang through the house so loudly that Layla knew there was no way she could claim she hadn't heard.

"LAYLA! LAYLA! COME DOWN HERE! CALL 911!"

Layla waited for a moment, and then the screaming resumed.

"LAYLA! LAYLA! LAYLA!"

She hurried down and made her way to the basement door. Celeste was halfway up the stairs. "Call 911 right now. Your sister's overdosed again." There was an old-fashioned rotary phone built into the kitchen wall. Layla dialed it while Celeste fished a bottle of Narcan out of the cupboard. The look Celeste gave her granddaughter as she passed her on the way back to the basement was undecipherable.

Layla was on hold for a couple of minutes, but she finally got through to a dispatcher, explained that her sister needed treatment for an opioid overdose, and was told that an ambulance would arrive in less than ten minutes. She climbed down the basement stairs and slowly walked towards Erika's room. Celeste was on the floor, performing CPR on a motionless Erika.

"The Narcan didn't work, then?"

"It did not. I gave her two sprays of it, there was no response."

"Do you want me to take over that for you?"

"No. Go up and keep an eye out for the ambulance. Go outside and wave to get their attention."

Layla did as she was told. The ambulance arrived in record time, and the paramedics rushed down to see if there was anything they could do. They performed all of the standard lifesaving measures, and after what felt like ages to Layla, they stood up and turned to Celeste with somber faces.

"We're sorry," the taller of the two paramedics said. "We'll take her to the hospital, but I'm afraid there's not much hope."

For a moment, Layla thought that Celeste was going to cry, but instead, she simply nodded. The paramedics brought in a gurney and carried Erika away.

"Should I call the bar and tell them that I won't be coming in tonight?" Layla asked.

Celeste's response was curt. "Do whatever you like." She did not make eye contact.

Layla offered to drive, but Celeste insisted that she would be the one to take them to the emergency room. Neither of them said a word during the trip.

The next few hours formed only fragmented memories in Layla's mind. They sat in uncomfortable plastic waiting room chairs for half an hour, until eventually a hospital official came up to them and sympathetically informed the pair that Erika was gone. When they were back home, Celeste brought a chair to the kitchen phone and began calling her church, the undertaker, and all of their relatives.

"Is there something I can do?" Layla asked.

"Why don't you call your mother and explain what happened? I'll get in touch with everybody else. Once you're done, take my credit card and go to the library. Get on the internet and find the website for the Monastery of the Peace of Christ. The order supports itself by making beautifully crafted wooden caskets. From what I've heard from friends, the simplest ones are about a thousand dollars each, made with various kinds of wood. Pick the nicest of the cheapest ones and have it shipped here. And then go to the thrift store on Oakland—it's open until nine—and see if you can find yourself a decent black dress." Celeste handed her granddaughter the car keys and immediately started dialing her next call.

Layla obeyed and dialed her cheap flip phone. Her mother didn't answer, so she decided to try again later. She drove to the library and ordered a varnished pine rectangular casket. She decided to spend an extra twenty-five dollars to have a cross carved into the lid, thinking her grandmother would appreciate it. As she left the library, she called her mother again, but once more, the phone went straight to voicemail. At the thrift store, she tried on five black dresses. Three of them didn't fit, and one that she really liked was priced at fifty dollars. She finally decided on a shapeless black gown that had probably been the property of a goth teenage girl or possibly part of a Halloween costume for someone going as a witch or Morticia Addams. The fabric was scratchy, and Layla thought it made her look like a sack of potatoes, but it was five dollars, and it would do.

The funeral Mass was held that Saturday afternoon. Neither Layla nor Erika had been inside a church in years, despite Celeste's fervent attempts to raise her granddaughters as devout Catholics. About thirty people attended, mostly friends of Celeste's who didn't know Erika but attended to support Celeste. Layla and Erika's father, Brice, had originally tried to sit next to their mother, Shelby, but she'd stood up and wordlessly moved to the opposite end of the pew. Nolan and Paige brought Juniper and sat in the back.

As soon as the Mass had ended, the family went to the graveyard for the interment. Celeste had given her granddaughter the gravesite originally meant for her, right next to her husband, who had passed away two years earlier.

Once the casket had been lowered into the ground and everyone present had thrown a rose into the grave (Paige had provided the flowers without being asked), Layla noticed that Juniper was standing about fifty yards away at the base of a clump of trees. She crossed over to talk to her daughter, but when she put her arm around Juniper, the little girl flinched.

"Mom, did you kill Auntie Erika?"

Several seconds passed before Layla could look at her four-year-old daughter. "Juniper, why would you ask me something horrible like that?"

"It's true then, isn't it? If you hadn't done it, you just would have said "no." You always answer questions with questions when you don't want me to know the truth. Like when my goldfish Murray died, and you wouldn't tell me what happened to him. You just kept asking, "Where do you think he is?" until I cried, and you finally told me he was dead."

Layla managed to open her mouth a little over an inch, but try as she might, she could produce no sound. *All I have to say is "no,"* she thought to herself. *Just say, "How dare you speak to your mother that way, young lady? No, I was not responsible for my sister's death, and you should be ashamed of yourself for asking me that. Shame on you! Now apologize to me right now!"* She tried to force herself to say those words, but even her strongest efforts could not produce an intelligible syllable. Repeated attempts produced nothing more audible than a very faint gasp.

Until that moment, Layla had not thought it possible for a little girl to cast

such a condemnatory and withering gaze. "It's true then, isn't it? You did it."
As tears began to run down the sides of her nose, Juniper whirled around
and sprinted across the graveyard to her father.

No matter how hard Layla attempted to will her legs to run after her
daughter, she was rooted to the ground in front of the trees. It wasn't until
Paige and Nolan led Juniper back to their car that Layla could finally walk
back to the others. Looking down into the open grave, gazing at the seven
red roses crisscrossing the top of the coffin where the mourners had tossed
them, Layla had a sudden mental image of being able to gaze through the
wooden lid and see her sister's face. Focusing on her imaginary picture of
her sibling, Layla whispered:

"You can't blame me for this. You did this to yourself."

They returned to the house for a reception featuring platters of cold cuts
and cheese from the supermarket. Juniper and her father and stepmother
did not attend. Layla's parents didn't stay very long, but Celeste's friends
stayed until dinnertime.

Once the last of the guests said her goodbyes, repeated the instructions for
warming up the tuna macaroni casserole she'd brought with her and walked
out into the night, Celeste locked the door and turned towards Layla. "Are
you going to tell me what Juniper screamed at you at the graveyard?"

"It was nothing. She was just having a temper tantrum."

Celeste grimaced, and her stare grew steadily colder. "Don't you dare lie
to me again, young lady. Not today. I want the truth right now."

"I'm telling you, Juniper wasn't feeling well!"

"Please. Don't. Lie." Celeste's voice grew louder with each word, and by
the time she said "Lie," the resonance of her tone made the family photos
vibrate on the walls.

Layla was about to evade her grandmother's request for information again,
but the pressure of Celeste's glower was too strong for her to fight anymore,
and she mumbled, "It's silly. Juniper accused me of killing Erika."

"What was that?"

"Juniper thinks I killed Erika!" Layla shouted even though she hadn't
meant to raise her voice at all.

Celeste nodded and stood silent for a full fifteen seconds. Finally, she said, "Well, Juniper is a very perceptive little girl then, isn't she?" She turned her back on Layla and climbed the stairs to her room without another word.

Chapter One—Is My Mommy A Murderess?

Here is where I enter the story. It was the Monday afternoon following Erika's funeral. Cuthbertson Hall needed to hire a new Spanish teacher, and HR was pretty certain that they'd found the right candidate for the job. They'd brought in a few members of the faculty, including myself, to give our opinions on the man. We'd had lunch with him that day, and he'd been friendly, even charming. But I didn't trust him. A while back, the actor Steve Schirripa had a recurring skit on Jay Leno's talk show where he went out on the street and took one look at some random person, and then made a number of snap judgments about that individual, such as their personal tastes, their backgrounds, and embarrassing stuff they might have done in the past. He claimed to have an uncanny ability to read people at a glance. I don't know how much of it was edited for television, but based on what was shown, he had a remarkably high accuracy rate. The skit was called "Steve Schirripa is a Judgmental Bastard." I like to think I have the same ability to get a strong sense of what people are like based on a very brief acquaintance with them. I'm not saying that I can know everything about a person with just one glimpse, but I get incredibly strong instinctive reactions, and when I do think I have an idea about the essence of a person, I'm right more often than I'm wrong.

And I did not care for this guy. He had the kind of smoothness that is incompatible with sincerity. He had that unsettlingly common self-delusion that he was completely irresistible in every way. But I didn't have anything solid I could use an excuse to convince them not to hire him. Fortunately, my boyfriend, Isaiah Funderburke, is Cuthbertson Hall's resident private investigator. Aside from his work as the Student Advocate, helping students with whatever problems they might have when they have no one else to turn to, Funderburke works with the school's security team, and he performs background checks.

"You're not going to hire him," Funderburke said.

The Assistant Head of the Upper School waited for a few moments. "Would you care to explain why not?"

"He's a fraud, that's why."

"He has excellent references from the last two schools where he's taught."

Funderburke shook his head and pulled out a stack of papers. "No, his *brother* has excellent references. His brother is the one who's a respected Spanish teacher in the Twin Cities. The guy who you seem to be so excited to hand a contract to is his younger sibling. Admittedly, they look a lot alike, but the real teacher has a couple of moles on his face that his little bro doesn't. Also, the guy who's currently applying for this job has been twice convicted for inappropriate behavior with young girls. Trust me, he is not the sort of fellow you want teaching at Cuthbertson Hall. There's more. It's all in my report."

He passed around some files, and everybody at the meeting flipped through them for a few moments. The Assistant Head wiped a few drops of perspiration from her brow with a tissue. "Funderburke, I think we've dodged a bullet thanks to you. I'll call him and tell him that his services will not be needed here."

"Actually, I already gave him a call and told him he was hired. He should arrive at your office to sign his contract any minute now."

"What?"

"The police are in your office waiting for him. He's got two outstanding warrants in Minnesota and another in South Dakota."

As we left the meeting and walked towards Funderburke's office, we saw the man in question being led away in handcuffs. He was making quite the scene with no thought at all regarding his personal dignity. About two dozen students were recording his angry shouts on their smartphones. Funderburke asked the students to send him copies of the videos, knowing that he would derive considerable amusement watching them.

When we arrived at his office, a little girl was sitting on the chair next to his door.

"Hello," I said to her.

"Hi. May I talk to you, please?"

"Absolutely," Funderburke told her. "Please come in." He unlocked his door. A tiny kid, she needed help getting into the comfy chair, so I lifted her up before taking my own seat.

"You're Mr. Funderburke and Miss Kaiming."

"Yes, we are. What's your name?"

"My name is Juniper. I'm in kindergarten."

"And how can we help you?" Funderburke asked.

"I think that my Mommy may have murdered my Auntie Erika." Juniper spoke very quietly, but we had no trouble hearing her.

Funderburke has a policy. When a student comes to him with a problem, no matter how unlikely or outrageous it may seem, he doesn't act incredulous. Every concern must be met with total seriousness and respect. "Could you please explain what happened and why you think that?" he asked.

Juniper explained to us how, even though her family tried to hide it from her, she knew that her Aunt Erika had a problem with pills. "She had an addition," she informed us, and we didn't have the heart to correct her.

She explained how Aunt Erika had overdosed, and even though her parents had tried to keep the cause of death hidden from her, she'd overheard them talking. "But at the funeral, when we were standing around the open coffin, I saw the look on my Mommy's face, and I got scared. By the way, I mean Mommy Layla, not Mommy Paige." Funderburke and I had the wrong idea for a moment, but Juniper quickly clarified her family situation.

"Just what sort of face did Mommy Layla make?" I inquired.

"A guilty face. And she lied."

"What did she lie about?" Funderburke asked.

"She said she came home and didn't go down to the basement to see Aunt

Erika. But she tugged at her left ear when she said it. That's what she does when she lies. Like two weeks ago, I asked her why she hated Mommy Paige, and she said she didn't, that she really liked her, and that they were really very good friends. But while she said it, she pulled at her ear like this." Juniper twisted her ear lobe with her thumb and forefinger.

"So she has a tell," Funderburke said.

"Tell what?"

"By "tell," Juniper, I mean something that someone does when they lie, even though they're not conscious of it. That's very observant of you to notice her tell. Is anybody else you know aware of what she does?"

"No one's mentioned it to me. But my great-grandmother is really good at realizing when I'm hiding something from her. I don't know if I have any tells, but she knew I was lying when I said that I'd eaten my broccoli when I'd actually dropped it in the big leafy potted plant near my chair when I thought no one was looking."

"Classic vegetable disposal technique." Funderburke made no effort to hide his approval.

"But what do you think your mother did?" I asked.

"I'm worried that she might have given Aunt Erika too much medicine, and that's how she died."

"Did you actually see your mom giving your aunt pills or anything like that?"

In response to my question, Juniper shook her head and flopped over, leaning over the arm of her chair. "No. I wasn't there when she died. I haven't been around much lately."

"Why not?"

"I'm not allowed at Mommy Layla's home. Mommy Paige said I wasn't safe there. I thought she was just being weird, but now I think she really was trying to protect me." Juniper started shaking, and tears started welling up in her eyes. "I'm worried. Could I be next? Is she going to try to poison me?" She started shaking, and I grabbed a couple of tissues and rushed forward to her. I cradled her in my arms and dabbed at her eyes, carefully maneuvering her so she wouldn't stain my silk blouse with her tears.

4

Just as I was getting her settled down and calm, there was a knock at the door. Funderburke crossed the room and opened it to reveal three women, who I would later learn were Layla, Paige, and Celeste. Funderburke was familiar with one of them, saying, "Celeste! What are you doing here?"

"My granddaughter and I came to pick up my great-granddaughter, but there seems to be some confusion," Celeste said as she walked into the office, followed by the other women.

"I was sure it was my day to pick up Juniper," Paige explained. My instincts pinged as I heard her speak. I got the sense that she wasn't being entirely truthful there, but I wasn't quite sure why she was making an excuse for driving up to Cuthbertson Hall.

"How do you two know each other?" I asked Funderburke. He explained that Celeste worked at one of his favorite Upper East Side bookstores, and they'd had many conversations about reading material.

After Celeste had made the proper introductions, Layla said, "Well, it's too bad that you had to make an unnecessary trip up here, Paige, but we'll be taking Juniper home tonight. You can pick her up after dinner."

"No!" Juniper pressed closer against me and wrapped her arms tightly around my midsection. "I don't want to! I'm scared!"

"Why are you scared, sweetheart?" Celeste leaned forward. "Honey, have you been crying?"

"Please, Great-Grandma, let me go home with Mommy Paige! I don't want to go back to that house!"

"I asked you not to call her "Mommy Paige." There was palpable venom in Layla's voice, and when I saw the anger flashing through her eyes, I started to wonder if Juniper's concerns were right on target.

Celeste placed a hand on Juniper's shoulder, and I noticed that she didn't recoil from her touch. "Sweetie, are you afraid because your auntie died? You know there's no such thing as ghosts, right? You're in no danger at my house."

The tears started coming back to Juniper's eyes. "Please. Please. Please."

"I think that I should take Juniper home with me," Paige said, walking forward and taking Juniper's hand. "We'll see how she's doing, and we'll reschedule later."

"Goodbye, Great-Grandma." Juniper gave her a hug, and started walking out with Paige, clutching her hand tightly.

Layla's voice was unsettlingly choked, like she was having trouble restraining her temper. "Don't I get a hug?"

Juniper looked at the rest of us with desperate eyes, and Paige stooped down and put her arms protectively around her and, with a little grunt, scooped her up into her arms. "She's not in the mood right now. I'll give you a call tomorrow."

Stepping in front of them, Layla quietly growled, "Why are you turning her against me?"

"It's not my fault she's reacting like she is to you."

"Whose fault is it, then?"

"I've no idea. She's been very upset the last several days. I suspect it has something to do with her aunt's passing. Perhaps she'll feel better when she gets home." Paige hurried away, carrying Juniper, and Layla stood still, looking like she wanted to bite someone.

"Who are you two, and what was she doing here?" Layla demanded.

Normally, Funderburke replies to an angry question with a proportionate attitude of his own, but today, he was much more diplomatic. "My name is Isaiah Funderburke, and I'm the Student Advocate here at Cuthbertson. This is my colleague and girlfriend, Nerissa Kaiming. Juniper came to us because she's been in kind of a bad way ever since her aunt passed away—my condolences, incidentally, I realize how difficult this must be for you—and she wanted our help. I think she's grieving, and she's having trouble dealing with the situation. Is this her first experience with death? Has anybody else close to her passed away?"

"My husband died a couple of years ago, but she was so young then, I don't think she really knew him or realized what was happening," Celeste replied. "Do you think she needs to talk to a professional?"

"I can set up an appointment with one of the school psychologists, if you like," Funderburke offered. He hadn't needed to outline his strategy to me. It was a sensible idea not to antagonize Layla right away by asking her if she'd poisoned her sister.

"I'd appreciate that, thank you, Funderburke."

"I guess it's just you and me for dinner tonight," Layla sulked against the doorway.

"Do you two live on the East Side?" I asked.

"Yes, just two minutes away from the bookstore."

"Just down the street from your house," Funderburke added, reading my mind.

"Would you like to join me and my family for dinner tonight?" I asked. "We have some concerns about Juniper, and it would be nice to talk about the situation over a home-cooked meal. She's a sweet kid, and we want to work with you to help her… through whatever she's going through now."

Layla's initial reaction was to decline, but Celeste was much more open to this possibility, and after a minute of coaxing, they agreed to come to my house at six-thirty that night.

When I say "my house," I should really say "my family's houses." For years, my adoptive great-grandfather lived alone in a big house on Milwaukee's East Side, right by Lake Park. Midway through his seventies, it became more difficult for him to live on his own, so his grandson Keith moved in with him after he graduated from college. I'll get to my personal autobiography later, but when Keith turned twenty-six, I was just shy of fourteen. I moved to Milwaukee in search of a decent education, and after my birth mother passed away, he adopted me and my daughter. No, I didn't make a mistake regarding my age. As I wrote, I'll explain everything later. Then Keith married his girlfriend Midge right before I went to college, and they bought the house next door to his grandfather's. They built a corridor connecting the homes, and now they share the two houses with their biological children, Keith's grandfather, Midge's grandmother, Midge's two younger siblings, my daughter Toby, and me. It's a little crowded, but it's the kind of family I dreamed of having when I was a little kid and basically raising myself.

I greeted Layla and Celeste when they arrived. Layla was wearing the same sweats she'd worn when I'd seen her last, but Celeste had changed from a sweater and slacks into a dark green dress. I was wearing the same cream silk blouse and navy-blue satin skirt I'd sported earlier, along with the soft ankle boots that are really easy on my feet, but I'd switched out my espresso-colored suede blazer for a caramel leather racer jacket, just because I thought it felt it suited my mood better. Celeste handed me a platter of little dinner rolls that looked like they'd been made from scratch, and our awkward pleasantries were interrupted by my three eldest little siblings rushing up to meet the guests. "These are Bernard, Eleanor, and Amara. They're triplets." I led them into the living room. "This is my father, Keith Kaiming." Mom came in from the kitchen. "And this is my mother, Midge." I saw the confusion in Layla's face. "I was adopted. That's why they're only about thirteen years older than I am. And half-Chinese." After the handshaking, I introduced them to Mrs. Stutschewsky, our ninety-six-year-old neighbor who still lives independently, but often eats dinner with us because she hates eating alone. "The others are all taking care of various business now, but I'll introduce you to them later."

The Dolaks sat down on the couch against the far wall. I was about to take a seat myself in the chair next to them when I heard Funderburke pulling into the driveway. I was a little disappointed when I saw him, because under his long walking coat he was wearing the same suit he wore at work, minus the tie. I believe that it's generally a risky and often terrible idea for one person in a relationship to try to change the other, but I have some particularly strong ideas about fashion that I realize not everybody supports. For example, I personally think that Funderburke looks incredible when he wears clothes that are basically masculine versions of what I wear, and I tend to focus on intense colors, interesting textures, shines and sparkles, metallic gleaming, cloud-soft knits, silky-smooth fabrics, and buttery-soft leather clothing. I dress pretty modestly, but I like to stand out in a crowd. And so, every now and then, I come across a suit or some other outfit that I want to see Funderburke wear. Problem is, not always, but usually, Funderburke believes that the wardrobe I've picked out for him is a little too… *flashy* for his tastes. So we have a deal. He wears the clothes I pick for him when we're hanging out at his place or when he comes to my home for dinner (which is usually three or four times a week), where none of my family ever comments on his clothes, but when he's out in public, he wears what he wants, which is either his work suits or a T-shirt and track pants. He believes in business formal for school, church, and certain social situations; and absolute comfort at every other time. I was hoping he'd wear the silver sweater I'd just found for five bucks online, but I realized that since we had guests, one of which was a murder suspect, it was probably best that he dress less distinctively than I'd like.

I greeted him with a peck on the cheek. We agreed earlier that it wasn't wise to attempt to extract a direct answer to Juniper's question "Is my mommy a murderess?," so the plan was to engage in ordinary conversation and see where *it* led.

"Thank you so much for inviting us," Celeste said. "It's only been a few days, but already I'm sick of our neighbor's condolence casseroles swimming in canned cream of mushroom soup."

"You're welcome. Those rolls smell great."

She smiled at my comment. "They're no trouble. I mix up the ingredients in bulk every few weeks. All I need to do is add water, stir, spoon them onto a cookie sheet, and bake."

Bernard was staring at Celeste. "You're blinking a lot. Is there something wrong with your eyes?"

She looked surprised at the question, but she answered him with a smile. "I had an eye appointment today, and they dilated my eyes. That means—"

"I know. It means they put drops in your eyes to make the pupils bigger." For a second, a guilty flash passed over Bernard's face as he caught Keith and Midge's expressions. "I'm sorry. I shouldn't have interrupted you."

"That's quite all right, dear."

"That's why I had to drive her. We thought we'd pick up Juniper on the way home, but it looks like I was wrong." Layla's arms and legs were crossed, and she didn't appear to be happy to be out having a meal with near strangers. I decided that now was the time to try to soften her up a bit. Normally I try complements about clothing choices, but if I'd said how much I liked her sweats, there's no way I could keep from sounding patronizing.

I started playing with my hair as I tried to think of something nice to say, when Layla surprised me with a positive comment. "You have nice hair. I used to have hair a lot like yours."

"Really? What happened?" I could've told Bernard that wasn't a diplomatic question to ask, but my little brother has never let tact get in the way of his curiosity.

"It got cut."

"It *got* cut? That's a weird way to phrase it. Normally people say, '*I* cut it.'" Bernard's a perceptive kid. "Did someone cut it without your permission?"

She hesitated, then replied, "Yes."

"What happened? It's pretty short now. Did your barber's hand slip and cut off too much? And then he or she had to chop off the rest to even it out? Or did it catch on fire? Or did someone steal it? I read about how, in South America, criminals are targeting women with long hair, cutting it off, and selling it for hair extensions. Apparently, there's big money in it."

"Huh. Looks like the crime wave has made its way up to Wisconsin."

Bernard was now standing next to the couch and was scrutinizing Layla's short locks. "Did you call the police? I don't think that they could get DNA off the stolen hair because you can only find that in the follicles, but they might be able to compare the hair samples, though Mommy says that's often not reliable forensic analysis. She says it's pseudoscience because you can't really tell if one hair matches another by staring through a microscope. All you can do is tell if one strand looks kind of like another, and that's why hundreds of innocent people may have gone to prison." Without taking a breath, he asked, "If they find out who bought your stolen hair and turned it into a wig or hair extensions, will you have it repossessed and reattached to your head? That's what I would do if I had long hair and someone stole it."

My parents were trying to repress the urge to tell Bernard to let up on the questions. Part of this was because they were also interested in Layla's answers. Also, Funderburke was attempting to be surreptitious with his hand signals. He was dangling one hand over the side of his chair that was blocked from Celeste and Layla's view, frantically trying to catch their gaze with one eye, all the while using a kind of pidgin sign language to tell them to *Let him keep talking.* Funderburke has said on many occasions that children

10

make terrific interrogators, because they ask questions that no adult could get away with querying.

I think Funderburke and I figured it out at the same time. I covered the side of my face that the Dolaks could see in with my tresses, turned to him, and mouthed *Her sister stole her hair and sold it for drug money.* He nodded, his tight-lipped smile relishing the fact that Bernard had ferreted out a potential motive.

Celeste started coughing, and Dad asked our guests if he could get them something to drink, apologizing for not offering earlier. Celeste asked for water, and Layla initially declined, but when Mom asked her if she was interested in the pitcher of iced coffee in the fridge, she immediately accepted a glass.

After Dad returned with the drinks, Funderburke, who keeps his beloved coat on longer than he really needs to indoors, fished around in one pocket and pulled out a little purple stuffed elephant that barely filled the palm of his hand. "By the way, I found this on the chair in my office after Juniper left. Is this hers?"

"Yes! That's Tunk-Trunk! She takes that everywhere!"

"Is that what she calls him? Does she often lose him?" Funderburke asked.

"All the time. I spent two hours searching last month and finally found her—Tunk-Trunk is a girl—in the little basket where we keep the newspapers."

"Tunk-Trunk doesn't have tusks. That's a sign that she's a female. Some African elephants have tusks, but Indian elephants don't. And elephants all over the world are growing smaller and smaller tusks as a means of naturally protecting themselves from ivory poachers," Bernard informed Funderburke.

"I read about that. Your father sent me a link to an article on elephants after talking about them with you."

"Funderburke, do you have any more of those tiny GPS devices?" Keith asked.

"Yes, right here." Funderburke dipped his hand into another pocket, sorted through a handful of change, safety pins, and mints from the restaurant where we had a pretty mediocre dinner the previous week, and held up a little black cube.

"You carry GPS devices in your pockets?" Layla asked.

"You'd be surprised how often they come in handy," he replied.

"I kept losing my stuff," Amara chimed in, "so Funderburke put some of the little tracking devices in my jacket and toys, and that helped us find them when I left them at school and at my friends' houses."

"And if I have your permission, I can put one in Tunk-Trunk. That way if Juniper misplaces her again, all you have to do is check your smartphone."

"That'd be great…" Layla's face soured. "But I don't have a smartphone. Not anymore. Not until I have a chance to save up for a new one."

Funderburke and I locked eyes again, both of us concluding that Erika had stolen Layla's smartphone as well. "Luckily, there's a little zipper here. There's room for me to slip the tracker in here…" Funderburke started tapping his smartphone. "I've activated the device on my own phone. When you get your own new phone, I can set it up for you."

"Thanks."

Celeste gestured towards my parents. "So, what do you two do? Midge, I suppose you're a housewife."

"Actually, no. I have my own business as a legal and forensic medicine consultant. I provide expertise and second opinions on autopsies, double-check reports, and challenge forensic science tactics, and I also write closing arguments for both prosecutors and defense attorneys who hire my services, depending on my thoughts on the case. I do work primarily from home, though."

"So you're both a doctor and a lawyer?" Celeste looked impressed.

"Yes. But courtrooms make me uncomfortable, and I don't want to spend my whole career in a morgue, so this way, I can pick and choose the jobs I want to take and still spend plenty of time with my kids."

"Well, I must say that it's very nice to see a woman making the most out of her intelligence, as well as putting a priority on family." Celeste turned to Layla. "Isn't that wonderful? To see a smart woman enjoying a successful career?" Layla didn't respond. I sensed that comments like these were a regular feature of their conversations. "Layla? Layla?" Celeste nudged her granddaughter with a sharp elbow jab, causing Layla to jump and spill half her iced coffee over her sweatshirt.

"Damn it, Grandma!" Layla froze under little Eleanor's shocked, judgmental scowl. "I mean, 'Darn it.' 'Dang it,' actually. I'm sorry."

"Quite all right," Midge replied. "It doesn't look like anything got on the furniture or the carpet."

"Do you have a place I can soak this? Maybe the stain won't set."

"That sweatshirt's no great loss," Celeste quipped.

"I can take care of it," I told her. "Follow me. I'll spray some stain remover, and then I'll get you something so you can stay warm."

She looked me up and down. "I don't think your clothes will fit me."

"I've got a great shawl. You'll love it. Please, follow me." As I left the room, Funderburke gave me a little nod. We both knew I could get more out of a one-on-one conversation.

Once we were upstairs, Layla pulled her sweatshirt over her head and checked her T-shirt. Luckily, the cold coffee hadn't soaked through it. I took it from her and tossed it into my bathroom sink to soak. I keep a little bottle of stain-removal spray on the shelf, and I doused the coffee stain with it, rubbed it in thoroughly, and set it back inside the water-filled sink. "All right, let's find that shawl."

Layla looked around my bedroom after I switched on the light. "You've got a lot of library books in your room."

"That comes with the territory when you're getting your doctorate in history. There's even more in my little office downstairs."

"You've got a lot of clothes, too." This is true. I ran out of space in my closets years ago, so I have a few two-story racks filled with some of my latest acquisitions.

"How many leather jackets and coats do you have?" she asked, running her hand along one of the racks.

I actually lost count a long time ago, so I evaded her question. "I don't see the shawl… I know I last wore it when I chaperoned the homecoming dance…"

"You must spend a fortune on clothes."

"Actually, I haven't spent more than forty-nine dollars and ninety-five cents on an article of clothing in a decade, and that includes shoes. The average price per garment is much less than that. Most of what's here was from sales, outlet malls, thrift shops, auction websites... some of it was given as payment by a friend of mine who runs a boutique. I tutored her daughter; she paid me in merchandise."

"Nice work if you can get it."

"Another acquaintance of mine is a costume designer in the Chicago theater district. A lot of times, they make outfits for productions and sell them cheap afterwards. That's how I got these four great velvet pantsuits last weekend. Ruby red, emerald green, sapphire blue, and amethyst purple."

"What show was that?"

"No idea. I think it was something experimental about female calculus professors or something like that." I opened up another pair of closet doors to reveal some more leather and suede clothes arranged by color. White on the left, followed by the brighter colors, moving on to various shades of brown (pale cream to mahogany), up to the numerous black jackets and coats of differing lengths and styles on the right.

"Wait! Let me see that one." Layla walked up to me and pulled down a glossy brown jacket. "Where did you get this?"

"At the Buy-Again Boutique about nine blocks from here. I know the manager. I ask her to give me a call when somebody sells them something really nice in my size. "

Layla ran her hand over the collar. "It's a resale clothing store?"

"Yeah. Alice, that's the manager's name. She gave me a call and said, "I've just got this great cognac lambskin jacket. You interested?" So I stopped by after work..."

The look on Layla's face stopped me. "This is mine."

"What?"

"Look!" She showed me the maker's label on the right inner pocket. Scrawled in the corner in blue ink were the tiny letters "L. D." "This was a high school graduation present from my grandfather. He knew I'd been admiring it in a shop window, and he surprised me." She laughed without a trace of joy and sank down on the foot of my bed. "So that's where she sold it."

"Your sister Erika?"

"Yep. How much did you pay for it?"

"I don't remember exactly. I know I negotiated... Maybe forty dollars?"

"So she probably got what, twenty dollars for it?"

"Maybe. Alice needs fairly substantial profit margins to stay in business, but I get special consideration for being a frequent customer. Twenty-ish dollars sounds about right."

Layla nodded and clutched the jacket to her chest. "I wonder how many pills that bought."

I wanted to ask some more questions about Erika, but I decided that it wasn't the right time to push. "Well, your jacket found its way back to you."

She looked up at me as if I was obviously insane. "It's yours now. You bought it."

"Standard property rights from a purchase do not apply when the goods in question have been stolen. You never relinquished title to your jacket. It belongs to you."

"I don't know—"

"Forty dollars isn't going to break me. Cuthbertson pays much more than most schools. I pay my rent by helping run the house and looking after my little siblings and elderly relatives, and when you see the massive spread on the table tonight, you'll know I'm in no danger of going hungry. Go on, consider it an early Halloween treat. I'm giving you your own jacket back."

"It doesn't even fit me anymore. Look." She wriggled her arms into it, but she couldn't lower them down to her sides once they were snugly ensconced in the sleeves. In any event, the two halves of the zipper were much too far apart to fasten. "See. I was five months along with Juniper the last time I could zip it up."

"But you kept it all these years because of its sentimental value, and someday it could fit again."

She snorted. "Yeah, that's not gonna happen. I gave up on that hope long

15

ago."

I helped pull the jacket off her arms and pressed it firmly back into her lowered hands. "It belongs in your closet. Stop arguing with me, okay?"

"Have you worn it often?"

"A few times. A couple of dates with Funderburke and one time when I gave a lecture at a library on the other side of town. It's really comfortable. Great lines, terrific material."

For a moment, it looked like she was going to say something to me, but instead, she started crying. I grabbed a couple of tissues and handed them to her. "I can't believe it wound up here, of all places," she mumbled.

"It's really not that much of a coincidence. Alice's Buy-Again Boutique is pretty close to both of our houses, so if your sister was looking for a place to sell it, that's a likely contender. And Alice knows that I rarely miss the opportunity to add to my leather jacket collection."

"I can't believe that I didn't think to call the nearest vintage clothing store right after she stole it," Layla muttered. "I just assumed it was gone forever. Grandma's right. I really do give up too easily." She sighed and wiped her eyes some more. "You didn't happen to buy a laptop or a smartphone secondhand not too long ago, did you?"

"Sorry. I did just buy a new laptop, but it was from the store, as my previous one died of old age."

"How about my hair? If I looked, would I find a big rope of my hair rolled up in your sock drawer?"

Laughing, I told her, "Sorry. No luck there. And this—" I tugged at my own lengthy locks—"is all mine."

The chuckle Layla gave was quiet, but it was a genuine expression of good humor. "I suppose that was too much to ask." She got up and looked over some more of the racks. "You could probably open your own vintage clothing store yourself here."

"I told you, everything in this room is a bargain."

"The six-dollar jeans I bought at the big box store, those are a bargain. By the way, all these clothes, I don't see any jeans here."

"Yeah, I'm not a big fan of denim. When I was younger, that was pretty much all my birth mother bought for me, and I kind of developed a loathing for it. I just never cared for the texture, either."

"Huh." She ran her hand over two dozen glossy pairs of my trousers. "Are these all genuine leather?"

"Yeah. I have an allergy to latex and polyurethane. One time, I bought a pair of pleather pants, and my legs broke into a horrible rash."

"Yikes."

"Itched like crazy. The silver lining, though, was that I didn't have to shave my legs for three months. But before you judge my clothing budget, I want you to know none of those pants cost me more than twenty dollars. These here–" I pulled out a tan pair. "They were only two bucks. Brand new, with tags. It's amazing what you can find on online clothing sites."

"Why were they being sold that cheap?"

"My room is filled with clothes other women have given up on ever wearing. They buy items like these pants, and they think, 'I'm going to wear these and be the bold style icon I've always dreamed of being. All the women will be jealous of me, and all the men will want me.' Every week, they say to themselves, '*This* will be the day I finally wear them outside.' And then, at the last minute, they chicken out and put on an old pair of jeans. They're afraid of what people will say. It's amazing what people don't do when they're worried that people will make fun of them. And so the pants hang in the closet for months that turn to years without ever being worn out of the house, and eventually the woman no longer fits into them or they become a symbol of her lack of nerve, so she gets rid of them. My fashion mantra is that I wear the clothes most women are afraid of wearing. I've lost track of how many times someone looked at my outfit and said, 'I wish I had the courage to wear that.' A lot of women fill their closets with regrets. There's a lot of garments here, but no missed opportunities due to lack of nerve."

"Huh." Layla let my speech sink in for a little bit. "How long have you known what your personal style is?"

"Since the start of high school. Cuthbertson makes all of its students wear a white dress shirt, a black blazer, and black pants. Girls can wear a black skirt that covers the knee, boys must sport a tie. I'm really not a fan of dress codes, but I realized pretty quickly that there was no explicit rule that said the uniform couldn't be made of leather. Pretty soon, everybody was calling it "the Nerissa loophole," and the school never got around to amending the rules. A few of my girls have adopted "the Nerissa loophole" themselves, at least some of the time."

My gut instincts told me that I should leave it there, but I was on a tear with one of my favorite topics, so I kept on going. "The six-dollar jeans you buy, how long do they last? A month?"

"The last pair I bought? Four months."

I could smell her lying. She was defensive about her cheap jeans for reasons I couldn't understand. I fastened a sharp look on her, the same one I use when I catch a student plagiarizing from Wikipedia in a book report. She crumbled like stale bread. "Two months." After I maintained the strength of my glower, she corrected herself further. "A little under six weeks."

"That's when they became unwearable?"

"Yep."

"So they started developing holes after two weeks?"

"A month."

"Six months out of the year, the temperature in Milwaukee's either barely above zero or well below freezing. And you're wearing jeans with holes with them a third of that time? Do you wear tights underneath?"

"Is there a point to this?"

"I hate fast fashion. When I buy clothes, I buy them to last. Look at these." I held up a different pair of lambskin pants. "These were ten dollars with tags. When I was sixteen, I bought them at a different thrift store—it closed three years ago when the owner retired—I still wear them at least every other week in cool weather. They hold back the winter wind better than Kevlar stops bullets. Now that's a good deal."

The iron curtain descending upon her face told me that I should have kept my big mouth shut. "You're still wearing the same size you did when you were halfway through high school?"

Just when I thought we were bonding. She muttered a derogatory two-word description of me under her breath, comparing me to an emaciated female dog, and I summoned up all my willpower in order not to take it personally.

I was formulating a devastating reply when her face morphed back from metal to flesh. "I'm sorry. That was rude. I'm a guest in your home, and my Grandma didn't raise me to insult my hosts." She started tearing up again, and I grabbed some more tissues for her. Suddenly I was in a forgiving mood.

"It's all right." I sat down next to her. "So, your Grandma raised you?"

"Yeah. Dad's a nice guy, but he was never cut out for the responsibilities of looking after children. And Mom's job had her travelling all the time, sometimes for weeks at a stretch. So Grandma took me in. Grandpa too. He just worked a lot, so I didn't spend as much time with him."

"The divorce must've been hard."

"Mom and Dad were never married."

"Oh."

"They split up two months before Erika was born." She shuddered. "From what we've discussed tonight, you've probably figured out that she stole a lot from me and Grandma."

"You don't have to be Sherlock Holmes to deduce that one."

"Well, we placed all of our valuables in either a safety deposit box or self-storage. Tomorrow morning, before my lunch shift at the bar, I'm heading down across town, loading them up and bringing them home. Then I'll spend my breaks between three-fifteen and six-forty-five for the next several days unpacking. Grandma's working double shifts at the bookstore to pay for the funeral expenses, and she'll be too tired to put her house back the way it should be, so it's on me."

I didn't think it through before I spoke, but in that brief flash of time, it seemed like a smart idea for more reconnaissance. "Would you like my help?"

"Are you serious?"

"I get off work at three-twenty tomorrow. I can be at your house a little before four." I had previously taken the liberty of checking the student directory to find their address. "I'm happy to offer an extra pair of hands."

I wouldn't say Layla looked suspicious so much as incredulous. "Why are you being so nice to me?"

"The tuition you pay for Cuthbertson, I feel you deserve your money's worth."

"Oh, I'm not the one paying for that. That's all Nolan and Paige."

"Nevertheless, Juniper's a really sweet kid, and I can tell she's going through a tough time now. Maybe if you and I talk a little more, we can figure out a way to help her through this sticky patch."

Her head slumped forward. "My daughter's afraid of me."

"Well, I've got a daughter of my own, and she's had a lot on her plate, with her mama being Cuthbertson's favorite target of gossip and innuendo. If we put our heads together, we may be able to fix the situation."

Her tears started coming back. "I'm losing custody of her. She doesn't even want to be around me anymore."

"Well, let's keep talking and see what happens."

She shrugged. "All right. I suppose the situation can't get any worse."

The pitter-patter of Bernard's little feet resonated up the stairwell as he rushed to my door. "Dinner's ready!"

"Thanks, little bro. We'll be right down."

Layla stood up, still holding her jacket against her chest. "It's all right. I'll be warm enough." A sudden shiver in her shoulders told me that wasn't the case.

"Hang on, let me check this last closet here…" I ran my finger along the line of assorted garments and couldn't find what I was seeking. "Wait a minute…" I saw a little bit of lavender sticking out between two of my full-length duster cardigans, the pearl-grey and the copper ones. I made a mental note to wear another one again that week, possibly the sky-blue one. I gently tugged at it, and a moment later, my shawl was in my hands. "Here we go. It must've slipped off the hanger and stuck between my cardigans with static electricity." I shook out the shawl, and the sounds of about a dozen little crackles were just barely audible. Wrapping the shawl around Layla, I said, "C'mon, let's get our dinner."

20

Chapter Two—Ten Things High School Should Warn You About Before College

D inner was pleasant, though not informative, as the Dolaks didn't provide us with any additional details regarding the death of Erika, which was to be expected. I should have figured that they wouldn't be in a hurry to discuss some of the seedier details of their lives, especially with two sets of triplets at the table, the elder trio being particularly inquisitive towards the guests.

A while back, when I chaperoned a trip to Milwaukee's Discovery World science museum with my daughter, we enjoyed a presentation on forensic investigation. The speaker informed us that many television shows utilize the trope of the angry cop screaming at the suspect, maybe even slapping the guy around until he confesses or gives up the desired information. But in real life, that's not an effective way to get somebody to talk to you and share potentially sensitive information. You have to make them *want* to talk to you, to make them feel so comfortable in your presence that they'll willingly share their secrets with you.

So, did I think that Layla had killed Erika? After the Dolaks left the house shortly after eight-thirty, Funderburke and I compared our mental notes on what we'd learned that evening, and as soon as we'd shut the door to my little research alcove, that was exactly the question he asked me.

"No. No, I don't."

Funderburke's facial expression made it clear that he and I weren't quite on the same page. "All right, why do you think that?"

"Because nothing about her gives me the sense that she could be a cold-blooded poisoner. Think about it. Poor little Juniper thinks that her mother injected drugs into her aunt's veins, or perhaps she worries that Layla put a gun to Erika's head and forced her to swallow a whole bottle of pills. But I don't think that Layla has the mental makeup to commit a murder like that."

"Why not?"

"Because she's miserable, and she doesn't have the gumption to dig her way out of the pit she's dug for herself. You talked to her tonight; you can tell she's not pleased with how her life has turned out. Celeste told us about her stellar high school academic career, how she was a triathlete, and how she got a partial scholarship at a prestigious little college out east."

"Yeah, I've been wondering why she didn't complete her degree."

"That's one of the details I want to find out. Maybe she lost her scholarship. Why? To be determined. But what stopped her from taking out a student loan,going to UW-Milwaukee, and wrapping up her remaining credits? She's been working at that bar ever since she dropped out. Why hasn't she found some other job? Something better, closer to what she'd rather be doing with her life? She's not making too much money. I mean, there are plenty of options for someone without a B.A. where there's room for advancement. I don't know her exact reasons, but maybe if I get to know her better, she'll open up more. You weren't there with us in my room, but from what she told me, she is not happy with her current physical condition. But she hasn't gone on a diet and exercise program. She told me that she didn't expect to ever lose weight. Worst of all, she seems to have resigned herself to losing custody of her daughter. Not because she doesn't want to be a mom, but because she doesn't have the strength to fight anymore. Why is this? What happened to her? Why is she so passive? I don't know, but that's the key. *She is a very passive person.* She hates her life, but there are at least four significant actions she could take to improve it. But she isn't going back to college or finding a new job or working out or fighting tooth and nail for her maternal rights. And that's why she didn't kill her sister. Her sister stole from her. Erika took Layla's favorite jacket and snipped off all of her hair. That's a lot to forgive, and a lot of people might not be able to let go of their anger.

But would she stoop to murder in order to get this thorn out of her life? I just don't think so. If she doesn't have the initiative to check the want ads, she's not going to steel her soul and plot a sororicide. It would be too much trouble. I think she's depressed, and I think she's given up on life. Not a great condition to be in, as everybody will agree. But that's the reason why she didn't kill Erika. No matter how much pain and strain her sister put upon her, Layla didn't have the motivation to commit murder. I think she's at the point where she's gotten sufficiently used to the misery that she actually nurtures it. The bleakness has become comforting and familiar to her, and making an effort to find happiness is just too darn much hard work."

At that point, my lungs needed a thorough replenishment of air, and I took the opportunity to revive myself with several long, deep breaths. Funderburke said nothing for about half a minute. He finally broke his silence, telling me, "Wow. You've put way more thought into crafting a psychological profile of Layla than I have."

"What's your assessment of her?"

"She's a liar."

The man does not mince words. I responded by saying, "Yeah, I saw her tugging her ear a lot, especially when she used the phrase 'accidental overdose.' But I think that there's more to ear-tugging than simple lying. I think she pulls at her earlobe when she's *nervous*, and sometimes, when she's nervous, she lies to avoid a subject or to move a conversation along. And that's not a sign of culpability, just discomfort." I pushed a stray lock of hair out of my eyes and asked Funderburke, "So do you think she's a murderess?"

He took a few moments to consider his answer. "No. I think that you're right. When she was talking about how much fun she had at her job, and how much she missed her sister, the aroma of cattle manure was thick in the air."

"Based on her ear tugging?"

"No. Based on the incredulous looks that her grandmother was shooting at her when she fired off statements like the ones I mentioned. Maybe it was different when she was just with you, but at the dinner table, Layla was all smiles about her life and all downcast looks about her sister's passing, even if she didn't go into many details. And Granny was having none of it. She didn't want to call her granddaughter out in front of us, but I'll wager you your next six months of clothing budget that the second they slammed the doors of their car, Celeste let Layla have it."

I shoved my hands into my jacket pockets. "No bet."

"My personal take on Layla? No, she's not a premeditated poisoner. But she's got a form of survivor's guilt. You know how many Cuthbertson students have someone they love wrestling with addiction. It tears them apart. They hope for the best and a full recovery. Some of them have their prayers answered. Others never see their dreams come true, and it's a constant source of pain. They all think there's something they could do to cure their loved ones, and they blame themselves—unfairly, of course—for not doing it. And I think that's what is happening with Layla. She believes that if she'd only talked to Erika more, or been smarter about providing support, or used a different form of positive reinforcement, or whatever, her love would have triumphed over the power of opiates. So the guilt is real because she places the burden for Erika's failure on her own shoulders."

I mulled over that for a minute. "I can see that. I think you're onto something there. That certainly *seems* like a reasonable interpretation of her mental state. I believe you've got it."

"It's a theory. Nothing provable, at the moment. I certainly don't feel comfortable going to Juniper and telling her that's what really happened between her mother and her aunt."

"And that's why I'm going to help Layla unpack her stuff tomorrow."

"Are you sure?"

I wondered why he had such a concerned expression on his face. "If we're right, and I'm pretty sure we are, then I'm in no danger, right? She's not a killer. It's not like she's going to throw pills down my throat while I'm putting the silverware back in the drawer."

"I'm not saying that your life is at risk, Nerissa."

"Oh. Because I had a whole spiel set for how I can take care of myself."

"I've seen you in action against those fake referees who tried to lift your wallet out of your purse at the Cedarburg River Day School soccer game.

I've never been more attracted to you. Not the issue here. I just want to make sure you're still focusing on our primary goal."

"Juniper's well-being." I sighed. "Yeah, I'm worried about that."

"Are you thinking about how we're going to break what we learn to her? Because frankly, I'm not sure how to explain my theory to a kid that young."

"I don't know either. I do think that Mom'll be able to help. Once they finish the toxicology screenings and whatnot, Mom can look over the reports, and she can explain what really happened, that it was an accidental overdose, not a murder."

"That's my concern. How are we going to prove it wasn't murder to Juniper? It's not like we're going to find a videotape of Erika taking too many pills all on her own."

"Yeah, I know." I turned and leaned against the wall. "I want Layla to patch up her relationship with her daughter. It's not right for a little girl to be scared of her mother. At least not without good reason, and I really do think that's not the case with Layla."

"So what do we do?"

"How about you come over for dinner tomorrow night, and we'll discuss the situation further then? I think I can get her to open up a lot while I'm helping her unpack her valuables."

"Sounds good. I'll see you in the morning, then."

"And I'll figure out what outfit I want you to wear at dinner tomorrow. It'll be just the family and Mrs. Stutschewsky. So you don't have an excuse. I'll tell you at the end of the school day tomorrow once I decide."

"Yippee."

So after we kissed goodnight, I helped get the kids scrubbed up and put to bed, checked Toby's homework, and then spent two hours grading quizzes before speed-reading through four chapters of a book for research and then hammering out two moderately decent pages of my doctoral dissertation, and crawling into bed with just enough time for six hours of sleep.

* * *

The following day passed like most other school days. My classes seemed to like my lectures on pre-colonial Africa and the marriage of John and Abigail Adams. Chili was on the lunch menu, which is one of my favorites, especially when they the cafeteria staff makes their own corn chips. At the end of the day, I dismissed class five minutes early so I could beat the crowds, and at three-forty, I was back home in my room, changing out of my emerald velvet pantsuit with the black satin blouse and pulling on my midnight blue and turquoise workout suit and sneakers. I tied my hair back in a ponytail, helped Mom change the younger set of triplets' diapers, and headed out to keep my appointment.

By ten to four, I was standing on Layla's doorstep, ringing the bell. I had a bit of a wait, but finally, she opened the door. She was wearing the same sweats she'd worn the previous night, but I was pleased to see that the iced coffee stain was mostly gone, at least in dim light.

After an exchange of hellos, she led me into the kitchen. She was unpacking all of the good china out of the boxes and piling it up on the butcher block. My task was to rinse off everything in a big basin of soapy water and set it all on towels to dry. I tried to prime the pump, asking her about her late shift at the bar that evening, after she'd finished dinner.

"It was fine. A lot of drunks, a lot of beers poured. Nothing out of the ordinary."

I asked her about her coworkers, and she was noncommittal, informing me that she really knew very little about them, just their names. "We don't have much time to chat at work. After all, when the bar's full—and it usually is at lunchtime and from dinnertime onwards—you can't hear yourself think."

"And the bar closes at two A.M.?"

"Two-thirty on weekends. I finish up my share of the cleaning between three and three-thirty. Then I hurry home as fast as I can in the dark, jump into the shower until the bar smells are all washed down the drain, and by the time I get what's left of my hair dry, I'm so worn out I collapse into my bed, and I'm out until it's time to get up for the lunch shift."

"What's your clientele like?"

"About half college students, half assorted people from around the neighborhood. Older people, blowing off steam after work. They tip way better than the undergrads." I thought I caught a trace of resentment in her voice at the college students and figured it was connected to her own incomplete degree. "It's the average blue-collar bar. Not fancy, but we sell plenty of drinks, the customers are friendly and appreciative, and we don't have too many conflicts or bar fights."

"Glad to hear that."

"How about you? How was your work today?"

I discussed my classes and talked about my work with the Bialowsky Fund and my work helping teen mothers with their high school degrees and beyond. "It's personal for me, as you probably figured."

"Was the Fund around when you went to Cuthbertson?"

"Oh, no, no, no. It's very new. Just a couple of years now. I helped create it, along with my parents and my Great-Aunt Scholastica. No, when I started high school, not a lot of people thought that I had any place at Cuthbertson. Just Great-Aunt Scholastica and my future family."

"What was it like raising a daughter through high school?"

I hesitated. I wasn't sure that I wanted to discuss my personal life, but then I realized that if I wanted to get, I had to give. "Often overwhelming. Freshman year was the hardest. I was in a new city, I'd never had anything even close to the mountain of work Cuthbertson assigns and I was the only one keeping infant Toby alive. My birth mother wasn't much help."

"What happened to her?"

"She died." I wasn't ready to give too many details. "We didn't have the best relationship, but because I was just a kid, I didn't realize how much she was suffering."

"From what?"

"The kind of wounds that don't show. I spent most of my life resenting her for her inadequacies as a mother. Then, with everything I learned about her after she passed, I was surprised that she was able to function at all." I wanted to move away from this topic as quickly as I could, without being too blatant about my redirection. "Probably the best thing she ever did as a mother was to ask Dad to be my guardian in her will. She didn't ask for him to formally adopt me, but I did. Thank God he agreed. So it wasn't easy, but

I made it through, thanks to my new family."

I rinsed off the sugar bowl, the last item of Celeste's good china to be washed, and set it off to the side. "All right! One job done. What's next?"

Layla stared at me for a bit, looking like she wanted to ask me for more information, but she didn't feel comfortable pressing. "Do you have any experience setting up a TV?"

"Absolutely."

We headed into the living room, removed a medium-sized flat-screen from a football field's worth of bubble wrap, and set it on a shelf. I pushed a tattered ottoman over and started untangling a Gordian Knot of wires while Layla pulled out a VCR and a DVD player. "Last time it took me two hours to get this working properly. So many plugs, it's hard to tell what's what."

It took me six minutes to untangle the cords. Plugging the cords into their proper places only took me three. After I successfully tested them out with a VHS of *Casablanca* from 1992 and a DVD of *What a Girl Wants*, Layla was shaking her head at me. "How did you do that so fast?"

"You get a lot of practice working with the AV equipment at Cuthbertson."

"Do you still use VCRs there?"

"Yes, we do. We pride ourselves on integrating the latest technology into our education, but we still have an extensive library of documentaries that are only available on VHS. Laserdisc, too. I just used one of those last week to give my class an overview of Ben Franklin's inventions."

"Wow." Layla flopped on the couch, causing a squeak on the plastic covering that made me break out in goosebumps. "I'm impressed, Kaiming."

"Thanks." I took a seat next to her, and we opened a pair of boxes of DVDs.

"Those will go in that cabinet over there," she pointed. "Above the videotapes."

"What's the order?"

"What do you mean?"

"Do you arrange them by genre, or are they just in alphabetical order?"

"I... used to just line them up in the order I bought them. Every time I bought a new one, I'd stick it at the end of the line. That order's all gone now."

"How did you find anything?"

"I used to always want to watch a movie without actually knowing what I wanted to see, so I'd just run my eyes along the spines of the cases until something struck my fancy. Usually, I'd just spin around, point, and watch something randomly."

I knew she was indecisive, I thought to myself, but didn't say. "Alphabetical it is, then." I started stacking the DVDs along the coffee table, sorting them.

"I should have known. Who else arranges her leather jacket collection by color? Come to think of it, I don't know anybody else who has a leather jacket collection."

"Well, postage stamps never really set my heart on fire." There were about sixty DVDs in the box. It took me less than two minutes to sort them from A to Y, and we filed them in the cabinet. "What's next?"

"How do you feel about cleaning the tarnish off silver? Everything turned nearly black in the storage unit."

"Sounds great." We picked up a large cardboard box each and carried them into the kitchen. Layla emptied out huge handfuls of silverware onto the butcher block, and I took out a six-piece silver tea set, four platters, and six candlesticks. Upon examination, they appeared to be silver plated rather than solid silver and not the best quality. Maybe worth about five hundred bucks for everything.

"We have a bottle of silver polish in the cupboard. It smells like it could mutate you and give you superpowers, so wear gloves."

"I know how to make an organic silver polish. All I need is a basin of water, some salt, and some aluminum foil. It's a chemical reaction. And a little dish soap, too, to take away the rest of the tarnish." I prepared the recipe, pulled on a pair of rubber gloves that didn't match my outfit at all, and started right on the silverware. "I can get the bulk of the stains off, but you can rub them with a cloth with a little dish soap on it to clean everything I miss."

The silverware was decorated with lots of little filigrees and patterns, all obscured by a covering of black crust. I was able to get the lion's share off with a little bit of scrubbing, and I figured that Layla could handle the last little bits.

"So," Layla said midway through the second fork. "What have you got planned for tonight?"

"When I'm done here, I have dinner with my family and Funderburke, and then I'm going to work on a presentation I have to give to the juniors and seniors tomorrow. "Ten Things High School Should Warn You About College."

"What?"

I repeated the title of my lecture, a little slower this time. "We spend four years training our students to get into their dream college. But once they get there, they're adrift. About a third of them transfer somewhere else, and some of them even drop out."

"Been there."

"And I realized a while back, we need to get to do more than just show them how to convince an admissions officer to give them the thumbs up. We need to prepare them to thrive in college. So, I'm working on a little speech, and I'm hoping that some of them will take it to heart. Hope springs eternal."

Layla looked far more interested than I thought she'd be to hear about my little presentation, and I said as much. "I can think of a lot of lessons I wish I'd learned before going off to college. You know that I got a partial scholarship?"

"Your grandmother mentioned that at last night's dinner, yes."

"Well, it wasn't quite as great a deal as I thought at the time. I was a triathlete in high school. Volleyball, basketball, soccer."

I couldn't help but laugh a little bit. "Two out of three."

"Huh?'

"I also played basketball in the winters and soccer in the spring, starting sophomore year.. I still coach soccer. But I ran cross-country in the fall."

Layla put down a spoon and leaned against the kitchen wall. "I used to love playing sports."

She was starting to talk about her past, and I realized it was a very delicate situation. If I pressed too hard, she'd clam up and kick me out of the house. So I had to coax, and a little lightning-fast emotional calculus told me that the best course of action was to continue with setting up a culture of reciprocity. I didn't want to get into anything too personal, so I chose my words carefully. "I love the rush of competition. After a big win on the basketball court or the soccer field, I'd be smiling the rest of the night."

After Layla recounted the results of some of her greatest last-second athletic triumphs, she turned to me. "I thought going to a prestigious college out east would set me up on the fast track to success the rest of my life. I didn't know that I'd be shooting myself in the foot."

"How so?"

"Like I said, that partial scholarship wasn't really the gift I thought it was. More of a poisoned chalice, really."

"Just how "partial" was it?"

"At the time I got it, I thought it was for half of the tuition. I didn't realize at the time, but it was only for the cost of classes. It didn't cover books, or the dorm fees, or the meal plan, and it certainly didn't cover the price of travel from Milwaukee to the East Coast. Even so, I figured that student loans would make up the rest, and once I graduated, I could pay off the debt in two, maybe three years. Then they jacked up the tuition forty percent the next year, but they told me that if the basketball and soccer teams did well, they could raise my scholarship. They never flat-out promised anything, but there was a strong implication that they really wanted me there, and I thought that the increase was just a formality." Her voice trailed off, and then she pulled a dishtowel off the oven and then dabbed at her eyes. "I was wrong. Not only did I not get the additional money, but they raised the tuition even more my junior year. So by Christmas…" She slumped against the wall again. I scrubbed at a butter knife, hoping that she'd continue, but instead, she changed the direction of the conversation. "What are you saying in your presentation? What's the first thing high school should warn you about college?

I realized Layla had lost interest in removing the tarnish from the silver, so I kept working on the butter knife myself. "Warning number one. You have to take care of yourself."

"Everybody knows that."

"In theory. In practice, it is different. Most teens have never taken care of themselves when they get sick. They can't count on their roommates to bring them a bowl of soup or buy them a bottle of cough syrup. Tons of them have no clue how to draw up a budget, either for money or time. Laundry, cleaning their rooms, even scheduling…" I was about to say "haircuts," but a quick mental red flag told me that word might rub Layla the wrong way, so with only a microsecond's delay, I changed my words to "dental appointments." I don't think she caught the alteration.

She nodded. "That's true. It's a big jump going from having your parents—or in my case, my grandparents—managing most of the major aspects of your life, and then—bang! You're on your own and can go to bed when you feel like sleeping and eat whatever you want at the cafeteria. Of course, Grandma was calling three times a day with advice and suspicious questions, but the point is the same. Looking back, for every good decision I made in college, I think I made one decision of dubious quality and one definitely harmful decision. Not a good average. My first week there, my worst decision was a sophomore named Laurent. How about you? Where did you go to college?"

"Lawrence University in Appleton. That's an hour forty-five minutes north of Milwaukee, in case you've never been there."

"I haven't."

"Well…I'm not trying to sound self-righteous and prissy—"

"Try harder."

I flinched a bit, but then she smiled and flicked her hand at me to show me that she was joking. She felt comfortable teasing me. I decided to take that as a positive sign. "Heh. I actually didn't have that much trouble starting out on my own. I mostly raised myself from about the age of six onwards. My birth mother wasn't much of one for cleaning or cooking, so once I was old enough, I took care of what I could."

"What did she do for a living?"

"She was a model. Not high-end fashion, but she got a lot of photographic work, a bunch of commercials, and a few clothing shows for department stores. No major designers. The menu at home was never great unless I made my own meals, or if I was able to make friends who invited me over for dinner. And that wasn't easy because we moved around so much—Chicago, Austin, New York City, Boston, Atlanta, San Francisco, Portland—the one in Oregon, Miami, then L.A., before we finally wound up in Milwaukee."

"Wow. But don't think you can avoid my question. What's your worst decision from college?"

I thought for a minute. "Well... that would be going out to dinner at a dive bar with a bunch of friends and then ordering a salad. The lettuce must have been covered with salmonella, because I was sick for a week and a half. No one who ordered their meal from the deep fryer took ill."

Jabbing me in the arm with the spoon handle, Layla scoffed. "Food poisoning is not a bad decision. I'm talking about hooking up with your roommate's boyfriend or passing out drunk in the snow, or getting a piercing or tattoo you instantly regretted. Two of those happened to me. I'm not telling you which ones."

"You already mentioned Laurent."

"Damn. I did. But he wasn't dating my roommate. So stop avoiding the question. What was your worst decision in high school?"

I considered making something up, but for reasons I can't explain, I decided to be honest. "I wouldn't call it a *bad* decision. Definitely a questionable one."

"And it was..."

"Posing naked."

"What?"

"Not for a dirty magazine or anything like that," I explained with undignified haste. "I was looking for a job, and as it turns out, the art department hired students for some nude modeling. Well, it paid better than scrubbing plates in the cafeteria kitchens, and the library wasn't hiring, and the hours fit my schedule...so..." I trailed off as Layla bent double and chortled until I thought she was going to dislocate her jaw. Once she quieted down, I defended myself. Feeling a burning sensation in my face, I said, "It was only for one term. And the classes I posed for were mostly girls, and I'm pretty sure most of the guys there weren't wired to take any interest in people with my attributes. It was art, not stripping."

A coy smile flashed across Layla's lips. "What do you consider the difference between the two?"

"Art is way less profitable." We were spending way more time on me than I wanted, but at least I felt like I had cracked her shell. "Can I get back to my "Ten Things" lecture?"

"For now. But we're coming back to this. Bet on that."

"Fine. Warning number two. Your metabolism changes. When you're a teenager, puberty does some messed up stuff to you, including filling your face with acne at the most inopportune time and pumping you full of hormones that play merry hell with your emotions. But there's one great benefit that lots—not all, but many—of teens enjoy, and that's a super-fast metabolism. These are the best eating years of your life. You can put an Old Country Buffet out of business and not gain an ounce. But once your growth spurts end—and for a lot of students, that's more or less the time you head off to college, give or take a year—the amazing calorie-burning machine in your stomach conks out, but your appetite's as ravenous as ever. So unless you're careful and adjust accordingly, the Freshmen Fifteen are all too real." I didn't say that I, personally, I'd managed to avoid any college weight gain, and I was wise to keep mum on that point.

Layla placed a hand on her belly. "I've been there. Even when I was playing sports, it didn't make up for all of the cafeteria fries. I was able to snap back into shape over sophomore year, though I had to start being more careful with my meals. After I had Juniper, though... That explains the first thirty-five pounds, the rest..." She turned to me. "How about you? Was it hard dropping the baby weight after having your daughter?"

"No." I shouldn't have been so blunt about it. I could feel her liking me less already. "And I didn't go back to the proportions I was before getting in the family way. I was so young. I was still growing. I had her in May, and by Labor Day, I was two and a quarter inches taller than I was a year earlier."

"But you didn't have to work very hard to get skinny again?"

Layla's asperity wasn't intense, but it was palpable. I tried to keep my defensiveness to a minimum, "I told you, growth spurt. I was changing diapers hourly, feeding frequently, cleaning an apartment, and trying to

34

keep my food-averse birth mother from wasting away, too. Plus, once I came to Milwaukee, my educational background was way below where it needed to be to be a Cuthbertson freshman. So when I wasn't busy keeping my daughter and mother alive, I was cramming my head full of algebra, global history, French, biology, and classic works of literature."

By the end of my little defense of myself, the irritation had slipped out significantly in my tone, posture, and eyes. At least Layla's expression had softened. She appeared to spend a few moments considering her reply before saying, "That's fair. Truce?"

"Truce."

"How did you manage to cram all of that self-taught summer school in three months?"

"It wasn't self-taught. The man who would become my Dad designed a condensed version of sixth, seventh, and eighth grades for me. The school I attended for those three years was good for nothing."

"I see. What's your daughter's name again?"

"Toby."

"How'd you decide on that?"

"She's named in honor of her paternal grandfather, who passed away while I was carrying her. He was a very kind man. His name was Tobe Komesuma. I Anglicized and feminized it. It seemed like a fitting tribute to a man who made sure I had plenty of food and supplies in the apartment when my birth mother forgot to leave me money for expenses."

It looked like Layla was struggling to keep herself from asking me more personal questions, so she just nodded. "What's the next warning?"

"Number three. You can't believe everything you learn. Now, I had a really good background in various courses at Cuthbertson. But the average student comes in as a total tabula rasa—no knowledge of anything, so if a professor is particularly dogmatic over history or politics or any moral issue…it's easy for a lot of young people to swallow a bucket of manure and accept it when they're told that it's chocolate pudding. This isn't just for college. Middle and high school, too. I know it sounds disloyal to my profession, but in general, I'm skeptical of educators. Don't get me wrong. I'm not saying I came into a classroom thinking I was smarter than the teacher, but in fourth grade, I had a teacher who insisted that the capital of New York was New York City, and when I showed the class an atlas that said it was Albany, she snapped at me and kept me in from recess for a week."

"Seriously?"

"Yep. I Googled her name a few years ago when I was reminiscing about people who have done me wrong in the past, and now she's an assistant principal. I thought about emailing some random students at her current school to see what they thought of her as an administrator, but I'm not sure if any of them can read or write. Thankfully, my education from the age of fourteen onwards has been amazing. The teachers at Cuthbertson are great, and I've had mostly positive experiences in college and graduate school, but… before I came to Milwaukee, I only liked twenty-five percent of all the teachers I ever had and respected only five percent of them. And most of the girls I mentor have had pretty crummy educational experiences, too. Just like you don't want an incompetent doctor holding a scalpel over you, it's not a joyous experience to have a misinformed, lackadaisical, or indoctrinating teacher in the classroom."

After a little laugh, Layla told me, "In both high school and college, the lion's share of my teachers and professors had an uncanny power to make you hate learning. I think there was a poll a few years back that revealed that about a quarter of Americans did not read or listen to a book over the past year. I'm deeply ashamed to say I'm one of them."

I should have tried harder to hide my shock and disapproval. "Really?"

"Frankly, I blame my instructors for making reading such a trial for their classes. Except for children's books. I read to Juniper. But I used to love reading. In high school, I'd pick out a novel at the library every week and finish it cover to cover. I don't know why I stopped. I just ran out of time."

"What kind of books do you enjoy?"

"I like novels about women who do impressive things, especially when they're told they shouldn't. I also enjoy biographies about women like that. How about you?"

"Well, as you saw in my room, I read a lot of history, and mysteries as well, but mostly Golden Age ones—I don't like violence. Agatha Christie and Dorothy L. Sayers. In other genres, I like the Inklings, Flannery O'Connor, Alice Thomas Ellis, Sigrid Undset..." I was deliberately focusing on the female authors in an attempt to appeal to Layla's sensibilities, leaving out some of my favorite male writers. "Have you read any of them?"

"No, I haven't. And unless something changes, I'm not going to get back in the habit anytime soon."

"I should get you a copy of Flannery O'Connor's collected short stories. Start small, and go on from there."

She shot me a wry little smile, as if she'd caught me trying to pull a fast one on her. "Are you trying to assign me homework?"

"No! Not exactly..."

She chuckled. "Going back to your third warning, the most respected professor at the college I went to was busted two years after I left for faking data in a science experiment."

"Yeah, the reproducibility crisis in academia is real. As for me, one of the best lessons I ever learned was by the man who would become my great-grandfather. The first week of class, he gave us a lecture on the history of the world, and he told us all to take notes and pay attention. Then he gave us a quiz on the lecture and handed it back to us the next day. We all got zeroes. Well, the class was about to raise holy hell, and he told us that every point he quizzed us on that he covered in his lecture was either a flat-out lie or a long-ago debunked myth made up by third-rate scholars. He pointed out the impossibilities of some of the points he raised, such as how the whole Great Wall of China couldn't possibly have been built in nine and a half years, like he'd said—but to think about how using an uneven number like "nine and a half" instead of "ten" somehow made it more convincing. Then he told us that the quiz wasn't going to count, unless we really ticked him off this term, and then he handed out donuts, so that quashed the potential uprising pretty effectively. But the lesson has stayed with me. I may not remember the capital of Gabon—" This isn't true. I knew that it was Libreville. I just said it as an example. I don't know why. "—but I will always remember to never swallow what a so-called educator tells you whole without thinking critically. Like when one lecturer at a conference I went to last month told us that more people die from gun violence in America every five years than were killed total in pre-Renaissance European wars, if you don't count the Battle of Hastings. This was total garbage, and I called her out on it, and I brought up the data on my phone to prove it. See, this woman just pulled that statistic out of her personal orifice, but all the other so-called professional historians in that lecture hall—admittedly, it wasn't very crowded—were nodding along with her. And then they glared at me as if I'd committed some horrific breach of etiquette by challenging her. The fraud tried to get me kicked out of the conference, but I managed to stick around. And she actually got tenure last year!" I shook my head. "But that just goes to show how it's easy to fool people with a lie. The audience believed that American gun violence deaths must be astronomically high, far worse than centuries-old warfare casualties. And none of them knew any of the actual statistics, so they bought into what she said hook, line, and sinker. That baloney line "if you leave out the Battle of Hastings" is just a cheap feint that somehow makes these ludicrous claims seem more convincing. I don't really understand why, but for whatever reason, it does."

"You know why those other audience members got mad at *you* and not her?" Layla asked. "Because they realized that they'd been fooled, and you hadn't. You just showed that you were smarter than they were, and they had no intention of forgiving you for that."

I laughed. "I bet you're right. I'm sure you're right. I'm just lucky that even though I'm getting my Ph.D., I have a job at Cuthbertson, and I want to stay there forever. If I tried to apply for a position at a university where any of those audience members were on the search committees, they'd toss my application into the garbage can with so much force it would dent the ground underneath the bin. And that leads into my fourth warning—a lot of career advice you get is terrible."

"Really?"

"Yes. Based on the experiences of friends all over the country, everybody has thoughts on what you need to do in order to be successful in later life, and even though a lot of it is common sense, a ton of it is hogwash. There's this scene in the movie *The Graduate*—have you seen that?"

"No."

"Well, in that scene, some random friend of Dustin Hoffman's parents tells him to go into "plastics." Turns out, everybody's got their own version of plastics advice. Go into this field. Don't do that. There's no money in it. I know no fewer than eight friends from college who studied in a field that bored them sick because they were told when they got their degree, they'd have their pick of great jobs. Well, they graduated, and some of them even got master's degrees in the fields their loved ones told them to pursue, and now all of those eight friends are either working in the service industry because they couldn't find a job in that field, or they're working just a bit above minimum wage in a profession they hate. People are always trying to steer you into a "hot" field, but once you've earned your credentials, the field has cooled down, and there are already thousands of young people just as qualified as you trying to break into the business. When I told people I wanted to teach high school, at least six different people told me I was too smart to be a mere teacher and that I'd be wasting my abilities. And only the accepted rules of social decorum kept me from pointing out that I'd seen their lives, and quite frankly, based on their experience, they had no right telling me how to live mine."

"You want to know the worst advice I ever got?" Layla said. "In college, my advisor told me not to worry about deciding on a career path or even a major until midway through junior year, when I absolutely had to make a choice. So I took all sorts of classes, sometimes just to have one with some of my friends, and by the time the deadline for declaring a major rolled around, I was already getting kicked out, and I didn't have enough courses in any discipline to make any employer think I had enough background to be competent in any field."

"Kicked out?"

"My...grade point average was too low." She tugged at her ear as she spoke, and though I knew it wasn't the whole story, I knew that the time wasn't right to ask follow-up questions. "What's the next one?" she asked in a blatant attempt to change the subject.

"Next, warning number five. You're separated from your family. Now, I realize that's not a downside for everybody. A lot of young people come from pretty dysfunctional backgrounds, and they're a lot happier once they go off on their own. But that's not the case for a lot of teens. I know there's a lot to be said for independence and learning how to live on our own, but the fact is, sometimes this is the start of fissures in families that never truly heal."

Layla started toying with the hem of her shirt, and I waited for her to say what was on her mind. I think after a little while, the impatience started to show in my face because she gave a little start before saying, "I just... wonder what would've happened if I'd stayed in Milwaukee for college."

"What do you mean?"

"Erika first developed her...*problem* when she was sixteen. From what she told us later, it started not long after I went off to college. If I'd stuck around, gone to UWM, lived at home, kept an eye on her...maybe she wouldn't have..."

Sympathetically, I told her, "You can drive yourself nuts with 'what ifs.'"

"Maybe. But Grandpa and Grandma were working... who knows what she was up to when no one else was around."

"Did she see your mom and dad often?"

"Dad probably came over for dinner a few times a week. When he was sober. He showed up about that often when I was in high school and when I came home for the holidays."

"Does he come by frequently now?"

"No. I told you...he only came to dinner when he was sober."

"Oh." After a moment's pause, I asked, "And your mother?"

"She saw us every now and then, but her job working in promotions had her travelling all over the world. Sometimes we wouldn't see her for months while she was developing projects in London and Paris and Berlin. And when she was in town for a few days... things were pretty tense at family dinners. She and Grandma did *not* get along. And after she decided Erika would be better off living with us, she barely came to Milwaukee at all." Just as I was about to press for more details, she turned the conversation back

40

around to me. "How about you? What was it like being separated from your family?"

I groaned. "If I hadn't been adopted, then I would probably have gone off to college and never gone home, not even for the summer if I could help it. Actually, the Fox Valley's an oven in the summer, and the dorms didn't have air conditioning, but you get the idea."

"So, you're okay with living with your parents? And little siblings? And all those other relatives?"

I nodded, projecting enough force to make it unequivocally clear that I meant what I said. "Definitely. I was cheated out of a proper family for the first fourteen years of my life, and now I want to make up for it with interest. Frankly, I have zero interest in having my own apartment with Toby, and Mom and Dad make it clear I'm welcome as long as I want. I love being surrounded by family, and for some reason, they seem to like me, so we're all happy."

"That's nice to hear."

"Do you and your grandmother get along well?"

A very slow, deep, exhale from Layla followed. "We used to." I must have touched a nerve, because she asked, "What's the sixth one?"

"College is full of cults."

"What?"

"I'm not saying every college campus is a Jonestown. I'm just saying that a lot of people are trying to mold minds and hearts in unhealthy ways. Have you ever read Saul Bellow's *Ravelstein*?"

"I'm pretty sure I told you about my reading habits."

"Right. Well, the title character of the book is a charismatic college professor who recruits students into his cult of personality. By the time he's done with them, he's estranged them from their families, molded them to think just like him, dress like him, and smoke the same cigarettes that he does. And after decades of teaching, he's managed to create a whole herd of clones of himself, only none of them have his intellectual acumen. Well, there are lots of wannabe Ravelsteins in college, trying to reshape students into their own preferred image. And there are all sorts of groups, whether it's activist causes, religious (or antireligious) groups, or political organizations…. When you're separated from your family, consciously or unconsciously, you wind up looking for another community to belong to, and it's often unhealthy."

"Did something like that happen to you?"

"No, but I know four high school colleagues who had to be deprogrammed in various ways. You?"

"No. Wait a minute, I'm wrong. Maybe the sports teams I played on. The coaches were always shouting, "You're a team! You have to support each other on everything!" If you had time, and one of your teammates hadn't written her term paper, you were expected to help her finish it so she could pass. That was how—"

"What?"

Layla broke down into a fit of fake coughs. I wanted to call her out on them—I have students trying to fake sick to get out of tests who are better at mimicking illness than Layla, but I stayed silent as she poured herself a glass of water and said, "Excuse me. Keep going."

"Warning seven. There are many opportunities for failure. You have to make a lot of decisions, and lots of young people are not ready for the consequences. You can hurt yourself financially, academically, emotionally, or professionally in so many ways—one unwise decision can have wide-ranging consequences."

"Like when I decided I wanted to go to a big party on the night before a big exam. I had a great time at the party, but I barely passed the test."

"Exactly."

"Did you ever prioritize partying over studying?"

I considered lying, as I figured it would make me more relatable to her. But I decided against fibbing if I could help it. "No."

She nodded. "You're a real goody-two-shoes, aren't you?"

I rarely get called that because of Toby. "It's not just being straitlaced. It's what I call pure bloody-mindedness. In the eyes of the world, I screwed up big time when I was thirteen. For whatever reason, a lot of people have been rooting for me to fail. And I refuse to give them that satisfaction. So for the second half of my life, I've been extra determined to never make a single mistake anybody could throw in my face."

"Have you succeeded?"

"Pretty much. Of course, that hasn't stopped gossipers from making up allegations out of whole cloth." A lot of people—especially mothers of Cuthbertson students—seem to be under the impression that I'm hyper-promiscuous. They couldn't be more wrong, but sometimes all confronting rumors does is make the situation worse.

Maybe I was making a face, but Layla shifted the topic again. "So, I'm not clear on this. Did Toby go to college with you?"

"No. I didn't think a dormitory was a safe environment for a small child, and anyway, she'd already finished nursery school at Cuthbertson, and she'd made a lot of friends, so after talking with my parents, we decided Toby'd stay in Milwaukee, and they'd look after her. But I came home every weekend except for a few when I had to attend conferences and the like, and a few terms, I even scheduled all my classes for Tuesdays and Thursdays, so I'd drive up to Appleton on Monday night, drive back home after my last class Tuesday afternoon, spend the next day with my family, drive back up Wednesday night, return Thursday evening, and repeat the process four days later. So I'd see Toby and the rest of my family every day then. I'd do something similar when I could fit all my courses on Monday, Wednesday, and Friday."

"It's nice that you're so close with your family." Layla sounded wistful.

"How would you describe your relationship with yours?" I asked, hoping that I hadn't gotten too personal.

"Grandpa and I totally understood each other. It hasn't been the same since he passed away. And my parents... Well, Dad has his own addiction that takes up most of his time, and Mom was so broken by her relationship with Dad that she's focused on her career ever since. Don't get me wrong, I love them both, but... I'm mad at Dad, and it's hard to make a connection with Mom."

"I see."

"So what's warning eight?"

"Higher education is a business. Yeah, you're there to learn and get the degree, but it's easy for expenses to pop up unexpectedly. That's why Cuthbertson's setting up classes to teach budgeting issues. I tell students, "You're not paying to party.""

Layla twisted her foot shamefacedly. "Guilty."

"Every time a student has to stick around for an extra term because that person couldn't take all the mandatory classes for a major within four years, the university makes tens of thousands of dollars. It's not a bug. It's a business plan. I'm just glad I had so many Advanced Placement credits. After I started taking an extra class every term, I was done in just ten trimesters. Two and a third years."

"Really?"

"Yep. I was back with my family and working on an independent honors project by Christmas of what was technically my junior year, and I came back for June Commencement."

"So you were in college about the same amount of time that I was. Only you got your degree because you were focused and had a plan. And I... didn't. And I'll be paying for it for at least seven more years, and I won't even have a diploma to show for it."

"That's all student loans?"

"Mostly. But there are also some Erika-related expenses. Don't you think that if a round of rehab doesn't take, they should refund your money, or at least part of it?"

"That does sound fair to me."

"Maybe I should consider the addiction treatment process a business as well. If they cure your loved one properly, they only send you one bill. But if the patient keeps relapsing, you come back again and again. Three stints, that's how many times Erika went to rehab." She twisted her polishing cloth in frustration. "What's the next one?"

"Warning number nine. Relationships can turn toxic fast. When you're off at college, with no family support system, students have a habit of attaching to a significant other who simply isn't good for you. High school romances are expected to fade out, but college romances are in some ways more dangerous because they have the potential to last way longer than they should. The judgment-warping hormones don't vanish on your eighteenth birthday."

"Hendrix."

"Was that one of your boyfriends?"

Layla nodded. "My only serious, long-term college relationship. It was great for three months. Then I thought it was fantastic for another two, but looking back, I can see all of the mold and rot set in with each passing week."

"What was Hendrix like?"

"Great smile. Five foot ten, but he told everybody he was six feet, which should have been a warning signal."

"Yeah, a man who lies about something that easy to check is a walking red flag."

"Did you ever go out with a guy like that?"

"In college, several, but never for more than one date. I dated a lot of guys casually, but I never had a serious relationship until I started grad school. I came close to making a terrible decision with the guy I dated before Funderburke, but thankfully, I decided to turn down his proposal. At the time, a lot of my friends told me I was crazy because, on paper, this guy was everything you're supposed to be looking for in a spouse. Looks, money, incredible career prospects. But there was always something missing with him. He always said the right things, but he never really meant them. He was outwardly charming to my family, but he didn't really like them. He was all glitter and no gold. So I turned him down, and he made another young woman of my acquaintance very happy for about six months before he broke her heart."

"So he was a bad guy."

"Mmm... not so much a villain as shallow and ersatz. He knew what he wanted and how he was supposed to behave to get it. Sincerity was not one of his strong points."

"So now you're with Funderburke."

"Yep. He's a guy who says what he means and means what he says."

"Huh."

I didn't like her tone. "What?"

"Nothing. It's just that, well…"

"Spit it out."

"Funderburke's not the kind of guy I'd like to date."

"Why not?"

"It's just… his looks and personality."

Now I was getting annoyed. Throwing the remaining silverware back in the basin, I asked, "Meaning?"

"Well, he's not what I'd call a hot guy."

"*I* think he's handsome. And he's in really good shape."

Layla was getting flustered. "He's just so… *intense*. That's what I mean. His expression all the time, that's what I mean by his personality. He just seems brooding and… I don't think 'obsessive' is the right word…"

"He's dedicated to his work and what he believes in. That's what matters to me."

"Private eyes don't make much."

"Cuthbertson takes care of its employees. He does all right."

"I saw his car. It must be older than I am."

This was true. "He keeps that Volvo for sentimental reasons. He holds onto everything he cares about, especially me."

"Yeah, that's obvious."

"How so?"

"I saw the way he looks at you. I wouldn't want to date him, but I want a guy who looks at me like that."

I wasn't quite sure how to respond to that, but I deeply appreciate the little glances and smiles that Funderburke gives me. I always consider them private moments, so I was a bit unsettled by the fact that other people noticed them. An electric shock went off in my belly when a couple of unsettling questions raced through my mind. *Do my students notice how Funderburke looks at me? And if so, what are they saying about us?*

"And number ten?" Layla interrupted my thoughts.

"It's possible to grow up wrong."

"What?"

"As you think you're developing and maturing, it's really easy to turn into a person you don't like and don't respect. That's happened to a lot of my peers. Did you ever read *The Chronicles of Narnia*? Specifically *The Last Battle*?" I was expecting another "no," but instead, she nodded and smiled.

"I read each of them at least ten times as a kid."

"Then I don't have to worry about spoilers. In the final book, there's a question that a lot of writers have responded to over the decades—the problem of Susan. How does a kind, brave, responsible girl turn into a flighty, shallow woman? She wasn't fated to turn out that way. In the one timeline, she grew up to be a just and distinguished queen. But back in the 'real' world, she got wrapped up in parties and silly stuff and began to see the best years of her life as a child's daydream. And that's what happens to a lot of people. They lose interest in the important stuff and get wrapped up in empty pleasures, and the years pass, and suddenly there's a hollow lump of froth where a really deep and interesting person used to be, and you start to wonder: how did the person I liked become this person who I don't respect?"

We were on the last spoon. Layla polished away the last of the tarnish and set it down with tears in her eyes. "It's true. I ask myself that question every day in the mirror. How did that bright, energetic, promising girl become this—" she pointed at herself—"blob of dough?"

"Don't talk about yourself like that."

"It's true. Physically, mentally, spiritually, morally… I'm nothing compared to what I used to be."

"I still say you should never—"

"Look, just forget I said that." She wiped her eyes with the back of her hand. "Let's put a few more knickknacks on the shelves and put away the boxes."

It didn't take long to redecorate the house, from a side parlor to Layla's bedroom, and the boxes were emptied in just over an hour. We carried them down to a small, dark room in the back of the basement. I nearly jumped out of my skin at the sound of the steps beneath my feet.

A few minutes later, as we walked back up, stairs creaking and wailing as we climbed, Layla suddenly said, "I just thought of an eleventh warning you should include."

"Oh?" I asked, emerging from the basement door and holding it open for her. "What's that?"

"It's a lot harder to make friends after you graduate."

Nodding, I said, "So true. In school, you see people every day, you get to know them in discussions, but when you're out of the classroom, you have to make a special effort to get to know people, except at work or grad school. About the only other place where I meet new people is church."

"Yeah. The other people at the bar are mostly okay, but I just don't connect with any of them." She smiled at me. "This is the first real, personal conversation I've had with someone around my own age in years, I think. I've been disconnected from all of my old friends. I don't want them to see what I'm like now."

Before I could reply, I heard a key in the lock, and Celeste walked inside. "Oh! Hello. Layla said you might stop by to help her unpack. Do you have much more to do tonight?"

"No," Layla answered. "In fact, we just finished. Nerissa was great. We took care of everything, and it's been less than two hours."

"Well, that's wonderful. Are you joining us for dinner? I just have an hour, and then I'll head back to the bookstore for another couple of hours to wrap up the night."

I shook my head. "Thanks, but I have to head back. I already have plans to eat with Funderburke and my family."

"Well, you'll all have to come over sometime so we can pay back your kindness from last night. We can have guests again now that I have my silverware and china back."

After chatting for another minute, I grabbed my purse from the table, said my goodbyes, and left. Halfway to my car, I realized that I'd left my wristwatch in the kitchen, having taken it off while I was cleaning the silver. I doubled back, but once I was inside the house, I heard the two of them talking in the hall.

"Did she ask you a lot of questions?"

"She wasn't interrogating me, Grandma. We just had a conversation."

"Good. You don't want to have a slip of the tongue and tell her exactly what you did to your sister."

"Grandma, I swear I didn't—"

"Don't lie to me. I'm going to take a twenty-minute nap and then make myself an omelet. I suppose you'll be eating at the bar again."

I heard Celeste heading upstairs. I grabbed my wristwatch as silently as I could and hurried outside again without being seen.

Chapter Three—I Hear What They Whisper About Me Behind My Back

Before I overheard that little snippet of Celeste's words to her granddaughter, I was almost certain that Layla hadn't done anything to harm her sister. Of course, I was waiting for Funderburke to wrap up his investigation, but I was sure he wasn't going to find proof of murder. The first time I left the Dolak house, I was ninety percent sure that Erika's death was nothing more than a tragic overdose. Then I heard Celeste's comment.

You don't want to have a slip of the tongue and tell her exactly what you did to your sister.

What did Layla do to Erika, and how did Celeste know about it? If Layla really was a killer, why hadn't Celeste gone to the police? Celeste struck me as the sort of woman who would never let anything stand in the way of her principles, though I supposed that she might make an exception for her only surviving granddaughter. But if Layla was a cold-blooded murderess, wouldn't Celeste be worried that she might be next? I didn't see any fear in Celeste's eyes. If anything, it was the granddaughter who was intimidated by the grandmother. And unless Celeste had sent some incriminating evidence to her lawyer, along with a note telling the attorney to turn it over to the police if she died or disappeared, I didn't see any reason how this family situation made any logical, psychological sense.

So, just what exactly was going on in that house? I thought about nothing else throughout the drive back home. Thankfully, it was a short distance, and with my mind on the case, I nearly hit a particularly slow-moving squirrel. Fortunately, I managed to swerve just in time, and as I glanced in my rearview mirror and saw he was unharmed, I could have sworn that the little furball stuck his nose up in the air and sneered at me as if I was beneath contempt.

As soon as I got home, Amara and Eleanor, who were lying on the floor drawing pictures of dragons, jumped up and both wrapped their arms around one of my legs, squeezing me so tightly that if I hadn't known, they were simply trying to give me an affectionate hug, I'd strongly suspect they were trying to shatter my bones and put me in a wheelchair.

"Hey, girls. How was your day?"

They both responded with a long list of pleasant events. "How about you? What were you doing the last couple of hours?" Amara asked.

"I was helping a...friend unpack some boxes."

"Are you talking about the lady who had dinner with us last night?"

"That's right. What do you think about her?"

"I'm not sure," Eleanor said. "She used to have a sister, right? Is she dead or in jail or something?"

You can't hide very much from my siblings. "Yes. Her sister passed away recently. How did you know?"

"Amara and I were playing, and she walked up to us and said, 'It's nice to see you two getting along so well. Sisters should be friends. They should be able to trust each other.'" Eleanor shrugged. "That was kind of weird. She looked kind of sad, and I wondered if she hadn't had a very good relationship with her sister, and it was too late to fix it now."

"Huh." My first thought was that it was lucky that Layla had stopped by on one of the evenings when the girls were pretty chummy. About half the time, their interactions can politely be described as "combustible," and I'm pretty sure there are microscopic cracks in all the windows from all of the high-pitched screaming between them. "That was very insightful of you, Eleanor. Good job."

Once I'd extricated myself from the clutching that could make a boa constrictor look weak, I followed my nose to the kitchen.

"Hey, Dad. Jambalaya tonight?"

"Mm-hmm." He gave the pot another stir. "It should be ready in another half-hour or so."

"Where's Mom?"

"Down the basement in her lab. She's running some sort of test to see if a prosecution's theory of how blood spatter could get on the inside of a cardigan sweater is feasible. I didn't get all the details. Amara and Eleanor were arguing over what Eleanor considered was an excessive use of the magenta crayon, and it took me a little bit of time to calm them down."

"They seem to be getting along much better now."

"Well, we'll see if that lasts until bedtime." Those unfamiliar with certain aspects of our family dynamic might have thought that Dad was being uncharitable towards his daughters, but I can assure anybody with such opinions that Dad was simply being realistic based on long, often eardrum-shattering experience.

I looked around the kitchen. "Is everybody else doing their own thing?"

"As far as I know."

"Bernard? Are you there?" I love that kid, but he has a habit of hiding behind or under furniture with a book, and he often overhears a lot of conversations that I deeply wish he wouldn't. So I gave the kitchen a quick once-over, making sure he wasn't quietly reading in the pantry or something like that, and then I shut the kitchen doors.

"What's going on?"

"Nothing, in particular, Dad. I just wanted to thank you for everything." I flung my arms around him and hugged him as tightly as Amara and Eleanor had embraced me a minute earlier.

"What brought this on?"

I brought him up to speed regarding my conversation with Layla, making the summary as concise as possible. "And all of that just made me grateful all over again. For you, and Mom, and everybody else, but especially you, for taking me in when I was fourteen."

"I think we all benefited from that decision."

"But you didn't have to, that's my point. You could have said no. Most people, when a fourteen-year-old girl with a snotty attitude and a ten-month-

52

old baby comes up to them and screams 'adopt me!' would say 'no, thank you' without missing a beat and send me off to foster care."

"You weren't *that* snotty."

"I'm still not proud of who I was back then."

"We're all works in progress in early adolescence. Besides, from the moment your plane landed in Milwaukee, you were a model student. With one brief exception your sophomore year."

"I was defending your reputation."

"I'm okay with that if you use your words. Just not your fists."

"Morwenna had no right to insinuate what she did. Besides, her father had already scheduled an appointment for her to get a nose job as a sweet sixteen present three weeks after our fight. All the damage was repaired pretty quick."

"And that makes it all fine, then?"

I sighed, reflecting on one of my less distinguished moments. "No. I know my methods were wrong, but my motives were pure. You know the rumors that were going around. A guy in his mid-twenties adopts a fourteen-year-old and her baby. No one who knew the first thing about you believed any of it, but still, when you hear your classmates confidently making false assertions...I still say I did the right thing."

"Really?"

I felt my face burning again, just as it did all those years ago when I'd walked by and heard Morwenna slandering Dad in front of a few of our peers. Originally, we'd tried to keep my exact relationship to Toby vague, letting people think she was my sister without actually openly lying about it, but the truth came out late in my freshman year, and since then, there wasn't much to do except confront it all head-on. For a long time, the general consensus was that I was basically Lolita with looser morals, and as anybody who has ever attended high school knows, a lot of teenagers could earn varsity letters in character assassination if rumor-spreading was considered a sport. So when the most straight-laced person who ever walked the earth is being cast in the role of Humbert Humbert, what do you do? Do you ignore the rumor? That doesn't work at a high school, which is basically a

Petri dish of innuendo. Sticking your head in the sand doesn't kill rumors. It only gives the gossip a chance to mutate. If I'd just let it go, the tittle-tattle would circulate until it was accepted as established fact. Then, the parents would hear the lies and decide that they didn't want a pervert teaching their children, and pretty soon, Dad would be told to start looking for a new line of work. That was an unacceptable outcome.

Of course, I wasn't actually following that line of reasoning when I threw my punch. All I was thinking about was how ticked off I was. I didn't realize it at the time, but I did exactly what was needed to shut up those girls. With that haymaker, I sent a clear, incontrovertible message. You can either gossip about me and my Dad, or you can be pretty. One or the other. You choose.

I know, I know, I know. Violence is wrong. I genuinely believe that. Now that I'm a teacher, I don't want my students settling their differences with wrestling matches. *But dammit, it worked.* After that day, no one ever spoke one word out of turn about Dad again, at least in my hearing. I told Dad that, and he gently informed me, "I don't know if it was the punch that quashed the rumors so much as what you said at assembly that day."

Dad had a point. Right after Morwenna was hurried off to the emergency room, the Dean of Students hustled me off to her office and informed me that I'd be suspended for a week. If I'd had a half-hour to cool down, I might possibly have meekly accepted my punishment. But I was still steaming, and instead, I snapped back at her.

"You filthy, cowardly, sanctimonious hypocrite."

If the Dean's eyes had bulged out any further, they would have bonked me in the face and broken *my* nose. "I beg your pardon, Miss Kaiming!"

"Damn right, you should be begging my pardon. You have failed in your job. You've endangered the well-being of a student, by which I mean me, and a teacher, my father, and you should be refunding your salary to the school. Have you or have you not heard the lying rumors about me and my Dad?"

She tried to quash me with a steely look, but my skin had turned to titanium, and I was having none of her unearned pretense of moral authority. I slammed my hand down on her desk. "Yes or no? Have you heard that gossip?"

After a bit of stammering, the words "I did, yes," barely managed to make it out of her mouth.

"Who said that manure? Was it a student? A teacher? A parent?"

"A parent..." she muttered.

"And what did you do when you heard it? Did you take that adult aside and say, 'Listen to me and listen well. Keith Kaiming is one of the finest, most upright, and most decent people to ever teach at this school, and when he adopted a teenage girl who had just lost her mother and had almost no one else in the world who cared enough about her to keep her from being jettisoned into an orphanage, Keith was there because he didn't see a grubby little slut who should be cast down into the gutter where she belonged. He saw a scared, anxious girl, barely in adolescence, who had made one questionable decision on one of the worst nights of her life and was now forever branded by tongue-clucking smug-faced Pharisees as beyond the pale and now had no future beyond providing a cautionary tale to all your dear little darlings who—sorry to break it to you—are up to way worse stuff when you aren't looking. You should be patting Keith Kaiming on the back for stepping up and seeing something worth saving in me when everybody else was looking down their noses and calling me trash. Now go buy Keith a gift certificate to a bookstore or something, because you've wronged him with your vile calumny. Learn a lesson from your grave mistake and never do it again.' That's what you should have told that parent. Did you say that? Huh? Did you? Because you have a job responsibility to look out for students and their teachers and to protect the reputation of the school. Did you do your job or not?"

The Dean gasped and spluttered for a while, and after a splattering of saliva landed on my blazer, I was so disgusted I slammed both my hands back down on the desk. "No! No you didn't! You failed in your job and are corrupt to the core. You have forfeited any and all right to respect from me, from my father, and from everybody else at this school. So don't you dare point a finger at me for standing up for what was right and doing the job that you couldn't be bothered to do. Shame on you. You should be suspending yourself for a month for dereliction of duty. So don't bother filling out a punishment form. You have zero moral authority to pass judgment on me. We're done here. I'm going to lunch."

As I stormed out, I realized that the door was open, and approximately ninety percent of the student body and faculty was standing out in the hall and had heard everything.

That day, we had assembly immediately after lunch, and at the end, students and teachers approached the podium to make announcements to the entire Upper School. I could feel the Dean's beady eyes on me across the theatre, and after the last person in line finished his announcement, I jumped up, ran to the microphone, and said, "I understand there are some rumors going around this school and my adopted Dad, Mr.—soon to be Dr.—Kaiming. So here's the truth." And I told them everything, from my exact relationship with Toby, to why I came to Milwaukee, to what happened to my birth mother, and why Dad had agreed to adopt me. I cut into the next class period by about nine minutes, but not a single teacher complained. By the time I'd finished, I cast my eyes over the silent, open-mouthed audience and told them, "If you have any questions, you know where to find me."

And there were questions. Plenty of them. But for reasons I can't explain, everybody who came up to me over the next several days turned out to be genuinely concerned about me, and all of them became friends. Prior to that, I hadn't exactly been Miss Popularity, though I did get a lot of attention from some guys who thought they might have some luck with me. They were disappointed.

But it meant a sea change for me socially. Over the course of the day, the whispers behind my back ended (at least, as far as I was aware), and if people wondered about what was going on in my life, they asked me to my face. I was probably way franker that I needed or wanted to be, but I figured that any prevarication would lead to more speculation, so I adopted a policy of total openness.

I suppose if I'm being completely open, I need to confess that today, I feel far guiltier over striking Morwenna than I admitted earlier. If I were face-to-face with the Dean today, my stubborn streak would not allow me to admit wrongdoing. In my private conversations with my conscience, it's a different matter, yet I have to say that the degree of guilt that I feel varies widely depending on the day. And even though, as I noted, a lot of good results came from that punch, it doesn't make what I did right. At least not wholly.

Incidentally, the Dean of Students left for a new job at a boarding school in Portland, Oregon, that summer. I'm not saying I was the deciding factor in her decision to move halfway across the country, but I'm not saying I wasn't, either.

What I can say with total certainty is that in the aftermath of the fight—no, not a fight—that implies that more than one person landed a blow—it was Dad who stepped up and taught me a lesson that left a deeper impression on me than almost anything else I picked up in the classroom. The next day, Morwenna was back in school with a bandage over her nose and sunglasses covering the black eyes that had developed from the blood vessels broken by the nose damage. During the midday break, Dad called us both into a conference room, along with his mother, who's a school psychologist at Cuthbertson.

Morwenna and I sat on opposite sides of the round table, both of us poised to respond if the other made the slightest movement that could be interpreted as an act of aggression. Dad and Grandma both took chairs ninety degrees from the two of us, and Dad looked first at me and then at Morwenna and said, "We need to discuss this situation."

"There's nothing I need to discuss." Morwenna was trying to make her voice sound tough, but the nasal whininess in her tone was comical rather than intimidating. I snickered, which didn't help the situation one tiny bit. We started snapping at each other before Dad and Grandma silenced us.

"Morwenna, we know the reason behind yesterday's altercation," Dad informed her. "What we don't know is why you said what you did. Is there a reason why you felt it necessary to present a false statement, one that could potentially have far-ranging consequences for me and members of my family, as fact to your friends?"

There was a brief flash of defiance in Morwenna's face, but it burned out quickly, and even with the bruising around her eyes, it was evident that she was feeling ashamed of herself. "I don't really believe what I said about you, Mr. Kaiming. Please believe that."

"All right, I'll accept that. But that raises the question of why you said that when you profess that you didn't believe it."

At this point, Morwenna started to fall apart, stuttering and twitching. She was obviously trying to keep herself from crying, as tears probably caused her pain.

Grandma is very perceptive, especially when it comes to the complex psyches of teenage girls. "I think you wanted to lash out and hurt someone, Morwenna. No one in particular. Anybody you could embarrass or cast in a poor light would do. And that makes me think that you were trying to spread your own pain around. Which causes me to suspect that someone hurt you very badly recently. Am I on the right track here?"

Morwenna started sobbing at this point and grabbed the tissues, wincing with agony with every sob. Dad and Grandma did the best they could to settle her down before she went through too much suffering. Eventually, Morwenna started to explain in brief, incomplete sentences how her situation at home wasn't going well. Her parents had just separated, and her mother was now dating a slimy man with two daughters whom she did not get along at all. Her father had returned to his first wife, a very nice woman with whom he had two grown sons and who he had left to marry Morwenna's mother. I don't need to go into all of the emotions that Morwenna felt, but she had so much anger and bitterness that it had to go out somewhere, so it spilled out into malicious gossip. Not just against me and Dad, but towards other teachers and other students and their parents. She didn't have anything against any of the people whose reputations had fallen victim to her mudslinging. All she had was vast quantities of rage and no place to direct it except for people who never did her any harm. These last few sentences are my words, not hers, but I think I phrased it much more eloquently than she did.

Ten minutes earlier, in my eyes, Morwenna was nothing more than a nasty, lying rat who should have her tongue removed via scalpel. Listening to her talk, I suddenly felt a level of pity towards her that I wouldn't have believed myself capable of experiencing the previous day.

And for reasons I didn't understand, I found myself spilling my guts to Morwenna, telling her about my own experiences and some bowdlerized details about my relationship with my birth mother. though with much more focus on my emotions than I'd revealed at my assembly announcement. When I saw the aggression slip away from her posture, I knew that we'd turned a corner. It's easy to despise someone when they're nothing more than a whining bag of meat that's done you wrong. When you start seeing that person as being capable of feeling emotions and wrestling with their own problems, it's harder to reduce them to nothing more than that individual's most prominent flaw.

I can't say that I forgave Morwenna that day, nor did she pardon my assault on her right away, but over the next few weeks, we spoke to each other every day. When she came back from her rhinoplasty (the doctor did a remarkable job, but by the way), the last of her fury towards me had dissipated. A month later, I realized that I actually liked her, and the two of us are close to this day.

If I'd been suspended, I'd have come back to school hating her even more than before I left. But when Dad forced me to look at her and her actions in a new light, he did the impossible by laying the path to making us friends. And it wasn't until halfway through high school that I started to build actual connections with more than just a few of my peers. It wasn't until right before I turned fourteen that I finally had a father and a parent who was actually *raising* me instead of letting me run wild because she was too wrapped up in her own cycle of misery to realize that I was flailing around, desperate for help.

My thoughts took over my mind, and I didn't say anything for a few minutes until Dad jarred me out of my reverie of memories and lessons learned. "What are you thinking of now?" he asked me.

"This afternoon, when I was talking with Layla…I think that her experiences with members of my family are a lot like the ones I had growing up."

"You mean with Lesley?" Dad asked. Lesley was my birth mother's name. I have trouble understanding why I think of her using the terms I do. "Birth mother" is sometimes the only phrase that fits. I can't refer to her by her first name—that doesn't feel right at all. And I never really called her "Mom" much, either. She didn't like it. She said it made her feel old, so I grew up avoiding referring to her by anything at all. When talking with classmates or teachers, every mention of her was qualified with "my," as in "*my* mother," as opposed to "Mom." She wasn't particularly interested in food, so I had to make a special effort to drag her to the supermarket, or on those occasions when we were living in a place where we had a grocery store in close proximity to the apartment, I would walk down there myself. In Miami, Gabriella, this super-nice checkout clerk, gave me two large canvas bags to carry my provisions back and forth the three blocks. My birth mother wasn't much of one for cooking or cleaning, and I found out later that she didn't handle most of her own bills, either. Her parents' accountant handled that sort of stuff for her. Most of her family hadn't exactly disowned her once she dropped out of high school and started her modeling career with me in tow, but any interactions with them were infrequent and terse. To them, I was, at best, an embarrassment and, at worst, the excrescence that had ruined Lesley's life. I can see the reasons behind their perspectives, however wrong-headed they may have been.

"Yes. She wasn't a great parent, but it wasn't until after she died that we found her diary that I realized just how many horrors she went through during her childhood and early adolescence. I don't know why I didn't see any of that…"

"You were thirteen, for crying out loud. There's no way you could have been expected to be able to identify signs of abuse and trauma. Quite a few people were to blame for Lesley's mental and emotional state, but you weren't one of them. That was one of the worst things that Lesley's parents ever did. They absolved themselves of their own parental shortcomings, and they laid all the burdens on you."

I nodded. "You're right. I'm fully aware of everything you just said. I just… I've been having a lot of flashbacks. Layla's story is a lot like mine. We both had a family member who was in a terrible way, but there was nothing we could do to help them. Even with Erika stealing her sister's hair... you know how that mirrors my own experiences."

"I know," Dad said. He was familiar with the story, but I need to explain it here, as anybody else reading my narrative won't understand the reference. I'm trying to phrase this as delicately as I can, because I don't want to sound like I'm condemning Lesley or shaming her for her behavior. The chain-smoking started as a way to stay waifishly thin, but the hypersexuality was, I now believe, a desperate way to feel anything at all. Over the years, I lost track of all the times she told me to stay in my room and not come out for any reason. And then I'd hear a man's footsteps alongside hers on the way to her bedroom. Frequently, it wasn't a man's footsteps. Occasionally, more than one pair of footsteps were walking beside her. When I was little, I had no idea what was going on, not until fifth-grade health class. I'll give her some credit. She always tried to shield me from the details of what was going on in her spare time. At least until around the time I turned thirteen. After that point, she lost all interest in sheltering me.

Doubling back a bit, one night when I was nine after I'd heard two pairs of footsteps leaving the apartment, I couldn't fall back to sleep due to an intense thunderstorm. I got up and made myself a mug of hot cocoa, and my birth mother wandered into the kitchenette and asked me how I was doing. When I told her I couldn't sleep, she was uncharacteristically maternal and invited me to sleep with her in her bed that night. It wasn't very pleasant. The scent of her floral shampoo and perfume was fine, but the sweaty musk, cheap cologne, a tackier perfume than my birth mother's, and a few other fumes left behind by her latest guests kept me awake. If they'd just spread around some odors, that would have been disgusting but forgettable, but one or both of them also left behind lice on the pillow. My birth mother had very fine hair, and a round of pesticide shampoo killed the infestation pretty quick, but the lice became entrenched in my thick locks, and no combination of chemical treatments, mayonnaise, or combing could destroy them all. The doctor kindly but firmly informed me that there was only one way to be rid of them, so after a few minutes with an electric razor buzzing over my head, I was a lice-free, bald little girl.

You can imagine, I put up with a lot of mockery and uncomfortable questions for a while, even after I started wearing a scarf around my head. For a while, I'd assumed that I'd picked it up at school, even though none of my classmates had itchy scalps, and it wasn't until I learned about the birds and the bees and cast my mind back to that night when I realized just how I'd caught the lice, and that my birth mother's choice of companions was to blame for my hair loss.

I never let go of that grudge during her lifetime, but the parallel with Layla should be obvious.

"That last year in L.A., things were spiraling out of control," I reminisced. "For some reason, I've been having nightmares flashing back to that hot, sticky July when I couldn't take the sounds of what was going on on the other side of my bedroom anymore, and I slept out on the fire escape for a week, until that fateful rainy night when I made a decision that changed my life forever." I sighed and shook my head. I don't like thinking about the night if I can possibly help it.

Leaning against the kitchen counter, I said, "You know what one of the best lessons you ever taught me was? Do the right thing, and to hell with anybody who gives you any grief over it."

"I don't recall using those words."

"Seriously, Dad, I've been thinking a lot lately about what you did for me. Without you—and Mom and the rest of the family, but especially you—I'd never be where I am now. I wouldn't be all but dissertation towards a doctorate in history. I'd be a high school dropout, working at a filthy gentlemen's club, providing lap dances to tipsy middle managers in exchange for dollar bills that had previously been rolled up and stuffed up people's noses to snort cocaine."

From the expression on his face, it was obvious that Dad didn't care for the mental picture I'd just painted, and a moment later, he made that point clear verbally as well. "I think you're exaggerating and selling yourself short."

"Am I? Dad, I don't think you realize how close I came to giving up on myself when I was fourteen. Look at the role model I had. My birth mother gave up on living. She just coasted along, taking a little allowance from her relatives to handle expenses and spending the rest of the time smoking and letting herself get picked up by strangers."

"You know that she was depressed."

"Yes, and she didn't have any strength or initiative to get better. I'm not judging her for that. But I know how easy it would have been for me to fall into the trap of resigning myself to a dismal level of unhappiness. And I think that's why I'm getting so concerned about Layla's life. She's a smart woman. She could do something really interesting or worthwhile. But she's completely out of gas. Layla is stuck in a rut where's she totally dissatisfied with every aspect of her life. She just needs to take the initiative and change something. Anything. A better job, getting a student loan and finishing her degree, fighting for shared custody of her daughter. But it's all just too much trouble for her. She's waving the white flag on a winnable fight, and it makes me mad."

Dad's glasses were splattered with droplets of broth from the jambalaya, and as he washed them in the sink, he said, "Traditionally, when a private investigator is digging into someone's background in connection to a crime, the goal is to put that person in prison. Now, you're trying to fix your target's life."

"Is that so wrong?"

"Nerissa, you just brought up a number of points of comparison between yourself and Layla. Bear with me here. As a thought experiment, I'd like you to think about some of the ways that you are very different from Layla."

"I have you. I have Mom. I have grandparents, great-grandparents, and adoptive siblings. I have people who care about me."

"Are you quite sure that Celeste doesn't care about her granddaughter? Because I'm positive that she does."

"Yeah...that's bothering me..." I briefly summed up what I'd overheard of Celeste's words to Layla less than an hour earlier. "So it seems like she thinks her granddaughter is responsible for her sister's death."

Dad drummed his fingers on the countertop. "Not necessarily. Are you sure you're quoting her verbatim?"

"Maybe I mixed up a word or two, but that's pretty darn close. Why?"

"Well, Celeste didn't come right out and accuse her, did she? She just said, "You don't want to have a slip of the tongue and tell her exactly what you did to your sister."

"Right..."

"So that doesn't necessarily mean murder. Whatever Layla did to Erika, it may not have been deliberately poisoning her. It could have been something else that reflects badly on Layla, or it could have happened years ago. No point in theorizing, the possibilities are infinite. Maybe it's just embarrassing, maybe it's criminal. But it's possible that part of the reason why Layla's stuck in a rut is because she's dealing with guilt. Perhaps she's punishing herself. Could Layla have been responsible for introducing her sister to drugs? I don't know. That's just a random theory I shouldn't repeat. But there's no reason to assume Celeste was directly accusing Layla of murder."

I took a minute to let this idea sink in, wondering if I'd imposed a false presumption on this snippet of conversation. My thoughts were disrupted by the sound of Mom and Bernard climbing up from the basement. Our basement stairs are much less creaky than the Dolaks', but Bernard's little legs make quite the clamor when he's racing up as fast as he can. When he saw me, he raced towards me and, with a flying leap, jumped into my arms for a big hug. I careened backwards and bumped into the spice cabinet. It wasn't so much the force of the blow to my chest, which didn't even knock the wind out of me. It was the fake blood splatter all over Bernard's face. Instinctively, I feared for my outfit and flinched at my little brother's expression of affection, but then I realized that I was wearing machine-washable athletic gear, and any red goo would vanish without a trace in the laundry, as I knew from cleaning Mom's clothes.

"Looks like somebody's been helping Mom with her lab experiments," I told him. Mom has a room to herself in the corner of the basement, where she runs tests to see if some theories connected to causes of death are plausible. Normally, she keeps it triple-locked, as a lot of what's in there isn't for kids. I wasn't sure what Bernard had said to be invited in, but it must have been particularly convincing.

"I'm so proud of him," Mom said. "I was stumped as to how the blood spatter could have gotten on the inside of that sweater there, and I'd gotten so frustrated I went out to run a bit on the basement elliptical machine. Bernard was lying on the weight bench reading—"

"I wanted a change of scene," Bernard shrugged.

"—and he asked if I'd been wearing the sweater during my experiments. Of course, I said "yes," and then he asked, "Have you tried tying the sweater around your waist?" Well, I hadn't, but then I realized that was the only way the blood could have gotten there." Mom picked up Bernard from my arms and hugged him herself. "You deserve a reward. Let me know if there's a book you want. I'll get it from the store before I pick you up from school tomorrow. But don't tell your sisters. They'll want something too, and they haven't helped me get a murderer convicted lately."

"Sounds good."

Mom beamed at us. "My little boy's solving forensic puzzles that left professional adults stumped. I'm not sure whether I should try to push him to be the next Doogie Houser and push him into med school or if I should report myself to social services for exposing him to an open homicide investigation." She lifted Bernard up to meet her gaze. "Please don't go telling your classmates that you got covered in fake blood while spending some quality time with Mommy."

"Deal," Bernard said as Dad wiped the red ooze from his face, then Mom's.

"Dinner will be ready in fifteen minutes," Dad informed him. "Go around the houses and tell the rest of the family—save Yeh-Yeh[1] for last, after you've changed into less gory clothes. He's napping, and you know how he doesn't like to be awakened until the very last minute."

"Okay."

"I'm going to take a quick shower and be right back." Mom pecked Dad on the cheek and left.

My phone chimed. "That's Funderburke. He says that he's just leaving his place, and yes, he is wearing the glossy suit I bought him because I really liked it when this Greek actor wore one like it on this European award show." I sighed. "I'll set the table, and then I'll change for dinner." I planned on putting on this new jumpsuit I really like, but I can't wear it out for more than a couple hours tops because one-piece jumpsuits are a nightmare if you have to use a public restroom, especially if they're made out of a dry-clean-only material like this one is. I explained all of this to Dad and watched his eyes glaze. If you took the combined interest Dad and Funderburke have in fashion and multiplied it by a million, the result would still be nil. Zero times any number is still zero.

As I started setting out the plates, Toby wandered into the room. "How long until dinner?"

"Fifteen—actually, fourteen minutes now."

"Is Dad coming tonight?" Toby started calling Funderburke "Dad" a while back.

"Yes, he is."

"You need help?"

I nodded, and she pulled some cloth napkins out of the buffet drawer and started putting one next to each plate. Our dining room table's so big that Yeh-Yeh says he only has to do three laps around it, and he's achieved his daily steps goal.

"Mom?"

"Yeah?"

"Can I borrow one of your leather jackets? One of the black ones with the wide lapels and cloth cuffs? I know just the one I want."

I nearly dropped the three plates I was holding. Toby barely has any more interest in fashion than Dad and Funderburke. I've tried to get her interested in some stylish outfits, but when she's not wearing her school uniform, she almost always wears a baggy sweater and a long sweatskirt. She only wears something else under duress. "Yeah, sure. Of course." I hesitated for a few seconds before asking, "Why?"

"I want it for my Halloween costume this year."

That tracked. "Oh. Sure. Who are you going as this year?"

"At school, they want us to dress as a fictional character we really like. I want to go as Naomi Masora."

I didn't know who that was, but I figured she was an anime or manga character. Toby's obsessed with those genres. "What series does she appear in?"

"*Death Note*. That's my favorite manga and anime series, and along with L, she's my favorite character." She started describing Naomi to me with astounding rapidity, and I tried my darnedest to keep up with her.

"So, can we pick out the jacket later?" she asked. "I know exactly the style it has to be, and you have one pretty close to it."

"Sure," I said, feeling dizzy after that overload of information regarding Naomi. She seemed like an interesting character, but getting her entire backstory at three hundred words a minute gave me a bit of a headache. "Toby?"

"Yeah?"

"I've been meaning to ask you. Do you ever get any flack about being my daughter? Have you ever heard any of your peers say anything about me behind your back?"

Toby toyed with the fork she was about to place on top of a napkin. "Sometimes...I hear some of the girls' mothers whispering sometimes, saying that I'm almost the age you and your birth mother were when they...you know."

"Which ones? I want names." Maybe I snapped that a bit too sharply, because she jumped backwards.

"I don't want to say. You'll make things weirder for me."

The anxiety in her face was so obvious I relented. "Of course. I just worry that I might—totally inadvertently—be causing you some unwanted social awkwardness and strife because of...well, everything."

"Yeah, you are. But I don't care."

"Are you sure?"

"I don't let mean people and idiots bother me."

She sounded so tough, and yet in my heart, I still worried that my past actions, and my birth mother's, might be causing my little girl pain.

I put my arms around Toby and felt her flinch. Toby is not a hugger. "I just want you to know that not a day goes by when I don't thank God that I had you. I'm always grateful you came into my life. Please, never forget that."

[1] Chinese for "paternal grandfather."

Chapter Four—That's A Good Theory

The next day was busy but exhilarating. My students were really engaged as we discussed the Revolutionary War era, and they seemed to enjoy my lecture on spycraft during that time period. My presentation on "Ten Things High School Should Warn You About Before College" was well-received, and afterwards, a dozen kids asked me if there were any plans to set up a presentation in the future to teach budgeting and other needed skills.

After seven hours of molding young minds, I was ready for a break. Mom picked up the elder triplets in her minivan, and Dad and I joined her as we drove half a mile down the road to the retirement community there. The Kaimings are a pretty religious family, and merely attending church on Sundays is, in our opinion, for slackers. The retirement home holds Mass at three-thirty every weekday, so quite frequently, we all pile in the van to attend. The priests there often act like they're worried that some of the residents will pass away in the middle of their sermons, so daily Mass only lasts between eighteen to twenty minutes, depending on how quickly some residents can make their way up the aisle for Communion. More often than not, Dad and I return to Cuthbertson to take care of some other work, such as in the spring, when I'm coaching soccer, or if there's a four o'clock faculty meeting.

Today, we were coming back to Cuthbertson for a family workout, but first, we were holding a conference to discuss the Layla situation. Funderburke texted me to explain that he was just wrapping up one last interview in his investigation, so he'd be back at Cuthbertson in ten minutes. This was just enough time for us to change our clothes. I hung up my cocoa suede blazer, matching maxi skirt, and bronze sweater in favor of a workout suit much like the one I wore the previous day; only this one was crimson with black detailing. By the time we were all ready, Bernard, Eleanor, and Amara were enjoying themselves on the playground with some of their peers, carefully watched by the after-school staff.

A second text from Funderburke asked us to meet him at his office, so my parents and I hung outside his door before he rushed back into the building, running so fast his long lambskin coat flew out behind him like a cape. "Did I keep you waiting long?"

"A couple minutes." I shrugged. "From the look on your face, I think it's going to be worth it."

As he unlocked his door and we all filed inside, Funderburke said, "I believe so. Nothing incontrovertibly incriminating, but it's enough to make me wonder."

Feeling my posture stiffen, I folded my arms across my chest and leaned against the wall. "Do you believe that Layla deliberately killed Erika?"

He sighed. "I'm not saying that, but I do believe that Layla is lying to us. But first of all, we should probably get confirmation on the cause of death."

Three of us turned towards Mom, who pulled a file folder out of her massive purse. "I managed to get a copy of the autopsy report, and I've looked over the results. Everything looks aboveboard, although as you know, final toxicology results can take months. Based on the initial analysis, Erika died of fentanyl poisoning. A massive overdose."

"Just how big a dose qualifies as "massive?" I asked.

"Two milligrams—that's a minuscule amount—can be enough to kill, depending on the size of the person. A tall, strongly built man like Keith or Funderburke just might be able to take three milligrams; a short and skinny woman like Erika, who wasn't in the best health, would succumb to far less. Due to several years of opioid abuse, many of Erika's organs had the functionality of a woman twice her age."

"Wait. Was she dying?" Funderburke asked.

"No, her health wasn't that severe yet. If she got clean, ate well, and generally took care of herself, she could have lived for decades. If she kept going along the path, she was… It's unlikely that she'd have made it much past thirty-five, if that." Mom shuddered. "When I first saw her, I thought she was forty. Older than I am. But she was only in her very early twenties…"

"Okay, we know she died of fentanyl poisoning. But was it murder?" I wondered.

"Well, the pills—we know she swallowed capsules as there were traces of gelatin shells in her stomach—weren't forced down her throat. There's no bruising or scraping to indicate they were anything other than willingly swallowed. When fentanyl pills are sold on the street, they're usually prepared so each pill only has a tiny amount of the drug in it, far below the lethal dose. The fentanyl is diluted with another substance, ranging from infant formula to rat poison. But it seems like this was very pure fentanyl. I can't tell how many capsules she swallowed, but there was over sixty milligrams of it in her. Maybe a bit more."

"So, over thirty times a fatal dose," Funderburke commented.

"Yes. She probably would have passed out within minutes after consuming them, and probably her breathing and heart stopped very soon afterwards. These drugs affect people in really different ways, especially if they're regular opioid users, but the end would probably have come very soon for poor Erika. Within half an hour after swallowing the pills, maybe several minutes less."

"Would she have recovered if she'd gotten a shot of antidote?" Dad asked.

"If it had been administered within minutes and she'd gotten proper medical care immediately, then maybe. There are a lot of variables, but given the humongous size of the dose…it's doubtful, but anything's possible. But with each passing minute, the odds of survival would decrease."

"All right," I said. "We know how she died. The question is, how did she get them? Did Layla give them to her? Or did she tamper with Erika's pills?"

Mom shrugged. "I can't say. There isn't enough evidence to say how obtained the pills. It's more likely than not it was supplied by some drug dealer or someone similarly shady. I doubt they'd be in a local pharmacy, so she wouldn't have been able to steal them, even if she was able to slip behind the counter. It's possible that Erika bought them herself from someone careless who had no regard for human life. I would say that this is almost certainly a homicide, because whoever prepared those capsules is responsible for Erika's death. Lately, there've been a few cases where some drug dealer tasks some underling with cutting pure fentanyl with baby formula or something like that, and then the lackey doesn't mix the powders up very well, or even forgets the baby formula entirely, so some capsules get nothing but formula, and others get all fentanyl, so people take the latter pills and die."

"Is that what happened here?" I asked.

"Maybe, maybe not. A much deeper investigation would be needed. I should point out that the theory I outlined would almost certainly serve as reasonable doubt in any case against Layla. I'm not saying I know for sure what happened, just that we can't prove what happened."

Nodding, I turned to Funderburke. "All right. Nothing definitive yet. What about your investigation?"

"Before I start, I should warn you, I haven't come up with anything conclusive yet either," Funderburke informed us. "May I walk you through my report, please?"

We all nodded, and Funderburke crossed over to the markerboard on his wall and uncapped the blue marker. "I managed to get a copy of Layla and Celeste's statements from a friend of mine on the force. I'm going to write them down here, and add the source of each point in red afterwards:

8:50 A.M. Celeste leaves the house and walks to the bookstore. Her granddaughters were still asleep, but two neighbors saw her leave. Celeste's statement.

9:00 A.M. Celeste arrives at the bookstore. Celeste's statement, confirmed by her fellow employees.

10:25 A.M. Erika leaves the house to go to a Narcotics Anonymous meeting at the church down the street. From Layla's statement.

10:30 A.M. Erika arrives at the church.

"Now, it's called Narcotics Anonymous for a reason," Funderburke explained. "So I recorded a short video and gave it to the pastor who oversees the meetings to play. I told them that I was looking into the death of Erika Dolak, and I held up a picture of her that I'd found on her online obituary and explained that she'd passed away recently of a drug overdose and I'd be grateful to anybody who could help me draw up a timeline of her actions. I provided my contact information, and only one person responded. This was a young woman, a college student who claimed to be a good friend of Erika's. We met at a coffee shop today. She told me to call her "Jane Doe," and I didn't push the matter. She wanted her privacy protected. Anyway, Jane told me that Erika showed up at the meetings to keep her grandmother happy, but she wasn't really committed to her sobriety. As far as Jane knew, Erika was still using on a daily basis, *and* she never spoke up at the meetings. She just sat with her arms folded and refused to share. She's been through multiple sponsors, but has never built a relationship with any of them. After the meeting ended, Erika said that she was all out of pills, but she was going to score some more later that afternoon and asked Jane if she wanted any. Jane claims she refused. I don't think I believe her. Based on the chip she was tossing in her hand, she's been clean for a little while, but I can tell that she's fighting valiantly against the urge to relapse. Anyway, Jane walked Erika back home, before heading home herself."

Funderburke added "Jane's statement" to the end of the 10:30 line and continued writing.

11:30 A.M. Erika and Jane leave the NA meeting. Jane's statement.

11:35 A.M. Jane leaves Erika at her house. Jane's statement.

"Now, I canvassed the neighborhood, and one woman, a Mrs. Böhm, is a retiree who has trouble moving around. She spends much of the day in her living room, watching television. Her set is in front of the window overlooking the street. Mrs. Böhm claims that she saw Layla return home just before noon. However, this contradicts Layla's statement."

"What do Layla's co-workers at the bar have to say about that?" I asked.

"Oddly enough, no one can definitively give her an alibi. There are a number of reasons for that. First of all, I asked my questions the better part of a week after the day in question, so no one's really sure which day is which. The weekdays all tend to blend together in that bar." Funderburke shook his head. "Not the nicest place. It's very dark, and it smells of stale beer, oil that's been used to deep-fry stuff too many times without being changed, and depression. And the bathrooms are worse. I was about to use it, but my nose was the only part of me that got inside that wretched place. I wound up going back to your house." He turned to Midge. "Your grandmother and aunt were there, watching the younger triplets, so they let me in. I hope that was all right."

"You're welcome to relieve yourself at our home any time," Mom said with a completely straight face.

"Thanks. Anyway, lunch is a very busy time there, Monday through Friday. A lot of people work at offices and shops and whatnot in the area, and the food is cheap, though not healthy or tasty." Funderburke shuddered. "Before the cook answered my questions, he made me order something, and he suggested the special of the day—a house-made veggie burger with fries. It was basically instant mashed potato mixed with frozen peas and some sort of sauce that dyed it brown and deep-fried until it started to burn. They were out of buns, so they stuck it between two slices of cellophane-bagged white bread. It's the sort of lunch you order when you hate yourself. I had one bite and spat it out immediately. It tasted like despair smothered in ketchup and mayonnaise. I took it to go and threw it out in the dumpster next to the parking lot."

"So, getting back to the alibi…" I prodded him as gently as I could.

"Right. Last week, it was Layla's turn to restock supplies in the basement, but when things got too busy, she was summoned upstairs to help with the waitressing, but no one can say for sure whether she was there or not around noon that day. Some are fairly sure she was. Others say she was almost definitely down the basement. So, in theory, she could have slipped out for fifteen or twenty minutes, hurried home, done something sinister, and rushed back. I politely asked them all not to tell Layla I was asking questions about her, and when good manners didn't work, I gave each of them twenty bucks. It'll all be covered in my expense report. Anyway, back to the timeline."

12:00 P.M. Mrs. Böhm claims she saw Layla come home. Layla denies this.

12:05 P.M. Mrs. Böhm claims she saw Layla leave the house.

12:15 P.M. Mrs. Böhm says she saw Erika leave the house, carrying a red plastic grocery store bag and heading south.

12:25 P.M. Mrs. Böhm observes Erika returning home, walking northwards. She does not see the red bag.

2:10 P.M. Stella, the college student who lives in the Dolaks' guest room in the garage, returns, has lunch there. Stella's own statement, confirmed by Mrs. Böhm. (Mrs. Böhm confirms Stella's return, not the fact that Stella ate lunch.)

3:15 P.M. Layla returns home. Layla's statement. Confirmed by Stella, who saw her out the window, though Layla didn't see her. Note: Stella says that Layla looked really disheveled, and that her jeans were torn to shreds. Further note: Mrs. Böhm did not see Layla return, though she may have dozed off around this time. Layla claims she went straight upstairs to nap and didn't see Erika. Stella, however, was concerned that something had happened to Layla and left her apartment to check on her. When she arrived at the back door, she could hear creaking and groaning from inside the house. She recognized this as the sound of the basement stairs. This contradicts Layla's statement that she didn't go down the basement. Before Stella could ring the bell, her phone rang, and she returned to her garage apartment to answer the call. She forgot about Layla and did not check in on her that evening.

3:45 P.M. Stella leaves for her next class, arrives ten minutes later. Departure confirmed by Mrs. Böhm, arrival confirmed by two of Stella's classmates.

5:10–5:40 P.M. Celeste returns home, confirmed by Mrs. Böhm. Celeste discovers Erika unresponsive in the basement. Celeste calls for Layla, attempts to revive Erika. Paramedics called, they arrive soon afterwards. Erika taken to the hospital, later pronounced dead. Celeste and Layla agree on this point, paramedics confirm the timeline.

Funderburke sighed and recapped the marker. "So, there you have the timeline of the last day of Erika's life. Any questions before I go over my findings?"

We all shook our heads. "No," I answered, "This looks pretty thorough."

"Then you see the issue. In the morning, Layla had no opiate pills, but she wanted them and planned to get them. Sometime after 11:35, she got them and swallowed them. Whether the capsules were prepared by someone who deliberately poisoned her with pure fentanyl, or if they were the result of shoddy craftsmanship caused by drug dealers who take no pride in their work, is unknown at present. Here's the big question. Did Layla swing by her house around noon? If she did, her denial of this is very suspicious. If she quietly left work and covered it up, then it makes me wonder if she played a role in giving Layla the deadly pills."

"Couldn't Mrs. Böhm have made a mistake about the day?" I asked. "Maybe she mixed things up and said Layla returned the day before Erika died, or even the day before that? How reliable a witness is she?"

"Mrs. Böhm is about seventy-five, but she's still pretty sharp. Her eyesight isn't great—she told me she can't read anymore, even large print, so she watches a lot of television. Her hearing is weaker than it used to be, too, which is why she had the sound cranked up as far as it could possibly go. She's also the self-appointed head of the Neighborhood Watch, so when she sees someone she recognizes walking by or anything suspicious, she jots it down in the notebook next to her chair. I checked, the date was correct. Also, she said when she saw Layla coming by the house at noon, Mrs. Böhm was watching a talk show where the interviewee was, quote, "that trashy blonde who's in all of those terrible movies and dates a new A-list actor every month." I ran through about a dozen names before I finally got the right actress, and I checked the television schedule and confirmed that she was on the show that day. So though I wouldn't say that Mrs. Böhm is one hundred percent reliable, I'd say her testimony would be more likely to be accurate than not."

I folded my arms across my chest and started dragging my toe along the carpet in front of me. "I still say that Layla isn't a killer."

"That leads me to something else I wanted to point out," Funderburke added. "If Layla had something to do with Erika's death, then she had to have gotten that fentanyl from somewhere. And as Midge said, it's not the sort of thing you can pick up over the counter at Walgreens. Layla doesn't have access to a medical research lab or a hospital dispensary. She would have to have bought it from some sort of shady dealer, and the bar owner made it clear that he doesn't allow anybody like that in his bar. The last fellow who tried to sell marijuana in that cesspool of a bathroom wound up losing two teeth and had all of his stash flushed down the john. The owner assured me that he doesn't know of any regular patrons who deal in selling opiates, and that begs the question, how would Layla have found someone to sell her pure fentanyl anyway? And even if she just happened to bump into someone who deals in such substances on her walk home from work, how would she have paid for it? Buying that much fentanyl in its purest form wouldn't be cheap, although it's not like she'd need to take out a mortgage to pay for it. A pal of mine who's a narcotics police officer says that a fentanyl pill can cost around forty dollars on the street, though both the price and the purity of the fentanyl can vary significantly. To the best of my knowledge, Layla hasn't got much in the way of disposable income. And she hasn't asked for an advance or borrowed anything from her co-workers."

"That's a good point," I noted. "Her clothes and shoes are strictly dollar and thrift store, and before they took everything back from the storage facility, she didn't have much she could pawn for more than a few bucks. Take a look. When I was at their house yesterday, I took some pictures." I passed around my phone. "That's Layla's room before she brought back her more valuable possessions. Nothing worth selling."

"If she sold something to buy fentanyl last week, it wouldn't have been there for you to photograph. Not only that, but she could have stopped by the storage facility, picked out a few items, and sold them..." Funderburke theorized.

"But if Erika bought the pills herself, where did she get the money?" Dad asked.

"Good question," Funderburke replied. "After talking to Mrs. Böhm, it seems that there have been some burglaries in the neighborhood recently. Usually, during the middle of the day, when residents are at work or school, someone has broken into houses—ones that don't have alarms—and smashed a window in order to enter the building. Nothing too big taken, like a giant TV. Mostly money or jewelry. So I called the local pawnshops, asked around to see if someone had stopped by a lot lately. None of them admitted to seeing a woman matching Erika's description, at least in the past couple of weeks. The police had already covered this ground before, I suppose. But there are other, less reputable ways to sell necklaces and bracelets or cash or drugs directly. I'm not aware of any fences who live in the area. I should point out that since Erika died, there have been no burglaries. Before, there were two or three a week, so they're overdue. Although… from what I could tell from Mrs. Böhm, the burglaries stopped a week before Erika passed away. At that time, several houses installed video cameras, and a few of the wealthier residents hired a security service to patrol the area. I think that a bunch of large dogs with very loud barks have been adopted in the past couple of weeks, as well."

"So we have two theories." I flopped into a chair and crossed my legs. "One. Erika bought her own pills. They were too strong and she died of an overdose. Layla wasn't responsible. Two. Layla bought some fentanyl, and made some super-strong capsules and gave them to Erika, deliberately poisoning her. Based on my conversation with Layla, I repeat, I just don't believe in the second theory."

"And didn't Celeste talk about how hard they worked to keep Layla away from drugs for as long as possible?" Mom noted. "If Layla had simply handed her sister a bottle of pills and said, "Here little sis, have some opiates! They're on me!" you'd think Erika would have been suspicious. Unless she was so desperate for her next fix that she simply swallowed the pills without asking questions."

"But that doesn't explain Celeste's comment," Funderburke argued. "She accused Layla of killing Erika. Layla denied it, but she wasn't angry and indignant, like an innocent person might be. Nerissa, I usually trust your instincts, but I watched Layla's mannerisms, and I really got a guilty vibe from her. Although… I also didn't get the sense that she was a cold-blooded poisoner. So, there are contradictory impressions here. And remember, she may have lied when she said she didn't go down the basement to check on her sister. Mrs. Böhm told me that Celeste insisted that Layla check on Erika constantly just in case she was in trouble. The tenant in the garage apartment heard her climbing down the stairs. That indicates she lied, which makes me suspect that theory two is more likely."

Dad drummed his fingers on the top of Funderburke's desk. "No... No, Funderburke, that's not what Celeste said." He turned to me and asked, "Nerissa, am I correct in thinking that you said Celeste's words were, 'You don't want to have a slip of the tongue and tell her exactly what you did to your sister?'"

"That's near enough, as far as my memory can be relied upon to recall verbatim. But like you said last night, that could mean any number of lesser misdeeds."

"Exactly what you did to your sister..." Yeah..." Dad took off his glasses, passed a hand over his face, replaced his eyewear, and continued speaking. "I can see how you interpreted that to mean deliberate murder. But like I asked Nerissa last night, what if it didn't? Yesterday, I thought it just meant something she'd done in the past, but what if it was more recent, but not murder? What if it meant...abandonment?"

"What do you mean, Dad?"

"Look at Layla's nightstand in this photo. I'll enlarge it." Dad handed the phone to me, and I studied it with Mom and Funderburke looking over my shoulders. "See that? The little white bottle?"

Mom adjusted her glasses as she squinted at my phone's screen. "I can't read the label, but that could be Narcan."

"Let's assume it is," Dad continued. "What if the truth is an amended version of Funderburke's first theory? Erika bought her own pills. She swallowed them, she overdosed, she passed out, and depending on how long she was unconscious, maybe she died. Then, at a quarter past three, Layla returns home and finds Erika dead or near dead. She rushes to wherever they keep the Narcan, and takes out a bottle. But before she can administer it, she stops herself. *If I bring her back from the brink of death, I'll just have to keep living with all my nice possessions in storage, and as soon as my hair grows out again, she'll chop it off and sell it for pills.* So what does Layla do? She decides not to rescue her sister. She brings the Narcan upstairs and waits a while to make sure the window for providing the antidote has closed. Layla didn't deliberately poison Erika. She did, however, refuse to provide potentially lifesaving treatment."

Dad paused to let us consider his ideas.

After a minute, Funderburke said, "That's a good theory. I think you might be on to something here."

"That would explain the most unusual part of the witness testimony—the girl who lives in the garage—Stella—saying she heard Layla walking down the stairs," Mom mused. "Why would Layla lie about going down the basement? Because she did go to check on her sister and found her lying there, either dying or already dead. She wouldn't know, although depending on when Erika took the fentanyl, it's quite possible she was beyond the point of no return. But Layla denied going downstairs for obvious reasons. That does make sense."

I didn't say anything for a little while, because I was trying to think through Dad's perspective on events logically. I realized right away that I really wanted this theory to be true, as it fit my own psychological assessment of Layla—or, if I'm being honest, my gut reaction of what sort of person she was. Layla wasn't a cold-blooded murderess. She was a deeply frustrated young woman at the end of her rope who made some ethically questionable decisions. This portrayal of her was likely heavily influenced by my own experiences, meaning that I was trying to paint Layla's character in my own image.

My thoughts were interrupted by a knock at the door. Dad opened it and found Paige and Juniper on the other side. After greeting them and offering them a seat, Paige shook her head. "We won't stay long. I picked Juniper up from her ballet lesson, and she asked if she could see if you were still there."

"Have you proven what Mommy did yet?" Juniper asked, lip trembling.

"Juniper told me her suspicions last night," Paige added before we could respond. "Is there any truth to it?"

"Right now, we don't think so," Funderburke said. "I need to keep investigating–"

"But you can't rule out the possibility, can you?" Paige asked.

"No, but we really think–"

"This whole ordeal is having a very harmful effect on Juniper," Paige interrupted. "She's been crying every night. She's been wetting the bed!"

"Mom!" Juniper squirmed, mortification covering her face.

"Sorry, darling. I'm just very concerned about you. But just so we're clear, you've been investigating Layla regarding her involvement in her sister's death, haven't you?"

Steeliness was now obvious in Funderburke's tone, and he clearly hadn't enjoyed being interrupted earlier, and now he was making darned sure it didn't happen again. "It is not appropriate to come to any conclusions given—"

"Thank you—I'm going to do whatever's necessary to shield Juniper from further harm. Have a good night." Paige turned and hustled Juniper out of the office.

Even though Paige had cut into his comments, Funderburke didn't stop talking, and his voice only grew louder as he said, "–the investigation is still ongoing, and it would be irresponsible to make any assumptions of guilt on Layla's part!" By the time he reached "part!" he was bellowing.

* * *

Fifteen minutes later, when Mom was spotting Dad at the bench press, Funderburke and I paired for medicine ball sit-up throws. Funderburke was still fuming. "Why did Paige bother bringing Juniper—UH!" he groaned as he caught the medicine ball. "–when she didn't want to take the time to listen to what we had to SAY?" he finished as he performed his sit-up and threw the ball back to me.

"I think—OOMPH—she just wanted to get confirmation that we were investigating Layla. Since we confirmed that in front of Juniper, she's going to TRY to bring it up at the upcoming custody hearing."

"UM! Of course." Funderburke's face soured. He despises divorce and custody cases that wind up putting terrible stress on the children involved.

81

"Do you know who Paige's lawyer IS?"

"Yeah, it's AH! Someone you know very well. Michelle LILITH." Layla had mentioned the name of Paige's attorney when we were transferring some gold-plated candleholders from a box to the china cabinet.

Funderburke caught the medicine ball with a grunt, but sat still and didn't complete the sit-up. "My mother?"

"Yes. How are you feeling about that?"

"I think I'm developing an emotional investment in this case. Especially now that Juniper is clearly displaying signs of distress."

I nodded. "Absolutely. Your standard policy applies, right?"

"Whenever there's a divorce or some other custody issue, I always take the side of kid or kids involved. Every single time. Because more often than not, nobody else is."

"And right now, we need to focus on the client. How do we help Juniper survive this situation?"

Funderburke slammed the medicine ball down into a niche on the wall and hopped off the decline bench. He took a step forward and held out his hands to help me off my own bench. "Let's get a drink of water and talk about this some more on the elliptical machines."

"Good." I didn't know how I was going to do it, but I found myself desperately wanting to find a way to bring Layla and Juniper to a reconciliation.

Chapter Five—The Party Boy and the Ice Queen

Much of the next day was devoted to putting out metaphorical fires connected to my girls. At that time, there were sixteen girls in the program for teen mothers, plus one spot for a single eighteen-year-old dad. Actually, to be precise, four of them were in their early twenties, but they'd dropped out of school when the babies came. Talia, for example, was twenty-two, but she was just starting her junior year of high school now. She informed me that aside from a few serpent-tongued students, she didn't have to deal with very much teasing. The main issue she had to wrestle with was the fact that a lot of students asked her to buy alcoholic beverages for them. She claimed she never acquiesced, but one time, a receipt fell out of her purse and onto the floor in front of me. I only got a fraction of a second's glimpse at it, but I was fairly certain that I saw the name of a nearby liquor store printed at the top before she snatched it up and crumbled it in her hand. I considered saying something, but I refrained because, after all, she was of legal age, and I didn't have any proof that she wasn't buying some drinks for her own responsible use. There's a rule that trial lawyers have about never asking questions if they don't already know the answers. The same goes for teachers. If there's a fair chance that you don't *want* to know the answer to a question, then trust your gut and let it pass, as long as you have no reason to assume that anybody's in peril.

Samantha, in contrast, was in danger. Her abusive stalker ex-boyfriend and father of her child was up for parole, so during a free period, I had a long phone conversation with the parole board, explaining all of the messed-up stuff he did a year earlier, including coming after Samantha with a butcher knife in one hand, and the other hand holding a beer bottle filled with gasoline and a rag stuffed into the neck. Luckily for Samantha, the latter weapon exploded in his hand immediately after he lit it using the gas oven burner, and the police arrested him after the paramedics rushed him to the hospital.I forwarded a half-dozen angry letters he'd scribbled to me and Samantha to the parole board, and this evidence managed to convince them that he might as well keep wearing his prison jumpsuit for a while longer. I knew his transgressions wouldn't keep him behind bars forever, but with a little luck, he wouldn't be out until summer, once Samantha had earned her diploma and was heading off to college with her kid.

Edith's parents were both addicted to methamphetamines, and they'd showed up at her foster home, camped out on the porch, and refused to leave until her foster mother paid them five hundred dollars. I sent Funderburke over to handle the situation, and when he returned half an hour later, he informed me that when he arrived, Edith's foster mother was just about to put the contents of her wallet into the hands of her uninvited guests, but he'd shown up just in time and snatched away the money, informing the foster mother that if she paid them a penny, they'd keep coming back forever. He'd asked them politely to leave, and when they refused, they asked him if he was going to turn the hose on them or use physical force, because if he did, they'd sue him and get the money that way. Fortunately, Funderburke has a remarkable skill that does not involve any sort of touching or physical intimidation. He has the ability to be superhumanly annoying. If he wants to, he can get on your last nerve and tap-dance upon it. Through a mixture of high-pitched whistling, off-key singing, and ranting about controversial topics upon which he has extremely strong opinions, the pair were only able to stand it for fifteen minutes before they surrendered and drove off in their rapidly disintegrating car.

I feel obligated to make it clear—Funderburke almost never annoys me, except when he's whining about having to wear something bold that I think looks incredible on him. Admittedly, my style's quite different from his—I spend a disproportionate amount of time choosing my outfits every week, and as Funderburke never tires of telling me, his strategy for selecting his clothing every morning is to stagger to his closet with his eyes still clouded by sleep, fumble around blindly for a couple of seconds, and then wear whatever shirt his hand touches first. I'll admit that his system works for him, but it still makes me irrationally angry.

What I am saying is that *Funderburke can choose to be unbearably annoying as a means of disconcerting people he either dislikes or is trying to gain a psychological advantage over for investigative or other work reasons.* He has a strict rule about never using violent means, both based upon moral principles and out of pure pragmatism. In the popular imagination, private detectives routinely solve problems with their fists, but Funderburke observes that in our litigious society, throwing a punch is a great way to get yourself sued and/or arrested. Even clear-cut cases of self-defense can get you into trouble if your attacker lies or a prosecutor is in a foul mood, so it's best to keep your fists unclenched except in life-or-death situations. There is, however, no law against being irritating, which is all for the best because otherwise, every cell on Death Row would be crammed as tightly as a can of sardines.

Doubling back to my hectic day, there were a couple of other minor issues, including a minor health scare for the one-year-old daughter of one of my best students, but somehow I managed to handle everything and my teaching duties as well, though I couldn't say for certain how I succeeded. By the time Funderburke and I had finished that day's afternoon workout, I'd assumed that the storm had passed and I'd be able to have a quiet dinner with my family and maybe even hammer out three or four pages of my dissertation before bedtime.

But circumstances rarely go easy on us simply because we've had our fill of hassles, and just after I'd gotten home after my workout and showered, I received a phone call from Layla.

"Hello, Nerissa?"

"Hi! What's up, Layla?"

"It's my Dad." Her voice quavered and cracked, and I knew at once something was terribly wrong. Her breath came out shaky, and I was pretty sure that she was starting to cry. "He's been in a terrible car accident. Actually, he's been hit by a speeding driver. He was walking to the—anyway, he's at Froedtert Hospital across town now. They say he's going to live, but he's badly injured. I've been trying to call Grandma, but she's not answering her phone, and she has the car. She probably can't leave work anyway because they've got a big author signing, but I need to get over there, and I can't afford a ride share, and the bus will take an hour and a half, and I was wondering—"

"Of course. I'll be there in ten minutes."

"I hate to bother you, but–"

"Don't worry about it. I just have to get dressed, and I'll be right there." I stumbled over to my clothing rack and debated for a moment before selecting a luxuriously soft black ribbed knit top and my most comfortable pair of black lambskin joggers. I realize that I don't often talk about my footwear, and that's because that's a sore point for me. There are a lot of pretty shoes I'd like to wear, but I can't.

During my senior year of high school, during the next-to-last game of the regular season, I was running down the soccer field, and Rally, Mom's little sister, who's the same age I am, passed the ball to me. I was about six yards away from the goal, and the other team's defense was breathing down my neck. A moment later, I was blocked off from my teammates, so acting on instinct, I reared back and delivered the most powerful kick of my soccer career. The ball soared over my opponents' heads, and it flew in a gorgeous parabola across the field and slipped through the goalkeeper's raised arms into the net. That was a glorious moment for me, but before I could even scream in victory, this Brobdingnagian girl on the other team, who looked like her bones were made of titanium and her muscles were sculpted from granite, stomped upon both my feet with her own cleated foot, which was so large that she was a half-inch away from needing to buy clown shoes in order to walk comfortably. Long story short, I hit the ground hard, unable to walk, and after Mom and Dad rushed me to the emergency room, the x-rays showed that I had multiple hairline fractures across my feet. I wound up getting two casts and a pair of crutches, and that canine with two X chromosomes didn't even get a yellow card. I'm pretty sure the referee was afraid of angering her.

The point is, even after my feet healed, I've had some problems with shoes. I can't wear high heels or any hard-soled footwear because it causes too much discomfort after a few steps. I can still run for hours if I have a reliable pair of sneakers, but most of the time, I have to wear athletic shoes that are designed to look like loafers, or perhaps some really nice boots with rubber soles. There are countless occasions when I wish I had a specifically-colored pair of stylish heels to match my outfit, and I'm stuck with my steadfast ankle boots or a simple pair of sturdy ballet flats. Yes, I am aware that a lot of people have much worse troubles, and I'm lucky to have shoes at all. First World problems, I know.

Anyway, I decided that I needed more color in my outfit, so I dug out my burgundy leather trench coat and slipped into it. As soon as I walked into the kitchen, Mom and Dad knew that I wouldn't be around for dinner that night, and they quickly turned a couple of that night's panko-crusted chicken breasts into sandwiches for me and Funderburke and wrapped them. Funderburke arrived a moment after I stuffed the sandwiches and some beverages into an insulated bag, and I explained the situation as quickly as I could.

After a long, mildly annoyed sigh, he told me, "I wish I knew that we were going out in public before I put on the outfit you selected for me tonight."

"Why? You look so sexy in it."

"I look like a recently disensouled vampire."

"A lot of guys would give twenty years of their lives to look as attractive as you do in those clothes. C'mon, let's go pick up Layla."

Funderburke looked at Dad as if he was about to ask to borrow a pair of Dad's sweatpants, but instead, he thanked them for the chicken sandwiches and zippered his coat up to his chin. I wrapped my arm around him and squeezed as we headed out to his car. After a moment, he reciprocated, removing his hand soon afterwards in order to open the car door for me. A minute later we pulled up into the Dolaks' driveway, and Layla leapt up from the patio furniture and raced over to us. I noticed she was wearing a new pair of jeans, but they appeared to be no more durable than your standard dollar-store clothing. I gave them a month before they disintegrated into lint.

"Thank you so much for this," Layla said as she climbed into the back seat of Funderburke's car. "You didn't have to do this. I don't know how I'm going to make this up to you."

"Don't worry about it. Let's just get you to your dad."

"Do you know the details of the accident?" Funderburke asked.

"Not really, no. Mom and Dad really haven't had much contact with each other ever since they split up, but there are some sort of papers that have to be signed. Something to do with Erika's passing. Anyway, a couple of hours ago, maybe a bit more than that, they were meeting up at a lawyer's office on the other side of town, and Dad showed up intoxicated, and the lawyer informed them he couldn't sign the papers, as in his condition it might not be legal. So my parents argued, and as they were leaving, Dad swore at Mom, and he staggered out into the street. Mom called at him and told him to come back, but he didn't listen, and a car came out of nowhere and struck him before speeding away."

"This happened two hours or so ago? That means around four P.M., give or take a bit?" Funderburke asked.

"That's right. About three-thirty. Why do you ask?"

"Nothing..."

Layla was distressed, but she was still pretty perceptive. "You were thinking that it was pretty early in the day for him to be intoxicated. Well, Dad's motto is 'It's always five o'clock somewhere.' Before the funeral, the last time I saw him was a month earlier. We had breakfast at George Webb's. We don't hang out often, but when we do, it's for breakfast. It's the only time of day when he's likely to be sober."

"Doesn't he ever come over to your house for dinner anymore?" I asked.

"No, not for a long time. He loves us, but he's ashamed to have me and Grandma see him after he's been drinking."

"He told you this?"

Layla rubbed her temples. "Well, that's what I'm choosing to assume."

I wanted to ask more questions, but I was afraid that if I asked too many personal and potentially embarrassing questions, Layla might clam up and become angry with me. I decided to switch to a question with a minimal chance of being considered offensive. "What's your father's name?"

"Brice Dolak. My mother's name is Shelby Wiersma, by the way, in case you were wondering. I think you two were already aware of this, but my parents were never married."

"How did they meet?"

"At a party when they were seniors in high school. They went to different schools, so they didn't know each other before they tapped a keg with a bunch of their friends on a beautiful early fall day." I could see her expression souring when I looked back at her in the rear-view mirror. "I was born nine months later."

I didn't press the point, as I didn't want to open myself up to reciprocal questions about my own conception, or Toby's, for that matter. I decided to move to a less explosive topic. "What do they do for a living?"

"Mom is a marketing consultant. She has to travel all over the country, even the world. She's spent a lot of time in England working on a major job the last few years. She never stays in the same place for long. Two weeks in Boston overseeing a project, a month in Miami helping a company climb out of bankruptcy. That sort of thing. She got the job when Erika and I were kids, and it means she's not in Milwaukee much, so I went to live with Grandma and Grandpa for stability, but Erika stuck with her for a few years, back when they lived in the same city for about a year at a time. When Mom had to move every few weeks, she shipped Erika back to Milwaukee. Since Dad has always scraped by doing odd jobs—he's never held a steady nine to five, it would get in the way of his drinking—his place was never an option, since the little refurbished tool shed Dad rents is no place to raise two kids."

"When did your parents split up?" I hoped that wouldn't touch a nerve.

"Well, they were never really together. For a few years after they had me, they would occasionally...you know.... That's how Erika came along. But Dad's drinking accelerated, and it got to be too much for Mom, so she eventually cut him off completely. He never paid her a cent in child support, although really, Grandma and Grandpa picked up his share of the slack and then some." Layla folded her arms across her chest. "I wonder if the hospital will call my little half-brother's parents."

"You have another sibling?"

"Yes. He's the result of a fling Dad had with a college student around the same time I had Juniper. She decided that she couldn't count on Dad for child support, and she wound up marrying her on-again-off-again boyfriend, and he adopted the kid, and she filed for full custody and won. They live in Madison, and they sent a restraining order to Grandma to deny her any contact with her grandson. As far as they're concerned, we don't exist. Grandma's heartbroken about it all, and I've never met the boy."

"Huh. I guess we all have half-siblings that aren't in our lives," I said.

"Really?"

"Yeah. My biological father made it clear that he had no interest in raising kids, and then at thirty-five, he married an heiress whose ancestors came over on the Mayflower, and they had two little girls in rapid succession. Their lawyers got in touch with me and sent me a very polite, threatening letter asking me not to communicate with them. Well, I don't mind never seeing him again, but I wonder about my half-sisters every day." I shrugged. "I shouldn't complain. I'm blessed with two sets of triplet siblings."

"How did that happen? The odds against that are astronomical."

"Mom and Dad had fertility issues. Then Dad's Yen-Yen[1] gave Mom some of this special Chinese tea that's supposed to work miracles, and clearly, it worked better than anybody expected. And then a few years later, when Mom had a twenty-four-hour cold, one of her cousins stopped by and made her a hot drink made with the tea that had sat in the back of the cupboard for four years, and you can guess what happened soon after she recovered."

"Oh." Layla looked a bit stunned by that story. "Funderburke, what about your half-sibling?"

"Half-siblings. Plural. My mother had three children by three different men. I entered the world through a one-night stand. I have no idea who my father is, and neither does she. She married her steady-ish boyfriend, and they had a son together. We have not spoken since I was fourteen years old, when I moved in with my grandparents. I understand that he now specializes in confidence schemes that are arguably legal. After her divorce from husband number one, my mother married a demon in human form, and before he ran off in order to escape abuse charges, he left her with my half-sister, who I met briefly when she was a baby, but I have not seen her since."

"Holy cow. I thought my family was messed up."

Funderburke tightened his hands around the steering wheel. "I'm glad that I can make you feel better about your loved ones."

Every time Funderburke talks about his mother and half-siblings, I start mentally telling myself, "I love my family, I love my family," repeatedly.

"I'm sorry, I don't want to talk about my father anymore. Can we please discuss something else?" Layla pleaded.

"Sure." I turned the conversation towards my day and how, over the last couple of years, I'd discovered some brilliant young women who just happened to have gotten in the family way and needed a little help getting a first-rate education in order to succeed in later life. Thanks to some sympathetic donors, I was able to provide them with full scholarships to Cuthbertson, but now I was dealing with some newly uncovered problems. Four of my girls were over eighteen, so they had aged out of foster care, but they didn't have any family members they could turn to for support and housing, so I had to find a way to keep them properly sheltered pronto, because they had one to three years of high school to go.

We got stuck in the tail end of rush hour traffic, but eventually, we made it to Froedert and hurried out in search of Layla's father. Funderburke had to unzip his coat to tuck his car keys back into his pants pocket. As the wind blew Funderburke's coat behind him, Layla caught a glimpse of his clothes and smirked. "Nice outfit."

"He's wearing it to please me, and I say he looks amazing. Lay off," I informed her as Funderburke zippered up his coat.

Layla mumbled something that vaguely sounded like an apology, and as we made our way into the lobby, a woman in a mahogany aviator jacket, designer jeans, and Italian high-heeled shoes strolled up to us. Her dark hair was pulled up and back in a clip, and I could see the family resemblance immediately.

"Hi, Mom."

"Hello, Lay-Lay. Your father will be fine. His life's not in any danger, but he's got two broken legs. Shattered legs, actually. It's not clear whether or not he'll be able to walk again without assistance." I got the impression she wasn't terribly upset about her ex's condition. If anything, Shelby's principal emotion seemed to be annoyance, and my judgmental gut feeling told me that this was due to the fact that her plans for the evening had been disrupted. She turned towards us. "Hello. Who are you?"

We introduced ourselves. It appeared that Shelby had lost interest in who we were by the time Funderburke reached the second syllable of his name.

"Why didn't you tell me you were back in town, Mom?" Layla asked.

"I didn't know I'd be coming back to Milwaukee until my bosses gave me a new assignment this morning."

"Was your appointment with the lawyers an impromptu meeting then?" Funderburke asked.

The expression on Shelby's face indicated that she was not pleased to have Funderburke enter the conversation. "The lawyer got in touch with me shortly after Erika's funeral passed and told me that Brice and I needed to come down to his office to sign a few documents. Well, I didn't think I'd have the opportunity to come back here for a month or two, but when my plans changed, I called the lawyer, and he had a spot free in his schedule." She arched her eyebrows to indicate that she hoped that would be the end of the questions.

"Where are you staying, Mom?"

"The company booked a room at the Potawatomi Hotel. I need to head back there in a moment. I'm meeting a couple of clients at the restaurant there, and I can't be late."

"Wait! Mom, I hardly ever get to see you. Can't you stick around for another couple of minutes, please? We really didn't talk at the funeral."

"Well, I wasn't in any condition to do much chatting that day."

"I understand. Please, can't you spare a little time to talk?"

Shelby checked the time on her phone and then sighed. "All right. Just a few minutes, though. I can't be late." She lowered her thin frame into one of the cushioned chairs off to the side of the lobby, and Layla sat next to her. It would have been awkward for us to get too close to them, but we sat down in a pair of chairs in a cluster about five feet away from them, where we could hear everything they were saying. Using a trick we've tried many times before, Funderburke and I pulled out our phones and stared fixedly at them, though we kept our ears completely focused on the two women.

"How was Dad doing this afternoon."

"The usual. Intoxicated and happy. He's still the party boy he was eighteen, and I don't think he'll ever change."

"When will I be able to see him?"

"They're working on setting his bones now. They may have splintered, so that may not work. If the damage is too severe, they may have to amputate." She sighed. "I don't believe that he has health insurance. He hasn't been working much since Erika died. He's been directing all of his focus on drinking. Someone will have to pay his bills. I really don't think that it can be me, I'm afraid. I can't be responsible for him. I sacrificed the best years of my youth cleaning up his messes, and he's on his own now."

An alarmed tone entered Layla's voice. "Mom, just how much will his medical expenses be? Grandma and I are going to be paying off Erika's funeral for months."

"You shouldn't have to worry about him. Leave him to his own devices. He's his own problem."

"But if he's very badly injured, he may have to move in with us."

"Well, you need to do what you need to do. Good luck to you. I don't want to sound unfeeling, but I have my own life and my own expenses, and I need to look out for myself. I've suffered too much from his selfishness. He drained me for years, and it's only recently that I've gotten my life back on track."

"I was wondering, if he's not working much, how's Dad getting money for drinking?"

"He has his ways. He's always had a talent for borrowing cash and never paying it back. Over the years, he's extracted four thousand bucks from me, and I'll never see it again. I hope that you haven't lent him anything."

Layla shifted uncomfortably in her chair. "A twenty every now and then."

"You'd have gotten better value if you simply set a match to your Jacksons. He's behind on his rent, too. The only reason he isn't out on the streets is because his landlord is worried about squatters' rights or something like that. I shouldn't tell you how he got to drink for free last night."

"What? Please, tell me."

"No, I mustn't. I really mustn't."

"Why not?"

"A young woman should be able to maintain some shred of respect for her father. It's not my place to take something so precious away from you."

"Mom, I'm begging you. What's going on?"

"Well, he's been teasing gay men in bars."

"*What?*"

"Your father's still a very attractive man, even if he isn't taking the best care of himself. So sometimes, when he's completely broke, he puts on his best clothes, finds a gay bar he hasn't visited in a while and waits for some fellow to pick him up. He doesn't actually *do* anything with any of them; he was very insistent on that point when he told me about it in the lawyer's waiting room. It was quite unsettling how he bragged about what he saw as his ingenuity. Anyway, sooner or later, a guy who's looking for love starts buying him drinks, and your father plays along for a while, stringing him along as he accepts beverage after beverage. Then, once he's sufficiently soused to *appear* pliable to his mark, but still in sufficient possession of his faculties to avoid going further than he'd like, he excuses himself, says something about he'll meet the other guy in a minute, and then he slips out into the night and makes his way home, tipsy and happy."

Layla looked stunned. "Does he do that often?"

"He told me that a couple of the bars in question have his picture behind the counter, and he's no longer welcome in those establishments." Shelby looked up at us. "Don't you two have somewhere to be?"

"How is Layla going to get back?" I asked. "I thought she'd want to stay a bit until she could see her father. If you're leaving soon, you won't be able to drive her home."

I'd made a strong point, and Shelby didn't like it. She pursed her lips for a moment, and then said, "Can't she take a rideshare home?"

"Those have gotten so expensive these days," Layla explained. I don't have the money for one. Do you have thirty or forty dollars for me, please?"

Shelby's hands tightened around her purse, as if she was afraid that Layla would snatch her precious cash from her. "I'm afraid I'm low on funds at the moment. I didn't have time to stop by the ATM." She rose to her feet and gripped a key chain that was clipped to the strap of her purse. I noticed that the key chain's fob was a poker chip encased in a golden circle. "I'd love to stay and chat longer, but I have to hurry to my meeting. If I don't get stuck in traffic, I'll just barely make it in time." Layla stood up and started to say something, but before she could manage to form more than two syllables, Shelby hugged her daughter. "Goodbye." Wrinkling her nose as she withdrew her arms, she murmured, "It's getting harder and harder to wrap my arms around you. You really should start doing something about that." After giving Layla a pat on the stomach that was more chastisement than a show of affection, Shelby hurried out through the waiting area and through the doors leading outside without a word or a glance in our direction.

Layla walked up to us with a slight trembling on her lips. "Go ahead and say what you're thinking."

I was trying to come up with something cutting to say about her mother, but Funderburke forestalled it with a much more prudent comment. "I think you should try to call your grandmother again. If she doesn't answer her cell phone, try the bookstore."

With a mumbled, "That's a good idea," Layla tried the first suggestion, went straight to voice mail, and then had more success with reaching the bookstore. After a minute's worth of conversation, she finally got through to Celeste. After explaining the situation in as calm a voice as possible, Layla started speaking solely in "uh-huhs" with the occasional "sounds good."

Ending the call, she turned to us. "Grandma's very upset. She's going to explain the situation to her boss and then drive straight here." Her face blanched. "My shift starts at the bar in half an hour. I've missed so much work in the past week, my boss said that if I skipped any more, I was fired. But I can't leave until I find out what's wrong with Dad." Her eyes started watering. "He's not a good father. Still, I don't want to lose him."

Funderburke excused himself to visit the front desk and try to find out where Layla's father was at the moment and who she could talk to about his condition. Meanwhile, I informed her, "You know, in college, I did a little work for the university catering department. I didn't work in an actual bar, but I served a lot of drinks to wealthy alumni. That's a classic fundraising strategy, you know. Colleges get their richest former students together in a room, ply them with moderate-quality wine and beer, and wait until the end of dinner when everybody's good and soused. Then, ask them for money, collect the checks from their tipsy hands, and hope that everybody's in sufficient control of their facilities so that their handwriting's legible enough to cash them. The rumor has it that most university presidents are picked due to how skilled they are at holding their liquor."

"What are you saying?"

"I can cover your shift for you tonight. At least the first part."

Layla's jaw dropped. "Are you serious?"

"Sure? This is a family crisis, and I'm willing to do what I can to help out someone in need. I mean, I can't stay until closing time because I have a class to teach in the morning, but I can give you a few more hours here at the hospital. If you can get back by ten or so to take over your shift, that'd be great. When your grandmother arrives, you can drive her car back across town."

She jumped forward and hugged me, pinning my arms to my sides so I couldn't reciprocate. After saying "thank you" approximately seventeen times in rapid succession, she released me just as Funderburke returned.

"Good news?" he asked.

"I just volunteered to take care of the first few hours of Layla's evening shift at the bar. We'd better hurry if we're going to make it in time."

"All right." Funderburke turned to Layla. "A doctor or a nurse will come here in about five minutes to take you to your father. The receptionist couldn't give me any more information about his condition, but keep an eye out—the person relaying the message has your description, but it's a busy lobby."

A few more declarations of gratitude later, and we were back in the car, heading back to the East Side. My stomach was growling in the least ladylike manner possible, and now I was devouring my sandwich as delicately as possible, trying not to let oily crumbs fall upon my clothing. As Funderburke was driving, he would eat his dinner later, after he had dropped me off at Groebel's Tavern.

"What did you think of Layla's mother? It's only me here, so don't hold back on your judgments," Funderburke asked.

"Ice queen. She had Layla and Erika young, and she resents her for existing and interrupting her plans for a self-indulgent early adulthood. As for Layla's father, Shelby considers him an overgrown party boy and hopeless drunkard, and blames him for the lion's share of the disappointments in her life. She wasn't the least bit upset that the father of her children is close to death. If anything, she resents him for interrupting her evening by being so inconsiderate as to be hit by a car."

"So you don't like her."

Swallowing a mouthful of chicken, I said, "There's something shady about her. I'm not sure what exactly, but I am positive that she wasn't being entirely honest about her plans for the evening. She was being much too brusque. And I don't think that she has a business meeting."

"Why not?"

"Those are expensive jeans, but they're not business attire. Yeah, maybe this supposed meeting is more casual than I think, but frankly, those shoes are more hot-date footwear than "conversation with a client." I suspect she's meeting a boyfriend. Something like that."

Funderburke drummed his fingers on the steering wheel. "What really struck me was just how much in a hurry Shelby was to get away. You'd think that having just lost one daughter, she might be all the more anxious to spend some more time with her one remaining child. I know that everybody processes grief differently, but I wonder if Shelby wasn't feeling comfortable around Layla."

"And you think that this is due to distrust of her daughter, don't you? I know that look. You think that Layla's mother suspects that she is responsible for Erika's death, and that explains why she couldn't be bothered to spend more than a couple of minutes with her."

He sighed and stared at the highway for a bit. "I just don't know. I liked your father's theory a lot. I think that Erika accidentally overdosing on pure fentanyl and Layla making a conscious decision to leave her alone makes sense. But just because Layla wasn't directly responsible for Erika's death doesn't mean that she doesn't feel guilt for leaving her to die. I believe that what we call intuition is partially based on our observational skills picking up on details we don't fully understand. You know the story of Clever Hans, right?"

"Refresh my memory, please." I wiped some crumbs from my lips with a tissue and hoped that I didn't smear my lipstick.

"Clever Hans was a horse that people thought could do math. Someone would ask Hans what two plus five was, and he'd stomp his hoof seven times. But then someone ran an experiment where someone would pose a math problem to Hans while being hidden from Hans's view. Hans would start stomping his hoof, but he wouldn't stop, even after he'd reached the number that was the answer to the question. See, Hans wasn't actually performing calculations in his head. After a bit of training, Hans could pick up on little signals from his questioners. Maybe an eye twitch, perhaps a change in posture. The humans asking the questions didn't realize that they were providing Hans with a sign to stop pounding his hoof. Without realizing it, they gave Hans a tell that stopped the stomping. When Hans couldn't see the human asking him questions, he never received the involuntary signal, so he kept on stomping. And I think that a lot of humans work similarly. Especially with people they know very well, they can pick up on little signals. Not always so blatant as tugging at an earlobe, but I'm not surprised if Layla's setting off all sorts of alarm bells in her family's heads by unconsciously signaling her feelings of culpability over her part in her sister's death."

I mulled over that for a bit. "I think there's something in that..."

"But you don't sound convinced."

"It's my judgmental instincts. I'm picking up some sort of vibe off of Layla's mother, and it tells me that there's something more to the story than what we're discussing. But I'm darned if I know what it could be."

We didn't share anything more than a few perfunctory comments for a while. As Funderburke dropped me off at the tavern, he informed me, "I'm still worrying about the pills. Where did Erika get them? I worry that there are a lot more capsules filled with pure fentanyl out there, and if we don't find the source of them, more people are going to wind up dead."

"So what's your plan?"

"There's another Narcotics Anonymous meeting at a different church tonight. I'm going to ask some more questions, but discreetly, in order to protect everybody's privacy. And I'm also planning to try to track down Erika's pal "Jane Doe" to see if she can provide anything else that can point me in a helpful direction. But first, I will pull into that parking lot over there and eat my sandwich."

"Sounds like a plan." I wiped my fingers on a paper napkin, leaned over, slipped a hand behind his head, and kissed Funderburke for a full minute, running his soft hair through my fingers and gently brushing the side of my hand against his cheek as I slowly pulled away. "I only ate half my sandwich. I'm full. You finish the rest. Thanks for driving across town on an empty stomach at my request. I want you to know how much the little sacrifices you make mean to me. That includes going out in public in the clothes I pick out for you. Remember, the secret is to make it clear through your posture and facial expression that any criticisms people may feel compelled to make about what you wear are irrelevant to you."

He blushed, and then he smiled at me in that puppyish manner that makes me feel all warm and fuzzy. I had the sense that it was a combination of his self-consciousness about his outfit, his reaction to the kiss, and the scent of chicken on my breath. "I'll call you when I know when Layla's coming to take over for me."

I hurried into the bar and felt depressed as soon as I crossed through the door. This was not the sort of warm and friendly neighborhood pub where everybody knows your name. This was a poorly lit, perfunctorily dusted hole in the wall, filled with depressed people who come there to drink alone while being surrounded by other individuals who are doing the same thing. Looking around, I suspected that this was also a popular hangout for college freshmen and sophomores who wanted to grab a beer at a place that didn't make a habit of checking IDs.

I asked one of the girls behind the bar where I could find the manager, and she pointed me towards a tiny office across from the bathrooms. I introduced myself to a man who was so large that he took up what seemed like half the space in the office, and he looked me up and down several times, leered, and said that I was a few steps up from Layla and that hopefully I was as good a cocktail waitress as she was.

I hung my trench coat up on a hook behind the bar, and I started serving customers. Most of them muttered their orders without even bothering to look at me. A few guys tried to lean across the bar and get handsy, but I was able to quash their advances without much difficulty. Most of them seemed so disgusted with themselves afterwards that they handed me five and ten-dollar tips by way of an apology.

A table of four boys who were clearly no older than eighteen asked for beers, and I asked for identification. After agreeing in voices so artificially deep I thought they were trying to do a poor imitation of James Earl Jones, I checked them and noticed at once that none of the photos matched the customers. One of the license cards was for a George Whittier. "George?" I asked. None of them responded. I called out the name again and received no reply. "I can bring you four sodas," I told them, tossing the fake IDs into a little bowl behind the bar.

"What? I have two kids and a mortgage!" said one of the boys, who appeared to be a couple of years away from his first shave. I shot him my best "stern teacher" look, and he crumbled. "I'll have a Sprite," he muttered.

As I placed the order, a thirty-something guy with an unfortunate goatee introduced himself as the assistant manager. "You know, we really don't check IDs here. If you want to work here, you have to be willing to let things slide."

"Do you see that guy over there?" I nodded my head towards no particular person in the crowded bar. "I went out with him once about a year ago," I lied. "Boring guy, but he takes a lot of pride in his work, and he's very ambitious. He's a police officer who goes undercover to bars and tries to catch establishments that aren't very assiduous about checking for underage drinkers. The more violations he identifies, the better his chances of promotion. He's got a grudge against me because I refused to sleep with him. He'd like nothing better than to bust me for serving a teenager hard liquor. Are you going to explain to your boss that the new girl warned you, but you ignored her, and the tavern got shut down?"

Scruffy Goatee Guy had nothing to say. He poured me four sodas, and I brought them over to the teens, who made no attempt to be grateful. I knew at once they'd be lousy tippers.

For the most part, the customers seemed to like me, and by ten o'clock, I'd made nearly four hundred dollars in gratuities. I had just finished calling a cab for a guy who was too soused to walk more than half a block when Layla walked into the bar.

I greeted her, saying, "Hi! I was expecting your call."

"Ooh, sorry about that. My cheap cell phone couldn't get a signal." She was clearly upset, and her eyes were crimson from prolonged crying.

"Is everything all right? Is your dad... is he?"

Layla sniffed, as the sobbing was causing her nose to run profusely. I grabbed a flimsy paper napkin from a dispenser on the table beside me. She accepted it with a brief "thanks" and dabbed her eyes with it before blowing her nose. I provided her with a couple more napkins and waited for her to regain her composure.

Apparently, ten seconds was too long to wait because the bar manager stormed over to us and bellowed, "I'm not paying you to stand there gossiping. Your job is to make sure the customers don't get a chance to get thirsty."

I turned to him. "Layla's father was just in a serious car accident, and–"

"Is your crying and hugging going to make him better? Is my losing money going to fix the problem? Huh? Get over to that table there and bring them more beers."

"Shut up, scumball!"

I hadn't expected that outburst from Layla. When I turned back to her, the tears had dried up, and her eyes were blazing with rage.

The manager took three steps towards her. "What did you call me?"

"I called you a scumball. Is that all you can think about? Selling watered-down cocktails to dipsomaniacs too wrapped up in their own misery to notice? This gin here–" She lunged across the room and grabbed a bottle that had just been placed on the countertop for the preparation of a martini. "This is spiked tap water. For crying out loud, do you have so little respect for the customers that you're willing to pick their pockets just to save a few measly bucks?" By now, every eye in the bar was on her.

The manager leaned down over her until his eyes were level with hers, and he glared. "Tell everybody you're lying," he hissed.

"I won't. It's all true."

The manager straightened up and shouted, "She's making it up, people. We serve top-quality liquor here. It's her time of the month, and she's not aware of what she's saying."

"Yes, I am! Yes, I am! And don't blame my damn period!" Layla flung the bottle in the manager's general direction. It sailed well over his head and smashed on the ceiling. The glass shards fell, glinting in the meager light, and danced on the floor, but fortunately, they didn't hit anybody on the way down.

Pointing a massive finger at Layla, the manager bellowed, "You're fired!"

"Good!" Layla trembled for a second, and then the reality of the situation hit, and her legs collapsed out from under her. I eased her into a chair.

"If you want her job, babe, it's yours." The manager told me. "Just throw her out the door and get back to serving the customers."

"I appreciate the offer," I informed him, "but this 'babe' has just gotten a brand-new appreciation for her teaching job. So thanks, but no thanks." I stomped behind the bar and retrieved my trench coat. I wriggled into it, fastened the belt, and helped Layla to her feet. Trying to make the most dramatic exit I could manage, I led her out the door, letting it slam behind me.

"Where's your grandmother's car?" I asked as we walked out into the chilly autumn night.

She pointed. "Just half a block down the street."

There were a couple of scruffy-looking men a few yards from us who were staring straight at me. They were giving me an unsettling premonition, so I grabbed Layla's hand and hustled her to the car as quickly as possible. "Get your keys ready," I whispered. She nearly dropped them, but she managed to catch them before they slipped from her fingers, unlocked the door, and we both climbed inside, I locked the doors seconds before the two of them came up to the car. One of them started tapping on the window as Layla hurriedly started the engine, and we pulled away. I heard one of them shouting, "C'mon! We just wanna talk t'ya!" as we cruised down the block.

Once we turned the corner and were out of their sight, Layla shook with emotion. "I needed this job."

"No, you don't," I informed her. "You need *a* job, one that will provide you with the cash you need to make ends meet and, preferably, a good deal more. Now, there's nothing wrong with working at a bar—a lot of people seem to derive a lot of pleasure from it, and I'm happy for them. But you don't strike me as one of those people."

"True. I always thought that I'd be working at this great nonprofit or some respected organization like Amnesty International or something like that. And lots of places are happy to accept the help of enthusiastic young people, but most of them don't offer positions that pay enough to keep body and soul together. I was offered a job at a homeless shelter a few years ago, but it paid less than a third of what I made at the tavern. You need a B.A. and even a master's degree, and a reputation for fundraising if you're going to have any shot at a decently-paying job in this field."

"Well, you don't work for a charity if you want to get rich. Actually, check that. If you have no scruples, running a nonprofit is a great way to make a profit, as long as your conscience isn't going to keep you up at night if you plan to funnel the cash that's supposed to help the less fortunate into your own pockets."

"I'm guessing that you don't dip into the funds that are supposed to support teen mothers to buy yourself new leather coats."

"No, I do not. Thank you for the vote of confidence as to my integrity. Just a sec. I need to check in with Funderburke." I checked my texts and saw several from him. The long and the short of it was that he was on the trail of "Jane Doe." I texted him back and wished him luck, informing him that Layla was driving me home.

A minute later, we pulled into my driveway. "Come on into the house. You look like you need to talk to someone."

"I don't want to impose."

"Good to know. Now, please, follow me. Have you had dinner?"

"No. I usually get my suppers free at the tavern. I get to eat what the customers send back."

"Yummy." Dad must have heard the car, because he had the door open for us.

"Toby went up to brush her teeth three minutes ago," he informed me. "I don't think she's asleep yet."

Thanking him, I ran upstairs. Toby had just turned off the light in her room as I reached her door, but it opened immediately at my knock, and she commented that I'd just barely made it in time to give her a goodnight hug and kiss. When I came back downstairs after tucking her in, I found that Mom and Dad had led Layla to the cozy little alcove that serves as my study, and Mom was bringing a freshly microwaved plate of chicken, buttered noodles, and carrots to her.

"Do you need anything?" Mom asked as she set a tumbler of water on the little table.

Slinging beers had worked up an appetite, so I asked for portions of everything Layla had just received, only half the size of what she'd gotten, and a glass of milk. We ate in silence for a bit. I finished while she still had plenty left on her plate, so I decided to bring up a subject that had been on my mind. "If you could do anything you wanted to advance your career, what would you do?"

Layla chewed thoughtfully for a moment and said, "I'd go back in time and tell myself not to let Erika distract me from my studies. You know why I got kicked out of college? Why I lost my scholarship?"

I didn't, and I tried to strike the perfect balance in my tone, making it clear that I'd be interested in what she had to say, but I didn't want to be so desperate for information that it put her off telling me.

There were still several bites of food left on her plate, but Layla tossed down her fork with a loud clatter, and she sighed. "This was when we discovered her addiction. We wanted to put her into rehab, but we didn't have much cash on hand at the moment. Most of Grandma and Grandpa's money was tied up in an annuity, so they couldn't withdraw enough to pay for the rehab fees. Holy cow, that's expensive. Anyway, Dad was no help, of course, and Mom had her own expenses—she'd used all of her savings to pay for one of her cousins' cancer treatments. Well, I didn't know what to do, and I started telling my classmates that I needed money, and then out of nowhere, I was recruited by this underground organization at the college. They told me I was a top student, and they'd pay me well to write essays and term papers for other students who weren't willing to do their own work. So I stayed up until four A.M. every night for two weeks, sipping cup after cup of black coffee and writing two reports a day on top of my own work. I got two hundred fifty dollars for each paper. Seven thousand dollars total. Combined with what my grandparents could contribute, it was enough to send her to the rehab clinic."

"And then you got caught?" I deduced.

Layla nodded. "One of the professors knew at once that the paper one bozo turned in was too well-written to be his own work. So the fellow was called into the professor's office, questioned with moderate intensity, and very quickly crumbled under the pressure. He confessed that he'd bought the paper, and a little investigation by the campus authorities led them to the group that sold the essays. Someone made a deal and gave up my name in order to avoid punishment. I never found out who it was, but the snitch's college career continued as if nothing had happened, whereas I was informed that my scholarship had been revoked and that I had the choice of quietly withdrawing from the college or being publicly expelled and possibly the matter would be turned over to the police. They said I could go to jail if I tried to fight the charges."

"The laws on selling work for grades vary from state to state," I noted. "I'd have to do a little research to see if you were really in any danger of legal punishment. Of course, nearly every college has rules against academic dishonesty, but unless their evidence is absolutely airtight, if a student bluffs and denies hard enough and threatens a lawsuit, the accused student has a gambler's chance of avoiding punishment. Although in many cases, a college can withdraw a scholarship at any time for any reason, especially if the recipient has signed a waiver saying they won't fight the decision to strip them of their financial aid should the situation arise."

"Well, at the time, I didn't have the strength to deny it, and my conscience was beating me up, because I was as guilty as sin. So I signed what they put in front of me, packed my bags, and came home to Milwaukee. At the time, I told myself it was worth it. I had sacrificed my college education so Erika could be cured of her addiction. I figured that was an acceptable trade. The problem was that Erika didn't live up to her side of the bargain." Layla slumped in her chair. "I know that addiction is a disease and that often the addict's brain chemistry is so severely dependent on the drug that no amount of rehab will break the opioid's hold on the addict. But if I'd known ahead of time that the rehab wasn't going to work, I'd have made a very different decision. That's the horrible thing. All the false hope. You blow your savings on a miracle cure for your loved one, and then when it doesn't materialize, you're broke, your sister's still getting high, and now you have no prospects. You'd think that the rehab clinics would have the decency to offer a money-back guarantee, but no. They clean you out whether they get results or not. And you don't just get cleaned out financially. You get obliterated emotionally as well. If you dare to complain, a self-righteous nurse will look at you like you're a mess a naughty dog has made on the carpet, and she will lecture you in a condescending tone that your sister is very ill and she doesn't need your anger and your judgments, she needs your understanding. But where was the understanding towards me? No one said, 'Layla, I know what you gave up to help Erika. I'm sorry we couldn't come through for you.' No, it was my fault. I was the wicked, selfish, grasping witch who didn't have enough love in her heart to shower Erika with love and support. The nurse implied that it was my fault that Erika couldn't kick the habit, because I wasn't providing her with enough no-strings-attached help. No, all Grandpa did was go back to work until he dropped dead to pay for more rehab that wound up doing nothing, and Grandma gave her free shelter and food, and still, Erika took and took and took. When she stole from us, her counselors told us that the missing items were just possessions, and we needed to care more about an actual human being and what she was suffering. Never mind all the pain she put us through, she had an illness, and she got a free pass, according to the counselors. They didn't say it in those words, but that's what they meant. So she took my computer, and my phone, and my jacket, but those were just possessions, so I wasn't supposed to care. Then she took my hair, and when I complained to her counselor, all I got was a wave of the hand and a blithe 'it'll grow back.' And she almost as good as took away my daughter, because it wasn't a safe place for her to live, not with Erika around. I tried. I tried to see my sister behind those dead, pinpoint eyes. But I never received anything from her, not a word of gratitude or even a comforting hug. All she did was take, take, take. Gimme, gimme, gimme, more, more, more. Until there was nothing left, I was hollow inside, and she was bringing me down with her. If she'd only once cried and begged for forgiveness, saying she was sorry for all the harm she'd done, but she just couldn't stop with the drugs, she was trying but failing, well, that would have been all I needed. But she couldn't even give me that. She ruined our lives. And if she hadn't died, it would have continued for years, maybe decades. Grandma would have passed away, working until her last breath supporting Erika, Juniper would have grown up barely knowing me, and I would be slinging beers for a living, my soul shriveling and my waistline expanding, until I dropped dead from a heart attack. She might have outlived me, you know, if I—I mean, if she hadn't overdosed."

I saw the look of fear on her face, hoping that I hadn't caught her little slip of the tongue. Of course, I had, but I tried to keep my own expression blank.

"It doesn't matter anyway," Layla mumbled as she ran her toe along the carpet. "My life's already gone down the toilet."

I waited for a minute, carefully choosing my words. "I don't want you to think about your answer to this question. Just answer on reflex. If you could do one thing now to change your life, what would it be?"

"Go back to college and get my degree," she replied immediately.

"In what?"

"Non-profit management, youth work, something like that."

"What if you had the chance to get that? Would you take that?"

"That's a moot point."

"No, it's not. How would you like a scholarship?"

"Are you offering me one?"

"Yes, I am."

She stared at me for a moment, as if I was playing an unfunny prank on her. "Be serious."

"I told you, the Bialowsky Fund is designed to help unwed mothers. We focus on teens, but over the past year, I've accepted some women in their early twenties who need to finish high school, and I've realized that to keep them on the path to success, we're going to need to help them through college as well. Your path's a little different from the ones others have taken, but that's not a disqualifying point. We've built up a decent endowment, and the job's getting to be too big for me, especially when I'm trying to wrap up my dissertation. I think I need to train an assistant, and I want to know if you're interested."

Layla did an excellent impression of a goldfish for a little bit before saying, "I thought that you gave these scholarships to genius girls who were victimized by their mothers' boyfriends, or who were kidnapped and sold into human trafficking. I just had a really bad day. I felt sorry for a guy who was mourning what he thought was the breakup of his marriage and hooked up in the back seat of his car."

"Well, intelligence is a prerequisite, but most of the young women accepted by the fund were in consenting relationships with boyfriends their own age. Speaking as someone who had a terrible week when she was barely thirteen years old, fled to the home of one of her closest friends after a huge fight with her mother, unloaded her emotions to that guy pal, and still isn't sure how it happened, but she wound up doing something she never thought she would that night, I'm not passing judgment when a woman with a young daughter asks for a little help. When I accept someone into the program, it's because I see something in them. Maybe it's ambition, often it's intellectual brilliance, and sometimes it's deep kindness. But I get impressions about people. I trust my instincts, and the vibe I get from you is that you made some decisions you regret and you are not happy with where you are in life. You could continue to write the obituary for your dreams, or you could say, 'No more of this. I'm tired of seeing my life as one huge jumble of disappointments. For the last few years, I've been trapped in a rut and miserable. Now, I'm taking steps to save myself. I want to finish my college education. Now, I'm being offered the opportunity on a silver platter. First, an education, then a job helping young women. Am I going to take a shot at achieving my goals of being a force for positivity in the world, or am I going to keep pouring watered-down beer down the throats of college boys with fake I.D.s?' The choice is yours."

"But–" Layla stopped herself and took a breath before speaking again. "You say you see something in me. What? I was a really good student in high school, but nothing super-special. My athletic skills got me a scholarship, but I wasn't Olympic material. So what are my qualifications?"

I shrugged. "The last several years have been rough for you. I deal with girls who've been in family situations that range from challenging to horrific. It seems that someone who's dealt with challenges of her own will connect with them. I had a lot of frustrations growing up, but compared to what a lot of those girls have survived, my early years were sunshine, lollipops, and rainbows. But I can't tell all of them to do what I did—'Find the nicest, most decent, most morally upright man you can and force him to adopt you.' I need them to see a different kind of role model, a woman who fought and clawed until she achieved the life she wanted."

"So...you're shaping me into your preferred image?"

"No, I'm asking you if you're willing to shape yourself into your own preferred image."

"And if I say no?"

"Well, I'm not sure why you'd refuse a scholarship, but if you decide you don't want it, then you and I will say "goodnight" with no hard feelings, and tomorrow you'll start looking for another job at another dive bar. There's plenty of them in Milwaukee."

Layla rose to her feet and crossed to the little window. She stared out it for a minute, but it was too dark to see anything but shadows. "I'm afraid I'm going to screw up again."

"Do you want fear of failure to control your life? And anyway, it's not like you're fearing cancer or an attack by a chainsaw-wielding madman, which are dangers that you have precious little control over, really. Fear of screwing up is something you do have control over. You've gotten into trouble in the past. Stay on the straight and narrow path, and you're set. Unless you want to self-sabotage. Do you want to torpedo your own chances?"

"Why would I do that?"

"Are you trying to punish yourself?"

I'd hit a nerve. She'd been slouching before, but she snapped up as straight as a flagpole, and I saw a spark in her eye that wasn't there earlier. "What are you saying? Do you think I've done something wrong?"

"Do you?" I replied, deftly avoiding the question and flipping it back upon her. "Because that's the only reason I can think of for why you'd say no to this opportunity."

She opened her mouth, thought better of it, and then fidgeted briefly. "If I said yes, what would happen?"

"Well, I don't have that much money to offer you, but it's enough to finish your undergraduate degree at the University of Wisconsin—Milwaukee. That's within walking distance of your house. You can apply to complete your college education. You had what? Two and a half years under your belt?"

"Yes. My grades weren't great that last term, though."

"Well, I'll work with you, and I'm pretty sure you can get in at UWM. They have a pretty quick turnaround time. I think you can get started in January. If you take classes during the summer, you can be finished with your undergraduate degree by next Christmas. Then we'll see if you want to get a master's or a certificate in something."

"But I have student loans and other debts to pay. Grandma gives me a rent-free home and meals, but I still need to make some money. Even if I go back to college, I'm going to need to bartend at night."

"Not necessarily. Cuthbertson is hiring coaches for the winter term. We need someone to coach fifth and sixth-grade girls' basketball. You played— how do you feel about coaching?"

"I guess… That does sound like fun."

"It doesn't pay too much, but it should cover your basic bills for student loans, plus a little extra. You could attend classes in the morning and early afternoon, then come up to Cuthbertson by three-thirty, spend two hours coaching, then go home, eat dinner, and take care of your homework."

She stared at me for a couple of moments. "You've put a lot of thought into this, haven't you?'

"I've spent a few minutes reflecting on the situation. Not to nag, but have you spent this amount of time pondering how to get what you want out of your life?"

Her lips twitched on and off as if she kept thinking of comments she wished to make and then decided it was better not to say anything. "No. No, I haven't."

"Why not?"

"I… just haven't had the energy to do anything." She folded her arms. "Apathy is a pretty big strike against me in your plans to launch my career in charity work, isn't it?"

"You'd be surprised," I informed her. "A few of the most brilliant girls in my group are so overwhelmed by the situations they're in—abusive parents, turbulent home lives, surviving horrific crimes…. Drawing on my own experience, when things are rough, a teenager barely has enough strength to survive. When they're dealing with puberty, tragedy, fear, and a baby to boot, that's a lot to endure. Who can blame them for needing a helping hand out of the morass?"

"But I haven't been a teenager for half a decade," Layla reminded me.

"No, I don't believe that turning eighteen, or twenty, or twenty-one, or whatever, means that because of a few questionable decisions, the remaining fifty-plus decades of your life should permanently be veiled in shadow. I mean, I was class salutatorian in high school, and I graduated from college in record time, earning summa cum laude and Phi Beta Kappa. I got straight A's while I worked on my master's degree, I'm ABD for my doctorate, I'm teaching at the top school in the state, I'm running an organization to help teen mothers, I go to Mass practically every day, my daughter's thriving at school, I have an amazing relationship with my adoptive family, and my boyfriend and I have helped dozens of children in crisis situations, but in so many supposedly non-judgmental, tolerant eyes, my defining characteristic is that I had sex just one single time in my life when I was thirteen, and I got pregnant because of it. So when I see young women who are in comparable or worse situations, I want to make sure they get the same fighting chance that I did."

I paused for breath, and after I regained some composure, Layla asked, "Just one time?" So that means you and Funderburke haven't…"

"Seriously? That's the one point you latched onto in my speech?" I said that approximately four times louder than was really necessary. "No, we're both hard-core Catholic, and Funderburke's witnessing the seamier side of society as a private investigator has turned him into a massive prude, and that's fine with me." I'm not sure because I couldn't see myself, but I'm fairly certain that I glared at her, and I was pleased to see the embarrassment streaming down Layla's face.

"Sorry, it's just…" She didn't bother finishing her sentence. "It's just—is there a morality clause that might make you rescind your support? Because I…went a little wild in college, and after I got kicked out and started bartending, I started assuaging my anger through casual relationships with guys. Nolan wasn't my first, not by a long shot. I'm not proud of how I've lived my life, but I'm not going to apologize for it, either. And even though I was raised Catholic, I consider myself 'in recovery' now. Grandma's really upset with me about that, but she doesn't control me."

I shrugged. "The girls in the program are from all sorts of backgrounds— different ethnicities, religions, classes. And I don't intend to chuck them to the curb if they go past second base with their boyfriends, either." A couple

112

of the girls have found religion since they started going to Cuthbertson, but I haven't put any pressure on them. I don't tell them they need to copy my fashion style, either, but they keep buying leather jackets, skirts, and pants.

Layla leaned forward. "What happens if UWM doesn't accept me? Or if I don't get the coaching job?"

"First, I'm pretty sure you'll be accepted, and if not, there are other colleges in Milwaukee. Admittedly, more expensive ones, but there are online schools as well. You're no fool. We'll find something. Secondly, there are other jobs. I do have a friend from college who just opened up a gastropub in the Third Ward. It's a much nicer place than Grobel's Tavern. It's clean, the food's great, and the clientele and staff are both friendly. I can get you an interview there. It's Milwaukee. There's no shortage of bars offering part-time work. But like I said, nice ones, the kind of places that don't make you feel like you have to shower and dry-clean your clothes after entering them. The neighborhood fixtures. Grobel's is the sort of place you go to when you drink when you're depressed and want your surroundings to match your mood."

"Or if you're twenty and under and want a beer," Layla nodded. "That's another thing. I've served a lot of drinks to students who were almost certainly using fake IDs. That's not exactly legal. Will that come back to bite me somewhere down the road?"

"Did you ever know for a definite fact that you were serving an underage kid?"

"No."

"It probably won't come up at all, but you've got plausible deniability. You should be fine."

A light seemed to flicker in her eyes, as if she was suddenly aware that her circumstances were about to head in a very different direction. "I'm not even sure what my major will be."

"Get me a copy of your transcripts. We'll discuss it."

She smiled with a level of warmth that I hadn't seen previously in our short acquaintance. "This is happening, isn't it?"

"Absolutely. Go home, gather up the information you'll need to apply for

UWM and come over for dinner tomorrow. We'll discuss our plan then."

"Yes, but—"

"What?"

"Nothing. I'll see you tomorrow, I guess."

I was sure that she was very close to talking about what really happened with Erika, but I didn't want to push it, knowing that too much pressure would cause her to retreat. I didn't mind. Part of the reason why I was offering her this opportunity is that I figured that eventually, she'd open up and admit that she'd refused to administer the Narcan to her sister. Then, I could convince her to explain the situation to Juniper, and ideally, that would lead to a reconciliation between the two of them.

It was all right if she wasn't ready to confess just then. With a little more time and gentle coaxing, I was pretty sure that sooner rather than later, she'd be willing to admit what happened that fateful afternoon, and once she had, I was sure that she'd be ready to rebuild her life.

[1] Paternal grandmother.

Chapter Six—I Hate It When We Fight

I can't explain why, but I really enjoy asking people for money. Not for me personally but for the Bialowsky Fund. Every successful charity depends on fundraising, and I've found some very useful allies. Mr. and Mrs. Tokay are big supporters of the Fund, especially since several young women in their family—including three of their daughters—have been in similar situations. The evening after I took over for Layla at the bar, the Tokays held a small cocktail party to raise money for the fund. The Tokays are also Lawrence University alumni, and I met them at a reception there when I was a freshman. they took a liking to me, and we've been in touch ever since. If you're not familiar with Lawrence, I should explain that it is home to a very respected conservatory, and the school is *extremely* music-oriented. Everywhere you go, there's live music playing and singing as the conservatory students rehearse or belt out their favorite songs just for the fun of it. Seriously, the place makes the high school from *Glee* look like the town from *Footloose*.

I haven't mentioned this fact about myself yet, but my favorite style of music is, beyond a doubt, Broadway shows, especially Stephen Sondheim, Richard Rogers and Oscar Hammerstein, Cole Porter, Frank Loesser, Leonard Bernstein, Jule Styne, and Marvin Hamlisch, though I'm a huge fan of some more contemporary shows as well. The Tokays are also avid musical theater fans, and they even produced some experimental musicals for a while before they realized that it would be a shrewder business decision to save a step and simply flush dollar bills down the toilet.

But the Tokays believe in keeping their money circulating, and believe me, they have plenty to circulate. So when they hosted the get-together at their Upper East Side mansion on a bluff overlooking Lake Michigan, I made sure to attend, and to drag Funderburke along as well. Like many of their parties, there was a musical theater theme, and they had a pianist and singer performing one classic song after another, with the Tokays jumping in for a duet every twenty minutes.

Due to the musical theater theme, I was wearing one of the gems of my clothing collection—a vintage gown from the 1950s. Stephen Sondheim's father, Herbert, was a well-respected dressmaker, and this iridescent blue full-length beauty was crafted by him. It makes for a great conversation starter, especially with the Tokays' friends, who share their musical interests. Our old acquaintance Tyler Coquina, who doesn't have any money to donate but who loves hanging out with people who do, was there, along with his wife Vianne, who seemed to hate the party, though the two of us managed to chat pleasantly for a few moments. Our conversation was interrupted when Tyler complemented my dress in a way that made me feel like he was staring right through the fabric, and he did it right in front of Vianne. Fortunately, the Coquinas had to leave early in order to attend a different fundraiser.

Funderburke wasn't nearly as pleased with his outfit as, at my insistence, he was wearing a gleaming metallic silver suit with a matching tie and a black silk shirt. He thought it made him look like the Tin Man, and I thought he was successfully pulling it off, especially because his involuntary scowl was giving him a dark, brooding aura that made me even more attracted to him. The suit was a big hit with the other party guests, although the constant requests to touch it and the askers neglecting to wait for Funderburke's permission weren't putting him in a better mood. I think that the guests could feel his discomfort and that this obvious unhappiness was so amusing to them that it put them in an even more generous spirit.

So I charmed the guests and laughed at their jokes, and by the time the evening was over, I'd sat on the piano and belted out "I Know Things Now," "Another Hundred People," and "The Miller's Son," and dragged Funderburke up to sing "It Takes Two," and despite his rapidly deteriorating attitude, he managed to nail the song. I'm not boasting when I say that we got four full minutes of applause. I don't believe it was because of our vocal prowess. The reaction was mainly due to the rosé champagne the Tokays served. I am not much of a drinker, and I only had three-quarters of a glass of champagne, but holy cow, it went to my head faster and harder than a bullet. I probably wouldn't have managed more than one song if I'd stuck to club soda like Funderburke. By eleven o'clock, the guests were exhausted and ready to head home, but not before they'd written out some absolutely massive checks. I was deathly afraid that they'd sober up and cancel them if I waited until morning to deposit them, so with the Tokays' permission, I took ten minutes, laid them out on top of the piano, endorsed them, pulled out my smartphone, opened my banking app, and deposited them all into the Bialowsky Fund account before I allowed Funderburke to help me into my shawl. After profuse thanks to the Tokays, I took Funderburke's arm and walked out into the night.

The Tokays only live four blocks from my home. On Milwaukee's Upper East Side, the eastern half of Lake Drive is lined with mansions standing above the water, but if you cross the street and go south a bit towards the park, you soon reach houses that are much more modest, like my family's. As it was a clear, beautiful night, I'd suggested that we save a little gas and walk down there. I admit that I didn't make that suggestion just for the exercise. I totally understand Funderburke's attachment to his decades-old non-classic car, but I thought it would look shabby compared to the luxury automobiles that would line the Tokay's driveway. My red sports car would fit in better, but I knew that they'd be serving bottomless glasses of rosé champagne, and I knew there was a very real chance that a tipsy guest might plow into my vehicle, leaving it severely dented. So we were travelling by footpower.

I had worn my hair down and loose, and the increasingly powerful breeze was blowing it every which way, but I was too triumphant to care. The night had been a success. The wind was blowing the champagne bubbles out of my head, and I was becoming more alert with every step. Even though I was wearing the shawl I'd loaned to Layla recently, the chill was slipping through, and I shivered involuntarily before crossing my arms and shaking more deliberately and ostentatiously. This is a habit of mine. Whenever I

117

do that, Funderburke takes off his own coat without a word and slips it over me. Yeah, it's childish, and it leaves him unprotected from the icy winds, but I love, love, love it when he does that, and I find myself pretending to shiver on our walks even when I'm not really cold.

Tonight, his coat stayed on his own shoulders. So I exaggerated my shivers, and said "Brrrrrrrrr" loudly and pointedly. He sighed, and after a moment's hesitation, he pulled off his coat and wrapped me in it. "Thank you," I told him in my sweetest possible voice.

"Welcome," he muttered.

"Is something wrong?"

"I'm just a little annoyed."

"Why?"

"You were getting into some personal topics at the party."

"Like what?"

"Like the fact that I don't know who my father is. Like the fact that my mother and I are estranged. Like the fact that my half-brother is a small-time confidence man who once accused me of the atrocious crimes my stepfather committed. Like the fact that you and I have never… you know."

"What's wrong with that? That last one's nothing to be ashamed of."

"No, but it's personal, and it's none of their business."

I started to feel a little annoyed myself. "I don't remember saying anything about your family life."

"Well, you did. You started drinking that champagne, and then you were babbling about all this stuff that strangers don't need to know."

"I'm sorry, okay? It must've just slipped out."

"Well, it's a good thing you don't drink very often. I–" Funderburke was interrupted when a car pulled up next to us. Inside were two guys who looked like they were in college.

"Hey!" The passenger side window rolled down, and some marijuana fumes blew out into the wind. "Nice suit!"

"Thank…you," Funderburke said with his jaw so tightly clenched I thought it would snap.

The stoned guys laughed hysterically, and the one closest to us whipped out his phone, took a picture of Funderburke, and then laughed like a hyena on nitrous oxide. He showed the picture to his friend, and they roared with delight before driving off into the night.

"Forget them," I said. "I think you look really hand—"

"Don't!" His face was reddening.

My temper was rising as well, so I snapped, "Fine!" back at him. I could and probably should have left it there, but I felt compelled to add, "If I'd known how you felt, I wouldn't have talked to Layla about our relationship."

"Wait, what?" He stopped and stepped in front of me. "You were gossiping about the two of us with a murder suspect?"

"She's not a murder suspect. She didn't deliberately poison her sister. She just chose not to administer Narcan at a time when it was probably too late, anyway."

"We don't know that. That's your dad's theory, and it's not a bad one, but it doesn't answer all of the remaining questions about that afternoon."

"Like what?"

"First, the fentanyl. Where'd she get it?"

"She bought it off a drug dealer who didn't bother to cut it with baby formula or whatever drug dealers do. There! Question answered."

"No, that doesn't answer the question. Not by a long shot. First of all, when drug dealers mix up pills, they almost never prepare one bottle's worth of them at a time. They'd fill up hundreds, maybe thousands of capsules filled with narcotics at a time. With all the care and precautions they'd have to take in order to not inhale the powdered fentanyl themselves, they wouldn't make up each bottle individually to order. No, most likely, they'd have dozens of bottles filled with capsules made with pure fentanyl, and they'd want to sell their product fast, take the money, and then prepare and sell more. Which means that there'd be at least two or three, and probably over a dozen or more, maybe even twenty-plus people who took the pure fentanyl pills, and were either found and rushed to the hospital (possibly after being given Narcan), or they died of an overdose. And these people were probably in this area of Milwaukee, because Erika didn't have access to a car, and based on what "Jane Doe" told me, her dealer lived within walking distance. So, that means the local hospitals should have seen an influx of fentanyl overdoses and deaths. The paramedics should have been called to more houses to treat fentanyl poisonings. The morgue should be more crowded. But I checked everywhere, and there has been no spike in fentanyl-related overdoses and deaths in our neighborhood in the past couple of weeks, going back well before Erika's death. Don't get me wrong, there are always plenty of overdoses, but there is no uptick in cases connected to pure fentanyl distributed in capsule form. This indicates that Erika's capsules were specially prepared with fentanyl. This was a deliberate murder."

I thought about this for a second and a half. "Not necessarily. What if the dealers caught their mistake right away and recalled the batch of capsules, so to speak? But Erika bought hers first, and it was too late?"

"Even if that were the case, what about Mrs. Böhm? She saw Layla returning home on the day Erika died. And Layla denies it."

"Mrs. Böhm could have been mistaken."

"Yeah, witnesses can always get details wrong. But I told you the other day, she's fairly certain, and I think that we need to take her observations seriously."

Part of me saw the justice in this, but I wasn't feeling conciliatory at the moment. "Why do you have it out for Layla? Why don't you like her?"

"I'm not trying to prove her guilty, and I actually do like her a little. But she's not my concern right now. Juniper is my client, and she's scared of what her mother is capable of, so I have a responsibility to cover every possible base so I can look her in the eye and convince her that her fears are either justified or not. The point is that a little kid has picked up on something that terrifies her. I'm the student advocate. I'm not going to pooh-pooh her concerns like most adults do when a kid's worries are inconvenient to them."

"'Most adults.' Are you referring to me? Are you saying I'm not properly troubled about a distressed child?"

"No. You know I'm not. But I have to keep digging until I'm positive I know the truth."

"Do you trust me or not?"

He stared at me for a second, as if he was expecting a trap. "Of course I trust you."

"Then I need you to listen to my instincts. Dad was right. She didn't poison Erika; she just was fed up from the strain of dealing with all the stress that came from living with an addict, and something snapped in her, and she chose not to administer the Narcan. Yes, it was wrong. She should have tried to save her sister, but she was under so much pressure that she broke and walked away. But Erika was probably dead already. Why are you fighting that solution?"

"I'm not fighting it. But I have to go all out to figure out if something's the truth or not. Why are you so obsessed with defending her?"

"I am not obsessed."

"Is it because she reminds her of you? Because you couldn't save your birth mother?"

Any other day, any other time, I would have admitted the truth of that remark. But not that night. "Don't try to psychoanalyze me."

"I'm just saying–"

"I don't want to hear anything else. I'm going home. Don't follow me."

Funderburke blocked my path. "I have to go back to your house to get my car."

Gritting my teeth, I replied, "Well, you can wait here for five minutes, and then you can pick up your car."

I stomped around him, and as I did, he called out, "May I have my coat back, please? Or are you afraid that you'll die of hypothermia without it?"

I yanked his coat off of my shoulders and threw it at him. The wind caught it and billowed through the air like a Nazgûl in a *Lord of the Rings* movie. Funderburke lunged at it, but it soared out of his reach, hovered over a nearby lawn, and then landed atop an eight-foot-tall tree that only had a couple of dozen leaves left on it. Funderburke sprinted across the grass and grabbed his coat just as the wind started to carry it off again. The swiftness with which he shoved his arms into it and zippered it up only made me angrier because it reminded me how much he hated being seen in public in that silver suit. As he brushed off a couple of leaf fragments, I turned around and hurried home as fast as I could, not bothering to look back.

A few minutes later, I was home. I slammed the door after entering the house. As I stomped into the living room, Dad came out of his study, saying, "I know you've missed Toby's bedtime, but if you wanted to wake her up, you could have just gone upstairs and knocked on her door."

Embarrassment set my face on fire. "Are you the only one still up?"

"No. Yeh-Yeh's on the phone with a former colleague complaining about his sciatica and Sino-American relations, but mostly his sciatica. Mom just managed to get Amara back in bed after she woke up screaming, and now she's taking a long bubble bath to cool down before retiring for the night. I've got a few more book reports to grade, and then I'm finished for the night."

"Ah. I need some time to cool down. Maybe I'll change clothes and take a run around the neighborhood."

"It's nearly midnight. Are you so desperate for exercise that you can't use the elliptical machine?"

"I need to clear my head. The night air will help."

Dad pushed his glasses up his nose and looked at me very carefully. "Did the fundraiser go very poorly, or did you and Funderburke fight? Or both?"

"The fundraiser went great. Take a look." I opened my handbag, fished out the stack of checks, and pressed them into Dad's hands.

He flipped through them. "Wow."

"The big problem we've been having has been finding living spaces for the girls who are about to age out of foster care. But if we could buy a nice house, they could all live there together with their kids. With these checks, we can do that."

"Any particular neighborhood?"

"Preferably something around here, of course. Someplace I can visit easily anytime."

"Well, I'm very proud of you. You're doing incredible work, and fundraising isn't easy."

"Thanks, Dad."

"So. Why did you and Funderburke fight?"

"Why are you so sure we fought?" I dissembled.

"He didn't walk you to the door. His car's still in the driveway, so I'm assuming that you walked home separately. And the way you slammed the door showed you needed an outlet for your rage." Dad folded his arms and leaned against the wall. "I knew a metaphorical storm was coming when you made him wear that silver suit in public."

I cracked, and with tiny tears forming, I told Dad all the details about the fight. Midway through, he led me into the study, shutting the door so our conversation wouldn't wake the kids. As I finished, the sound of Funderburke's car starting led Dad to the window. "Do you want to run out and talk to him?"

"No. I'm not ready yet."

"Well, don't put your reconciliation off too late. Neither of you is going to get any sleep if you're mad at each other, and you've got work in the morning."

"There's no reason why you should lose your precious rest because of what's going on with me. Why don't you call it a night?"

"Because my daughter's upset, and I want to help her get back on track. You know, I wouldn't have shared my theory about what Layla really did that afternoon if I'd known that it'd lead to friction between you two."

I slumped back in my chair. "Dad, do you trust my ability to read people?"

"I think that, more often than not, you've got a remarkable knack for sizing up the character of certain individuals. Nobody's perfect, though."

"So you're saying I'm wrong."

"No, I'm saying that even though I have the deepest respect for your intuition, I think that Funderburke's determination to keep investigating is valid."

"You're on his side then."

"Nerissa, Funderburke is always on the side of the kids who come to him for help. And you've made it your mission to cheer for young women with babies who want to continue their education. Both of you want to champion people in dire need of assistance, and I love you both for that. Normally, there's no conflict between the two of you. But now you're trying to fix a young mother's life for her, and Funderburke can't shake the feeling that the young mother in question belongs behind bars. You two work really well together most of the time. And now, you both need to reevaluate what you're doing to find a way to start investigating in tandem again. Funderburke has a taste for seeing criminals get punished, and you like to see basically good people who've made a mistake get back on the right track. And now you're both subconsciously hoping that your preferred resolution to the case is the right one. But if you're going to convince little Juniper of the truth, your gut feelings aren't enough. You need the kind of hard evidence you can take into court."

I ran my hands through my horrifically wind-mussed hair. "I know in the marrow of my bones that Layla didn't deliberately feed her sister fentanyl. And yes, Funderburke is right. I see a lot of myself in Layla."

"There's one major difference, you know."

"What's that?"

"You never stopped fighting to make things better for yourself and Toby."

"But I didn't fight to help my birth mother snap out of her dark spiral."

"That's not how I remember it. You kept yelling at her, begging her to try doing something different in order to be happy. You were barely a teenager. You were up to your ears in your own problems. You weren't trained to deal with this situation. But darn it, you tried."

"I guess…." I smoothed out the hem of my gown. I didn't want it wrinkling.

"What's the matter?"

"I'm trying to understand how people can make the decisions they do. I mean, Erika practically shaved Layla's head, took away her possessions, and put her family in a constant state of high alert. I can rationalize why she got to the point where she decided that she just couldn't bear to keep her sister in her life anymore. But I keep flashing back to that sticky summer night when I was barely thirteen, and I don't know why I let everything… get to the point it did."

"Do you blame Toby's father?"

"No. He was just a horny teenager. He was a good guy, really. We were friends. He was just beset by raging hormones. And he'd been through a lot, what with his family losing their business in the L.A. riots and his father getting sick." After I told him Toby was on the way, he completely freaked out and never had another full-fledged conversation. We never really got the chance. By the time we started eighth grade, he'd joined a group of other angry young men that wasn't sufficiently organized to justify being called a gang but was dedicated to getting revenge against the people who they believed had wronged them and their families. I can't go into details because I might provide information that might lead to extralegal repercussions for the former members of the gang, most of whom grew up, matured, and led respectable lives. But Denji—" That's Toby's father—"—never got the chance. He tried to track down the people behind the destruction of his family's business, found some—or at least thought he did—and when he tried to get revenge through an eye-for-an-eye level of destruction, he wound up getting severely beaten. Denji's still alive, but the blows inflicted were so severe they caused irreversible brain damage. On a good day, he can feed and dress himself, but his mother has to take care of everything else. He can't speak or write, so no one knows for sure what he's really thinking. Mrs. Komesuma's been through a lot, and I talk to her and her daughter on the phone at least twice a week. Toby has a warm relationship with them as well, but she's only met her biological father once. She was so distraught by his condition I never made her go back. Thank God Dad and Funderburke have filled the paternal role for her.

I must have gotten caught up in my thoughts, because Dad asked me what was going through my mind. "I'm thinking a lot about that night—*the* night— that changed my life. You know what I mean." Dad nodded. Up to that point, I'd never really discussed it with him—it's not the sort of topic you feel comfortable talking about with your father—but maybe the pink champagne was still having an effect on me, because I started spilling details. "That car tonight, the one with the stoners who took a picture of Funderburke—the smell took me back to that awful week during the dog days of summer, when I was sleeping—or rather, unsuccessfully trying to sleep—on the fire escape to avoid the sounds coming from my birth mother's bedroom and the sickly smell of cheap weed provided by her boyfriend of the moment. There was precious little food in the house, and I didn't have the money to buy more. I did have too much pride to beg from the neighbors, so I was eating cereal for dinner with no milk. That night, when the rain drove me back inside, and I knew I couldn't stay in the apartment, I was starving. I couldn't believe my luck when I saw a little plastic tub of brownies on the kitchen island. My birth mother didn't like having sweets in the apartment, so I wasn't sure how they got there, but I was too hungry to care. I wolfed down one, then another, and then grabbed my keys, pillow, and blanket and walked down the hall to the Komesumas' apartment, little realizing that I was heading down a path that would alter the trajectory of my entire life.

I told all of these heretofore unmentioned details to Dad, naturally stopping there. Even if I'd chugged an entire magnum of champagne, I could never describe certain details from that night to him.

Dad frowned at me, but it wasn't a disapproving expression. The look he was making indicated that all the little gears in his head were whirring and clicking. I waited for him to start talking, but after six seconds, the reserves of my patience were exhausted, and I was inappropriately loud when he asked what he was thinking.

"The man who was spending the night in the apartment...was he a drug dealer or just a user?"

"I don't know. Based on my recollections, I don't think he had the motivation, intelligence, or business savvy to be a drug dealer himself, so I think he was just a marijuana enthusiast. Why do you ask?"

"Well, Lesley was a model who was obsessed with slimness. She didn't eat sugary baked goods like brownies. She didn't buy or bake them."

"I assumed that someone else in the building made them and shared them. I got to the brownies before she could toss them in the trash."

"Nerissa, you're still looking at that night through a thirteen-year-old's eyes. Consider what happened with all you know about the world now. Isn't it more likely that Lesley's boyfriend brought the brownies?"

"I suppose..." The penny dropped. "Dear Lord, how did I never see this before?"

"I just told you. Your perspective is so fixed in your mind that you haven't been able to look at that night critically. You never consider that the sweets might have been... tainted."

Running my hands over my head, I muttered, "The brownies were tainted. I knew I felt funny that night, but I never thought..."

"If my theory's right, and you were unknowingly high, well, that changes a lot, doesn't it?"

"What do you mean?"

"This is the first time you've ever mentioned those brownies to me, even after all these years. On the rare occasions you've referred to that night, you've said you have no idea why you made the choices you did that night. Well, once again, I may not be correct here, but if I am, you didn't make a choice. You cannot consent if you've unknowingly consumed a mind-altering substance. Not only that, but you'd barely slept a wink for a week, and sleep deprivation can impair your judgment as badly as alcohol."

I said nothing. This was all too much for me to process at the moment. "I know what you're saying, and I don't know how to respond."

"There's certainly no reason why you should respond in any particular way, is there? Whatever emotions you're feeling are certainly justified."

"All those years, I thought I'd protected myself from her never-ending parade of bed partners. I've lost track of all those nights I shoved my dresser in front of my door and was wakened at two in the morning when I heard a hand at the doorknob, trying to get inside. Maybe I'm doing some of those people an injustice. Maybe they were just looking for the bathroom, I don't know."

"You're the one who keeps talking about how great your instincts are. I really don't think now is the time to start doubting them."

"I slept with a kitchen knife under my pillow and a frying pan under my bed, just in case someone managed to get inside. Back when we lived in an apartment that didn't have a fire escape outside my window, I kept a spare of sheets knotted together just in case there was an emergency, and I needed to climb down them. And my alarm bell didn't go off. Brought down by a brownie."

Dad put his hand on my shoulder, and I squeezed his wrist. "Never blame yourself. You survived much more than any child should have to endure."

"All right, but who do I blame? I can't blame my birth mother because the only way I'm able to not seethe with rage over her failures to protect me is to acknowledge that she was barely holding it together after dealing with her own battalions of troubles and traumas, so I just have to repeat the mantra, 'It's not her fault, she was barely holding it together.' I'm not blaming Denji. He wasn't a predator. He was my friend who had his own share of problems. The pothead who brought the brownies? He was too stoned to think that I might come across them, and I don't even remember his name. I'm not sure I ever knew it. So what do I do now?"

"What do you want to do?" Dad asked me.

I stood up, started to speak, and then stopped. I paced back and forth for a few moments and then turned back to him. "I want to make things right with Funderburke. I'm going to his place now to patch up everything."

"Are you sure you're O.K. to drive?"

"What? Of course, I am. I only had three-quarters of a glass of champagne, and that was nearly two hours ago."

"How much did you eat at the party?"

I cast my mind back, and realized that I'd gone pretty light the hors d'oeuvres. "I had a deviled egg, some celery sticks..."

"So basically, no dinner. No wonder why the champagne went straight to your head."

"I was not drunk."

"No, but your temper always flares when you don't get enough to eat. C'mon." He led me into the kitchen. "What do you want on your sandwich?"

"I don't need a sandwich."

"A deviled egg and celery is not dinner. It's not even an appetizer. You need a sandwich." He cut two slices of brown bread from the loaf my great-grandmother (Mom's grandmother) had baked that morning and spread butter on them before layering slices of turkey and cheddar and provolone cheese. Then he poured me a glass of milk, pulled a bowl of grapes from the fridge, and set it on the kitchen table. "Eat, and then go make things right with Funderburke."

"I don't like being told what to do, Dad."

"I've noticed. Now eat your sandwich."

"What if I say 'no?'"

"Then you're grounded."

"For what? Wasting food? And I'm way over twenty-one, in case you forgot."

"You're wasting time. Eat your sandwich."

I surrendered, even though I tried to hide how much I was enjoying my meal out of pure obstinacy. I tried to call it quits after eating half, but Dad was having none of it, and I finished the rest. After I drained my glass of milk, I popped a handful of grapes into my mouth. "All right?"

"Yes."

"Good." I tried to think of something sharper to say, but instead, I found myself jumping forward and throwing my arms around Dad, squeezing him. I didn't realize I was crying until Dad tore a paper towel off the roll and pressed it into my hand.

"Do you want me to go with you?" he asked when my eyes were dry.

"What? No, no, I'll be fine." I looked down and made sure I hadn't wrinkled my Sondheim gown or left crumbs on it.

Dad walked me to the door and watched me until I'd gotten into my car. Seven minutes later, I was knocking on Funderburke's door.

"I was wondering when you'd get here." I turned around and saw Mrs. Zwidecker standing in the doorway of her house. Mrs. Zwidecker is a Lower School teacher at Cuthbertson. She taught Funderburke when he was younger, and they've been close ever since. Now, Funderburke rents the little guest house in her backyard. Drawing her dressing gown with the peacock-feather pattern closer around her, Mrs. Zwidecker said, "I heard him slamming his car door, and when I reached the window, I saw him storming into the house, clearly seething. I figured you'd been fighting."

"Have you spoken with him?"

"Yes. I asked him if he wanted some of the strawberry cheesecake I made tonight. I figured it would make him feel better."

"Did it work?"

"It had a very soothing effect on him. He said he was going to take a shower,

SHE RUINED OUR LIVES

and I don't hear the water rushing through the pipes anymore." I thanked her, politely declined her offer of cheesecake, and knocked on his door. He opened it about fifteen seconds later, wearing a T-shirt and cotton shorts, his hair still pretty damp.

"Hi," I said. "I want to put everything right between us. Please tell me that you are, too."

It wasn't a big smile, but it was warm enough to tell me that he was ready to make up. "Come on in." He looked up at Mrs. Zwidecker. "Good night. You can get some rest now. We won't be long."

"Good night." I knew immediately that Mrs. Zwidecker wasn't going to go to bed until she saw my car pulling out of her driveway. It's not that she doesn't trust us. She just likes to know exactly what's happening.

I stepped into the little house. It's basically a one-room studio, not counting the bathroom. The tiny kitchenette is right next to the door, and the living area consists of a computer desk against the wall, with a recliner and couch facing the television. Funderburke installed compact shelving against the far wall a year ago to hold his massive book and DVD collection, though there are still a bunch of other jam-packed bookshelves against every wall. His bed was two steps up on a raised platform, along with a chest of drawers for his comfortable clothes, a walnut armoire for his dress and work clothes, and a pine armoire for the clothes I bought him that he'd rather not wear. The silver suit had been tossed over the back of the sofa. "You can give that to the poor if you'd like," I told him.

"I can't think of a poor person I dislike enough to inflict that suit upon him," Funderburke told me without any anger.

I decided to cut straight to the chase. "I hate it when we fight, and I'm sorry I snapped at you."

He sighed. "I've been on edge all day. I didn't get home until one-forty last night because I was trying to track down the source of the fentanyl, and you know how important it is for me to get my nine hours. So I was running on fumes tonight, and I wasn't up for the party. I'm sorry. I should have tried harder to win over the guests. I know how important this fundraiser was to you and the Bialowsky Fund. I hope I didn't cost you too much money."

"I'm pretty sure you didn't."

"I hope not, but my mind was elsewhere. I was really distracted because that silver suit gets really hot."

"Well, thank you for wearing it. Seven people told me how great you looked in it."

"Seriously?"

"Hand to God. And thank you for singing with me."

"I was off-key."

"Only a little midway through, then you corrected nicely." I hoped I wasn't going to anger him with my request. "I really like singing with you. Can we do karaoke one night soon?"

"If you want," he replied with the martyred air of a man who's willing to subject himself to a night of hell because the woman he loves will enjoy it. "Are you sure that I didn't turn off any donors?"

Pulling out my phone, I tapped it and showed him the amount I'd deposited just over an hour earlier. "Take a look. We're going to be able to get that house I wanted for the over-eighteen girls."

His eyebrows bumped up against his hairline. "Holy cow! If I'd known this much money was involved, I would've stripped naked and sung the entire libretto of *Les Misérables* in the original French."

I enjoyed that mental picture for a few moments. "So, are you and I good?"

"I really, really hope so. Are you okay with my continuing my investigation into Layla?"

"I know you're doing what you think you have to, so even though I'm sure she didn't deliberately poison Erika, I've no right to be mad at you for looking for proof."

"I don't *want* to lock her in a filthy prison cell. I just have to *know*. I have a responsibility–"

"To Juniper. I get it. I shouldn't have gotten mad at you about that. And I shouldn't have thrown your coat like that. That was not cool."

"And I was behaving like a sulky little boy tonight. I hate these parties, but this was your night, and I should have gone all out to help you."

"You can make up for it by promising to do everything you can avoid another argument for as long as possible. At least a year. Sound all right?"

"I'll do my best."

I smiled at him and tilted my head. "Can we kiss and make up?"

He made no effort to disguise his eagerness as he stepped forward. Mrs. Zwidecker couldn't have seen us through the closed shades, but her instincts were preternatural. The moment our lips touched, she started flashing the house lights on and off to signal that it was time to wrap it up and go to bed. I pulled away reflexively, but Funderburke drew me in for a lengthy, proper kiss.

"I was not going to get any sleep tonight with things not right between us," he sighed. "I'm still going to be dragging due to insufficient rest tomorrow, but this will help."

"Same here."

He must've seen that my mind was drifting. "Are you all right?"

"Yeah. Dad and I had a great talk tonight. It's too late to talk about it tonight, and I need time to unpack everything mentally and emotionally. But we will discuss it later. I'm just thinking about how Edith was really distraught with PTSD flashbacks, and she was talking about how her parents took so much from her and turned her into a prostitute. I explained that she never consented to anything, so she was still morally a virgin, even if she did have a baby. That really had a profound effect on her. I just never realized I'd be in a similar position."

"What do you mean?"

"I think my Dad may have found my virginity tonight."

"Huh?"

"Don't think about it tonight, please. It'll only cost you more precious sleep you can't afford to lose. Meanwhile, Dad's probably waiting up for me, so I need to get back so he can get his rest."

Mrs. Zwidecker flashed the lights again, and Funderburke gave me one more passionate kiss before walking me outside to my car. I tapped my key fob, and he pulled the door open for me.

"All in?"

"I'm all in. Thanks, Funderburke."

He leaned in for one more kiss before shutting the door and stepping backwards out of the way, and I smiled at him before driving out into the night, my heart infinitely lighter than when I arrived.

Chapter Seven—Custody Battle

The next few days were jam-packed with all sorts of tasks that had nothing to do with the Dolak family. My usual teaching duties took up most of my time. Amara had to be rushed to the emergency room after playing a new game for just one person she'd invented including a basketball, a soccer ball, three tennis balls, a tennis racket, an inflatable raft, and a hula hoop. Luckily, the X-rays showed that she hadn't broken any bones, but she did dislocate her left arm, which was easily fixed. One of my girls—Brigitta—was confronted by her aunts who wanted to drag her back to the doomsday compound in northern California where she'd been trapped from ages fifteen to seventeen after her parents were killed in a fire. Funderburke had them arrested on two outstanding warrants for child endangerment. We were hoping that Brigitta could get custody of her three younger sisters and move them to Milwaukee before what happened to her happened to them, but the California family court system was dragging its heels.

So, between the routine challenges and the unexpected crises, my plate was pretty full, especially with my dissertation director politely but insistently demanding a revised draft of chapter four by Sunday night. So, with the help of about fifteen gallons of iced triple-strength coffee with milk, I managed to make it to Monday afternoon alive and with all of the items on my to-do list checked.

After finishing my second U.S. History course of the day, I was hoping to get down to lunch in order to beat the rush for the chicken enchiladas. The cafeteria food at Cuthbertson is far superior to the stereotype about school lunches, but even with a menu full of high-quality meals, the enchiladas are among the best of the best.

Halfway down the stairs, I nearly collided with Layla. Following the standard apologies and greetings, she explained that she was here to ask for a favor. I invited her to lunch, and soon we were talking over plates of enchiladas. Fortunately, one of the students at my lunch table was out sick, so there was an empty chair. The six students at the table were completely wrapped up in their own conversations, so they weren't interested in what Layla and I were discussing. Cuthbertson, incidentally, assigns students to lunch tables. The seating arrangements change on a monthly basis.

"Do you have any plans for four o'clock this afternoon?" she asked.

"I was going to Mass with my family and Funderburke, followed by a workout," I informed her. "Why? What's up?"

"Mass? On a Monday?"

"You call yourself a 'recovering Catholic,' I call myself a 'recovering nothing-in-particular.' My upbringing was pretty unreligious- though not antireligious—until I was adopted. Don't roll your eyes, please."

"I wasn't—" She decided that the attempt at denial wasn't worth it. Maybe my glare dissuaded her. Maybe it was just her conscience. "I'm sorry. But I need your help. Can you come to a custody meeting at four? I don't have a lawyer, and Paige and Nolan have hired the top attorney in town. Her office is just a few minutes away from Cuthbertson Hall."

"Michelle Lilith." It was a statement, not a question.

"Yes! Do you know her?"

"Oh, yeah. Trust me. Funderburke will be happy to join us."

"I don't need him there, just you. If you can tell them about the scholarship and my going back to college, and even though I'm unemployed right now, I'm—"

"Believe me. You want Funderburke there. He's already involved, remember. As the Student Advocate, he's Juniper's personal representative for her interests."

"But does that mean he's on my side?"

"No. Not at all. Not even close. He's on Juniper's side."

Layla sagged. "I don't think he likes me very much. He could destroy my chances at retaining at least some level of custody."

"Layla, ask any lawyer in town. Funderburke is a J.D. himself, and anybody in the business will tell you that he's the one man in town who can get under Ms. Lilith's skin."

"Are you sure?"

"I've seen it happen countless times. It's glorious."

She poked a piece of enchilada with her fork and pushed it around the pool of red sauce covering her plate. "You have a lot of confidence in him."

"He's never let me down, and I'd like to believe that I've managed to avoid disappointing him as well."

After staring at the morsel on her fork for an awkwardly long amount of time, she finally placed it in her mouth. Once she'd swallowed it, she said, "I think it'd be very nice to have someone in your life like that."

"It is."

Her lunch was almost completely gone at this point, and now she was drawing little lines in the sauce with her fork. "I've let Juniper down. A lot of times. I've been so wrapped up in my own mistakes, disappointments, and frustrations I've forgotten to look out for her. Do you think I'll ever get her to trust me again?"

I decided to demur a bit. "What have you done to make her distrust you?"

The response was sharp and curt, and I knew that Layla wasn't ready to be completely open. "She's a very bright little girl with an overactive imagination, and she's seeing darkness in me that isn't there. She's confusing me with the monsters under her bed." It was an indignant comment, and it rang so hollow in my ears that I began to wonder if I'd made an error in judgment by offering her a way out of the morass. Then I saw her tugging at her earlobe, and the corners of her lips trembled. Maybe my imagination was fogging my perception, but I sensed that she didn't really believe the line she was trying to sell me. And that, I reasoned, was a step in the right direction. If she'd managed to convince herself that she was blameless, then maybe Layla was too far gone to help. But if Layla realized how unconvincing her lies were…then maybe she'd conclude just how necessary it was to tell the truth.

"Look, you don't have to be a perfect parent, but it's critical to be an honest one. When Toby was little, I had to avoid some of the questions she had because they weren't appropriate for a child. I thought I was protecting her with an evasion here, a borderline lie there. I didn't want her to know all the details about her biological father, her biological grandmother, or their fates. I thought she'd be happier not knowing all the details about my past. I was partly right. You can't spring all of that on a tiny kid. She couldn't grasp it all when she was three. But Toby could always tell when I was holding back on her, and every time I dodged and prevaricated, it put another brick on the wall between us. Thankfully, I had Mom and Dad and all my other adopted family members to help with the situation. Sometimes, 'I'll tell you when you're older' is the only line you can possibly say. But when she turned ten and she learned a little more about the facts of life, I could tell her a lot more, and it really repaired our relationship. It was fine when she was a toddler, but then I went away to college, and I realize now she resented it. At least I wasn't gone the full four years, and I was back at least three days a week, much more some terms. But I had to make a choice. Was I protecting her by hiding the truth? Yes, to a certain extent. And yet…the growing distrust was hurting her in a way I didn't understand at the time, but if I had to do it over again…I'd find a different way to reach out and answer her questions much earlier, truthfully and in a way that wouldn't harm her."

I was trying to be subtle. Hopefully, I had put so much stress on my relationship with my own daughter that it wasn't too blatant that I was providing some advice regarding repairing the bond between Layla and Juniper.

She stared at her plate for an inordinately long time and then met my gaze. "Have you ever done something that you feared that Toby would never forgive?"

I took a couple of moments to mull that question over in my mind. "No. No, I haven't. I've made my share of mistakes—and goodness knows a teenager with a kid and a jam-packed schedule of classes is bound to slip up more often than she'd like. But I knew my daughter would always forgive

SHE RUINED OUR LIVES

me for being a young, flawed human being who was still trying to figure out how to survive in a crazy world. What she would never be able to accept was cruelty, duplicitousness, and a patronizing attitude. I never inflicted any of those curses on her, but other people, including family members who do not bear the Kaiming name, have done their best to wear her down to a nub with their sneers and lies."

Nodding, Layla asked me, "Mind if I ask a very personal question?"

"Why not? Those are the most interesting kind, most of the time."

"Perhaps you're right." She sighed, then plunged forward. "When did you first realize that you loved Toby? I mean, that incredibly all-consuming love mothers have for their children?"

"From the moment my pediatrician told me I was going to have her. How about you?"

Leaning back in her chair and folding her arms, Layla spoke in just barely above a whisper. "For me, it took a lot longer. When I first found out, I panicked. I was scared of what would happen to my life, and I was sure that Grandma would throw me out of the house. So I thought about it for a little under an hour, and I made an appointment, thinking that would solve the problem. And then, that night, Grandma made dinner, including most of my favorite foods and three kinds of dessert, and she filled a plate so high it nearly touched the ceiling and placed it in front of me.

She picked up the cup of tea that she'd made for herself, sipped it, and said, 'Sweetheart, I want you to know something. I am not what most people would call a tolerant woman. I don't enjoy excusing other people's shortcomings and sins. What gives me pleasure is pointing out the flaws of individuals I dislike and those who have wronged me. And that is not a virtue. It's a serious shortcoming that I really ought to work at improving, and I suppose that now is as good a time as any to begin. I'm aware of how difficult the last few years have been for you. Your sister's addiction has taken a toll on both of us. No one's ever been able to accuse me of being soft, but I realize that I've forced myself to become harder and tougher to keep what remains of this family together. And in doing so, I think I may have been colder, more distant to you than I ought to have been. I realize that you've been struggling, and I regret every moment when I haven't been the grandmother I should be. I want you to know that if you're in trouble, you can always turn to me, and I'll be there to support you and any new members of this family that may be coming in the near future.'

I started crying, and the first words I could manage after regaining some level of composure were, 'How did you know?'

'I saw the pregnancy test in the bathroom garbage. I suspect that subconsciously, you wanted me to see it.'

And we talked. It was the most heartfelt, honest, and supportive conversation the two of us have ever had with each other. By the end, after we'd finished our meals, I knew that there was going to be a change of plans and that I'd need to find Nolan and tell him everything.

'I think I need to cancel an appointment,' I said, wondering if Grandma would be angry at me for even considering that possibility.

She drained her cup of tea and, in the most matter-of-fact tone possible, informed me, 'I read the note in your day planner. I already called and cancelled it this afternoon. And I found a highly-rated OB-GHN. You'll be seeing her at ten tomorrow morning. Now have some dessert.'"

I had gotten so caught up in Layla's story that I didn't realize until that moment that, at some point, all of the students at the table had become very interested in what we had to say. Layla belatedly made the same observation, and before she could say any more, the end-of-lunch announcements were read at the podium at the front of the room, and the students started filing out to their next class.

"I should get going, too," Layla told me.

"Are you going to go down to the pre-primary wing and talk to Juniper?" I asked.

"No. I'm not ready yet. I don't know what to say. I'm just going to walk down to the park down the street and think for a few hours."

"Wait, you don't have a car. Did you take the bus here?"

"I did. There's another bus that'll take me from the park to within three blocks of the law office. I'll see you there at four."

* * *

At the appointed time, Funderburke and I drove from Mass at the retirement home to the law offices of Lilith and Associates. I saw the muscles in his back stiffen, as if he was preparing for battle. Layla was already there, sitting on a bench in a little garden area. She was wearing a black dress that didn't look very durable, and I later learned she'd bought it for her sister's funeral. I realized that it was probably the nicest, most professional-looking item of clothing she owned, as ripped jeans wouldn't be an adequate wardrobe choice for a meeting that might decide the fate of her daughter. She had a frayed hoodie on over it, and it didn't look like it was doing much to protect her from the October wind, which had more invisible frost in it every day as the days grew steadily shorter. A couple of weeks earlier, it was bright daylight at four in the afternoon. At this point in the month, the sun was heading towards the horizon at surprising speed, and in another few weeks darkness would be falling across the sky at this time. If I'd known more about her clothing situation, I would've told her to go to my house and borrow my shawl. Or maybe we could have found her something better in the Cuthbertson theater department's costume collection.

"Hi!" She hurried over to us, shivering as she moved.

"Hi, Layla. Have Paige and Nolan arrived yet?"

"I haven't seen them. They're picking up Juniper and they should be here at any moment."

"Let's go inside, then. It's getting blustery." As I said that, I saw Funderburke's hands move to unzip his coat, thinking that I was signaling, so I quickly shook my head to tell him that I wasn't asking for an extra layer of warmth. Actually, I could have used it, but we were just a few steps from the door, so there was really no point.

The moment we were inside, Layla peeled off her shabby hoodie and then rolled it up, and stuck it under her arm in a futile attempt to hide it. I offered to tuck it inside my purse, and she gratefully accepted. I felt like I had to do something to give her some more confidence. I would have lent her my black leather blazer to smarten up her outfit, but it was much too small for her. I rummaged around my purse and found a silk scarf. I couldn't remember when or why I had put it in there, but I figured that I had it, and I ought to make use of it. "Here." I tied it loosely around her neck. The pop of color did a lot to brighten up her appearance. There was not much else I could do. I don't use much makeup, and the little bit I had with me didn't fit her coloring. The lipstick in my purse wouldn't suit her. As for her hair, it was at that awkward stage where it was too short to style nicely but too long to lie neatly on her head. "Hold still." I fluffed and teased her locks for a minute, reasoning that if I didn't have the time to make her hair look elegant, I could at least make the messiness look somewhat stylish. I twisted with my fingers and puffed up the lank patches, and by the time I was finished, she went from looking embarrassingly dowdy to attempting a bold style that didn't quite pay off. I led her over to a mirror in the corner of the foyer. "What do you think?"

She tugged at the scarf. "It looks...*better*." Truly, the result wasn't *good*, but it was a strong step up from where it had been two minutes earlier.

The receptionist flinched as we pushed our way through the heavy wooden doors into the main office. We'd only met her a few times, but whenever our paths crossed, there'd been varying levels of trouble, and she was now prepared for friction.

"Ms. Lilith is in a conference call right now. Will you please wait in the green conference room?"

"We will, thank you. Don't get up. We know the way." The receptionist nodded, clearly distrustful of us, but the ringing phone prevented her from following us. As Funderburke led the way through the office, the law firm's young associates stared at us and then hurriedly looked away when Funderburke returned their gaze. They all knew that a storm was coming, and they were all reacting as if they were trying to ensure they wouldn't get wet.

Turning the corner, the entryway to the green conference room was hidden from the view of the rest of the office. Layla and I immediately sat on one side of the long table, but Funderburke crossed to the little break room through the open doorway in the far corner.

"What are you doing?" Layla asked.

141

"Making a snack," Funderburke replied with amused airiness. He reached into the pocket of his walking coat and withdrew a packet of microwave popcorn. He disappeared into the break room. After the sounds of plastic wrap being removed and a little beeping, I heard the microwave begin running, and Funderburke strode out, whistling a few notes.

"Will they mind if you're eating during the meeting?" Layla asked, clearly unaware of Funderburke's tactics.

""I'm not going to be eating. But yes, I'm pretty sure Ms. Lilith will mind." Funderburke flopped into the chair at the head of the table, kicked back, and threw his feet upon the table. "This is a power play, as much on her part as it is on mine. She told you to be here at four. I'm certain she told Paige and Nolan not to come until four-twenty and not a minute earlier. She wants us waiting, you see. She is waiting and anticipating and getting nervous. It's a tried and tested psychological tactic to establish dominance. Of course, she didn't expect us to be here." Funderburke waved at a potted plant on a ledge in the far upper corner of the room.

"Did you just greet that fern?" Layla asked.

"Of course not. I greeted Ms. Lilith. She's watching us through a little video camera. She's not expecting us. She wanted you here, alone and growing more nervous by the minute. After twenty minutes in these chairs— notice how steadily uncomfortable they get the more you sit in them. A third of an hour later, you'd be so frazzled you'd agree to any custody proposal she put forward. Forty minutes in one of them, you'd sign away everything you own for a chance to stand up and walk off the cramps. But if you tried to stand up, she'd snap and say that if you rose from the table, all negotiations would be off, and you'd go straight to court. You two should stand up, by the way. No sense in staying there a second more than necessary."

"You're still seated," Layla noted as we rose.

"This is Ms. Lilith's personal chair. Notice how the design is different? It's like sitting on a cloud upon which an angel with a freshly talcum-powdered bottom recently reclined."

"Wouldn't her clients also get the uncomfortable chairs?" Layla asked.

"A moment before they came in, the office manager would come in with a carafe of water and "accidentally" spill some on the empty chairs. The staff would swap them out for comfier ones."

Layla gaped. "That's manipulative."

"Yes, it is. It's the divorce industry. It's not about client happiness, it's not about the wellbeing of the children, it's not about justice for the wronged. It's about lawyers making sweet, sweet stacks of cash off of their targets and punishing people they dislike."

"Well, I haven't got any money, so what do they want with me?"

"This isn't about you," Funderburke's tone sharpened. "It's about Juniper."

As we talked, the popcorn popped, and by this point, the sound of bursting kernels slowed. Layla's nose wrinkled. "Your popcorn's burning."

"It's meant to. Let the microwave keep running."

"Do you like your popcorn charred?"

"No, but Ms. Lilith can't stand the smell of microwave popcorn, and she definitely can't take the scent after it burns."

"I don't care much for it either."

"Well, please endure it for a bit longer. If all goes as planned, it'll only be for a few more minutes."

Eventually, the microwave dinged. "Nerissa, will you please take over sitting in this chair for me?"

"Absolutely." Funderburke stood up, and I flopped down into the chair and placed my boots on the conference table. Funderburke removed the popcorn from the microwave, tore open the bag, and smiled with satisfaction. He scooped four handfuls into little plastic cups taken from the break room cabinet and then placed the bag, still fairly full, in front of a desk fan. He switched on the fan, nodding appreciatively as the scent further circulated around the room. He then took a cup into each hand, placing two behind silk potted plants atop tall bookcases where they couldn't be seen and repeating the process atop another bookcase on the other end of the room.

A couple of moments after he finished, the doors opened, and Ms. Lilith and two of her young associates entered the room. "Hello, Isaiah. Nerissa. Layla," she added as an afterthought. Looking at us, she said, "I wasn't expecting you two today."

143

"Well, you did say that you wanted to spend more time together."

Ms. Lilith took a deep breath and shuddered. "There's been a change of plans. We're going to meet in the blue conference room. Follow me, please." We left the room and headed down the corridor. As we turned the corner, the receptionist hurried past us, holding a can of air freshener and a container of disinfectant wipes.

Paige and Nolan were seated at the conference table as we were ushered into the blue conference room. I hadn't met Nolan before, but he appeared nervous and uncomfortable. Juniper was sitting in his lap, and she looked similarly anxious. Paige wasn't looking any too calm herself. From her posture and fidgeting, I would have said that she looked rather guilty to me, though whatever was troubling her conscience was unclear to me.

"Hello." Paige's voice was soft and shaky.

"There's coffee, soda, and bottled water," Ms. Lilith offered, pointing to a little table in the corner. "Try not to throw the bottles," she quipped with a sly little side glance at Layla.

"I want a word with my client, please," Funderburke told her.

"You had several minutes to speak to her in the green room."

"Layla is not my client. Juniper is."

"What do you want to say to her?" Paige placed a hand on Juniper's wrist.

"It's what she has to say to me that's important," he explained. "You're holding a conference to discuss custody of her, presumably hoping to iron out everything so you don't have to take this matter to court. But what you two want and what Layla wants may not match Juniper's thoughts on the matter."

Paige's hand squeezed around Juniper's wrist. "I don't want you putting ideas in my daughter's head."

"She's *my* daughter," Layla shouted.

Funderburke was calmer. "Are you denying your daughter her right to counsel?"

"I don't think that a three-year-old girl's rights are being violated here," Ms. Lilith answered.

"Are your clients afraid of Juniper's wishes being known?" Funderburke

144

countered.

"Maybe we should let him talk to her," Nolan muttered.

Paige's back stiffened, and her shoulders thrust backwards. "Are you turning on me?"

"Honey, you know I'm on your side, but Juniper's been scared lately. She hasn't been sleeping through the night, she's crying all the time, and she won't talk to us. We need to find out what's wrong."

"We know what's wrong! She's scared of Layla!"

After Paige's outburst, Juniper burst into uncontrollable tears. Nolan and Paige immediately leaned over her, trying to comfort her. Paige fished a tissue out of her purse, but by the time she held it, Layla had crossed around the table and snatched it from her. "I'll do that." Layla brought the tissue to Juniper's eyes, but the little girl flinched.

"What's wrong, sweetie?"

Juniper said nothing, but the fear on her face, as she looked at Layla, was palpable.

"What's the matter?" Now, there was a faintly aggressive tone underneath the question. In response, Juniper clung tighter to her father, and Paige slipped an arm around her.

"You're turning her against me!" Layla practically spat out the words.

"Make a note of that," Ms. Lilith said to the young associate on her left, a young woman with an auburn pixie cut and an olive-green pantsuit that probably cost upwards of eight hundred dollars but it hadn't been tailored to her figure, and her shoulders were totally lost in the jacket. The pixie cut, incidentally, didn't fit her face properly, either. Given the size and shape of her head, the shortest suitable haircut for her was a chin-length bob. Cutting in on my musings, Ms. Lilith added, "Ms. Dolak is paranoid."

"I want to talk to Funderburke and Miss Kaiming!" Juniper shouted. The exclamation was so sudden that all the adults in the room jumped. Nolan and Paige looked at each other, unsure of what to do.

Ms. Lilith broke the silence. "Perhaps that would be a good idea, actually. You can use the pink conference room. Will five minutes be enough?"

"Ten at most," Funderburke countered. "All right, Juniper?"

She nodded, and as I followed him out of the room, I abruptly changed course and took five quick steps to make my way to Layla. "Say nothing except the most basic pleasantries until we get back," I whispered into her ear.

The other young associate, her black hair shingle bobbed and wearing a midnight blue pantsuit, led us into a much smaller conference room. As the name suggested, the interior decorator had gone with a color scheme that was perfect for Divorce Attorney Barbie.

As Funderburke shut the door behind us, Juniper opened her mouth to speak. "Just a moment," he told her. He crossed to a mahogany table where a coffeemaker was standing against the wall. He pushed it to one side, revealing a little intercom panel. An orange light glowed in the center of the bottom of the panel. "I'm sure it was *totally accidental* that this was left on," he bellowed into the speaker at the top of his lungs before flipping the little switch in the corner.

Once the last bit of the orange glow had faded from the tiny bulb, Funderburke nodded and turned back to Juniper. "All right, whenever you're ready, please feel free to talk."

"Did Mommy kill Aunt Erika?"

Funderburke hesitated, and I stepped in and answered, "I do not believe that she did. Based on what we've found so far, we think that your aunt simply died of an overdose. Your mother isn't to blame."

"Are you sure?" Juniper pulled Tunk-Trunk out of her pocket and held her toy against her chest.

"I haven't completed my investigation yet," Funderburke cut in, shooting me a warning glance, telling me that he didn't want me to commit to a version of events before he was dead certain.

"If she didn't kill her, why is she acting so weird?"

Funderburke and I looked at each other, trying to think of an adequate response. Finally, Funderburke spoke. "Juniper, we strongly suspect that your mother, though innocent of cold-bloodedly poisoning your Aunt Erika, still blames herself for her sister's death. You know that your aunt had a problem with drugs. Your mother spent years trying to help her and ultimately failed.to break her of her habit. This wasn't her fault—it's notoriously difficult to break the hold addictive chemicals have over people, and no matter how much you love them, no one else can lift that terrible burden from someone else. Now, the fact that your mother can't give voice to the guilt she's feeling is affecting her behavior, and I'm hoping that with your help, we can help her to give voice to what she's feeling."

I thought that Funderburke had phrased that rather well. I looked at Juniper's face, hoping that his explanation assuaged her worries. From the change in her expression, Juniper's wasn't entirely convinced that her mother had not committed premeditated murder, but at least she was now open to that possibility.

"I hope you're right," Juniper finally replied. "I would like to have my Mommy back."

Nodding, I asked her, "Do you have a preference as to where you'd prefer to live?"

"I don't mind moving back and forth. I love Daddy and Mommy—Mommy Paige, I mean, but I really love Great-Grandma. I used to be a little afraid at her house because Aunt Erika was always acting so weird. But Mommy has been so weird lately, and then so strange since Aunt Erika died, I haven't felt safe around her."

"If we could make sure that you felt safe, would you prefer joint custody? By that, I mean spending some time at one home and the rest of your time at the other. Perhaps switching back and forth weekly? Or whatever plan is convenient for your families?" Funderburke asked.

"Yes…" Juniper didn't look quite pleased with that suggestion.

"Is there something you'd prefer?"

"I'd really like it if Mommy could be friends with Mommy Paige. I know they don't like each other much… but I wish they could get along better. I don't understand. I asked Daddy if he was married to Mommy before Mommy Paige, and he said "no," and then he wouldn't say anything else to me. It was weird."

"Well, grown-ups aren't as skilled at organizing their lives as they like to think they are," Funderburke explained. "It's not my place to tell some of your parents' secrets, but all you need to know right now is that even though your parents' relationships aren't as neat and tidy and friendly as you'd like them to be, you're luckier than many kids because you have a lot of people in your life who love you and want you in their lives. A lot of kids who get caught up in the divorce blender aren't as lucky."

Juniper frowned. "Great-Grandma seems to think I already have enough family members."

"What do you mean?"

"Yesterday, my grandma came to the house. She played a game with me for half an hour and said she'd take me out for ice cream later this week. Afterwards, I talked to Great-Grandma on the phone, and she got crazy upset. She said that I was not to go out with Grandma for any reason, and that I had to listen to her. I don't understand. Why don't my family members like each other?"

I wanted to make sure that I had this straight. "When you say "grandma," you mean Layla's mother?"

"That's right. I haven't seen her much before, but she was really nice to me."

"I wonder why—"

We were interrupted by Layla throwing open the door and charging into the room. "You've been investigating me the entire time?"

Paige appeared behind her. "I'm sorry. I didn't think. I mentioned that Juniper was worried about Erika, and I mentioned that she'd gone to you to look into it. I never thought it would upset—"

Layla screamed. "Is this what you've been trying to do all this time? Pretend to befriend me so you can throw me in prison?" Before I could respond, she ripped off the scarf I'd loaned her and threw it to the ground. Tears started flowing down her face, and she whirled around and stormed towards the exit.

Chapter Eight—You Faked Being My Friend

I hurried after Layla. "Wait a minute. Please, listen to me."

Funderburke was right behind me. "Don't speak to her inside the building. Go outside."

A millisecond of consideration led me to realize that this was a shrewd idea. I didn't want the lawyers to hear whatever Layla had to say. But Layla didn't head outside. She rushed through the large plate glass doors with "Lilith & Associates" etched into them and headed straight for the little one-person bathroom off to the side in the foyer. When I reached the door, it was locked.

I debated my options for a moment. Knocking wouldn't help. I could ask for the janitor's passkey, but there was no point in trying to speak to her until she'd had a chance to cool down a bit. I could stand outside the door and wait for her to leave, but that could be a long time just to stand around a lobby, especially when the sight of me might cause her to go storming back inside the bathroom. I could go someplace else to wait, but I didn't want her to slip out without my seeing her. Though, when she left, I knew that her destination was the bus stop.

As I considered what to do, the associate in the olive-green pantsuit sidled up to me. "Popular, aren't you?" I didn't respond, as I knew that any attempt to engage with her could escalate rapidly in directions that I didn't want to journey. So I turned my back on her, and as I stepped away, I heard her hiss at me, "Slut."

SHE RUINED OUR LIVES

I'm called worse on a regular basis, but her mocking tone made my temper flare. I decided to count to ten before doing anything. As I mentally thought the number "one," I saw Funderburke reflected in the polished windows and his whole body clenched. Momentarily, I feared what his reaction might be, but before he could say a word or move another muscle, Ms. Lilith's voice reverberated around the foyer, cold anger in her tone. "I heard that, Elodie."

I saw the reflection of an olive pantsuit, whose name I now knew was Elodie, in the window, jumping and whirling around. I turned to get a better look at her and saw Ms. Lilith looking glacially furious. "Why did you say that?" she snapped.

"I...I just..."

"You do not speak to someone here on business like that. It is completely unprofessional, and it reflects horribly not just on yourself but on the entire law firm. Your comments were rude, cruel, and unworthy of Lilith and Associates."

"Yes, Ms. Lilith. I'm very sorry."

"Your apologies are inadequate. I no longer trust your judgment, and I now believe that you have no place at this firm. Your employment here is terminated. Gather up your belongings. I want you out of here by five."

"What?" Elodie's expression indicated that she didn't believe that Ms. Lilith had actually said what she'd heard.

"You heard me. Don't expect a positive reference."

"But... I just bought a condo."

"I don't know why you act like that's any concern of mine. You know how much I charge for my time, and you will not receive another second of it. Gather your things. Now!"

Elodie staggered back through the doors, and theoretically, I should have felt sorry for her, but I just wasn't able to muster any level of sympathy. I just watched her shoulders droop in the jacket that sagged in the wrong places.

Once the door had closed behind Elodie, I walked over to Ms. Lilith, who was still standing in the foyer with her arms crossed. Paige, Nolan, and Juniper were standing off to one side. "Thank you," I told Ms. Lilith. "That wasn't necessary, but I appreciate it."

"You're welcome."

"If you decide she deserves a second chance, I won't hold it against you if you give her one."

"She's already on her third chance. I caught her padding her expense reports, engaging in some of the unethical behavior my son likes to call out divorce lawyers for indulging in." She gave Funderburke a little nod.

"Your son?" Paige asked.

"Yes. Isaiah—Funderburke—here is my son. He doesn't advertise the fact."

I gave Funderburke an encouraging look and a tilt of the head towards his mother. "Thank you for standing up for Nerissa," he told her with more grace than he usually uses towards her. "That was quick. You even beat me to a response."

"You're welcome. If you really want to thank me, don't ever microwave popcorn in my offices again."

"How about fish? Can I microwave that?"

A horrified look flashed across Ms. Lilith's face, and then, for the first time in our acquaintance, she laughed. Funderburke opened his mouth, shut it again, and walked back towards me. I took him by the elbow and led him to a corner.

"Do you want to know what my greatest regret is?"

"The burgundy leather jumpsuit you wore to parent-teacher conferences last year, and after several cups of iced coffee, you found the need to answer nature's call, only to find that the zipper was stuck?"

"No." I could tell that his contact with his mother had rattled him more than he wished to let on, as he was trying to lighten the mood with a smart remark, but any attempt at merriment had failed to reach his eyes. "It's the fact that I never managed to smooth out my relationship with my birth mother. With the short-sighted, judgmental arrogance of a fourteen-year-old, I always hoped that we'd be able to work out our differences somewhere down the road, once she finally earned a certain degree of emotional maturity and took some responsibility for her life. I was so busy loathing her shortcomings that I never thought that I could do something to help her. I kept her at arm's length emotionally, waiting for her to fix her own problems. I thought we'd have decades to put everything right, and then, that one terrible March night our freshman year, I walked into the living room of our apartment and found her lying face down on the floor. I never got the reconciliation I wanted. And I know you want to punish her for all of the hell she put you through during the divorce and for not believing you after your stepfather blamed you for his own dirty misdeeds. But you don't know how much time you have left to fix everything. Trust me, you don't want to spend your life wondering, "If only…" It's a wound that never heals. I know you're not ready to let go of all of your grievances, but maybe you never will be until you actually take some steps towards forgiving her."

I could tell that I'd gotten through to Funderburke because he couldn't manage to come up with a smart remark. He looked at me for a little while, gently placed a hand on my shoulder, and walked over to his mother.

"I heard everything she said," Ms. Lilith informed him. "Nerissa doesn't realize that her whisper is actually a stage whisper, and the acoustics in this foyer don't lend themselves to private conversations."

"So, do you have a response to Nerissa's comments?" Funderburke asked.

"I've told you before. I would very much appreciate an invitation to one of those famous dinners at the Kaiming family dinner table. But I'd also like some private time with you. If I had my secretary get in touch with you regarding my availability, might you be willing to go out to dinner with me? There are a couple of very nice restaurants around here."

It was obvious that Funderburke was struggling with complex emotions, but he finally answered, "All right."

"Thank you." Ms. Lilith paused. "Your half-sister won't be able to join us. After another eardrum-bursting argument between us two weeks ago, we've decided that boarding school is worth a try. I've made arrangements with an academy in Chicago with an excellent reputation. And a hefty price tag."

"Oh." I could tell that Funderburke was making a supreme effort not to say anything that might spoil the moment.

"I'd like a hug, if you don't mind."

After a quarter-second pause, Funderburke stepped forward and placed his arms around his mother. He held her against his chest and looked at me with a face that wordlessly said, "You see? I'm trying."

When he released her, for the first time, I saw Ms. Lilith's eyes glistening with a small amount of dampness. "That's the first time you've hugged me since you were fourteen."

Her secretary stuck her head out of the glass doors. "Ms. Lilith? There's an urgent phone call from Judge Ravensmythe."

"Thank you, Twyla." With a little nod to both of us, she hurried back inside the office.

Nolan, Paige, and Juniper had been watching the scene, and Paige approached us. "Can we have a word outside, please?"

Agreeing, we led her outside while Nolan and Juniper stayed in the foyer. She wrapped her camel-colored wool coat around her, and with the sun rapidly fading and the wind growing stronger, my blazer wasn't enough to protect me from the chill. A completely genuine shiver shot through my body, and on cue, Funderburke slipped out of his walking coat and wrapped it around me.

"What do you think of me?" Paige asked.

I took a deep breath and chose my words with excruciating care. "I know that Juniper loves you and trusts you. That counts for a lot."

"Do you think I'm being cruel by asking for full custody?"

Evasion seemed like the wisest response. "I notice you're saying 'I'm' instead of 'we're.' Are you saying that you're the primary driving force in these proceedings?"

She hesitated and responded extremely slowly. "I...don't...know... actually, yes."

"Does Nolan not want full responsibility for Juniper's care?" I asked.

"It's not that. He loves her. But what I saw just now... made me wonder if I'm imposing my wants on her and not seeing her for what she is."

I waited a minute for her to continue, and when she remained silent, I provided a little prodding. "How do you prefer to view her?"

"As a terrible mother who doesn't deserve Juniper."

Funderburke joined the conversation, "By implication, that means that you deeply want to believe that you deserve her as a daughter."

"Yes."

"Why?"

She didn't hesitate to answer my question. "Because I believe I want her in my life more. At least, I thought I did. And now I wonder if I'm doing her an injustice."

I kept prodding. "And this is because...?"

"I have to explain. I can't have children of my own. And I blame my mother for that."

Another long pause. Paige was trying my patience, but she was clearly in the middle of some emotional turmoil, so I realized that it was best to be more understanding than I felt like being. "Please, go on."

"My parents divorced when I was fourteen, and soon afterwards my mother moved in with a really sleazy guy. She thought he was wonderful; everybody else knew better, and when they confronted her about him, she cut them from her life. But he wasn't really interested in her. He was interested... in me."

I've heard versions of this story a hundred times before, and it never fails to make my stomach lurch. "Oh, no."

"When I told my mother, she didn't believe me, and when I realized I was going to have a baby, she freaked out. She called me all the names you'd expect, and when I told her how it happened, she slapped me across the face and called me a liar."

"Where was your father during all of this?" Funderburke asked.

"Boston, with his new wife and baby daughter. He stopped visiting and calling after the wedding. I'm not sure why, but I'd guess his second spouse wanted him to focus on his current family. Anyway, my mother told me she wasn't going to allow me to turn her into a grandmother before she was forty, and I had a choice. I could do as she said, or I'd be out on the streets. It wasn't really a choice, as I had nowhere to go and no other family. So she took me to an appointment, and I'm not sure what happened, but there was a serious infection, and the next thing I knew, a doctor was telling me that I'd never be able to have children of my own. And when I cried and screamed at my mother for putting me in this situation, she turned very cold and hissed at me that it was my own fault. I had no one to listen to me, and my mother's boyfriend didn't stop, and it kept on going until I got a scholarship to college, moved out, and never looked back."

It's always awkward when someone you barely know suddenly starts pouring out her heart and her life's story to you. Watching her emote and gush, I couldn't stop asking myself: *Why us? Why now? Why is she telling all of these incredibly personal details to near strangers?* The cynical side of me considered the possibility that she was trying to manipulate us. Then, my more rational side wondered just what she would have to gain by attempting to sway our emotions. As far as I knew, her only goal was to receive full custody of Juniper. And from what I could tell, she already had a pretty strong hand to play. She had plenty of disposable income, and Layla had next to none. She was married to Juniper's father, and both of them were well-paid lawyers, compared to Layla a newly unemployed bartender who was hoping to go back to college. They'd hired one of the most successful attorneys in town, and Layla had no legal representation. Add on the fact that Juniper was palpably frightened of Layla, and based on my experience with family courts, I thought it was a slam-dunk that Paige and Nolan would be awarded permanent full custody unless Layla threw herself to the floor of the courtroom cried enough tears to get people gathering up two of every animal, and begged the judge for sympathy. I'd seen that tactic work in the past.

Having a legal background herself, I was sure that Paige knew that her best tactic was to just sit back and let Ms. Lilith do what she did best and use her knowledge of the legal system to achieve a favorable outcome for her clients. Layla had just dropped a gift-wrapped present in Paige's lap with her recent antics. Judges are not in the habit of awarding custody to young women who throw temper tantrums in public and then lock themselves in a bathroom. There was no need for Paige to negotiate. She'd as good as won.

But just what did "winning" mean for her? Would minimizing Layla's presence in Juniper's life be in the girl's best interests? If I was right about Layla's involvement in Erika's death, then the answer was *definitely not.* And I wondered if Paige had come to a similar conclusion. And the more I studied

Paige, the surer I was that she was completely sincere.

All these thoughts flashed through my head in a matter of moments. Paige interrupted the flow of my reasoning by saying, "I was watching what you were saying to Ms. Lilith. I had no idea you were her son."

"It's pretty common knowledge in the local legal community. I've been told that it's a popular subject of gossip at meetings of the Milwaukee Bar Association."

"I know this is personal, but do you mind if I ask just what caused the rift between you two?"

Funderburke folded his arms and leaned against the wall of the building. Normally, he wouldn't reveal the sadder details of his past with strangers, but as Paige had overshared, he felt like she deserved a reciprocal show of backstory. "My mother's second husband was cut from the same cloth as your mother's boyfriend. Only he wasn't interested in girls. I don't know why he left me alone, but thank God he did. My half-brother wasn't so lucky. And when I, as a pre-teen, found out what was going on, my wicked stepfather shifted the blame to me. I don't fully understand the power and manipulative influence an abuser can have on a child, but my half-brother backed up my stepfather's lies, and my mother believed them. I moved in with my grandparents, who supported me wholeheartedly. By the time my innocence was proven, and my stepfather fled for parts unknown, my relationship with my mother was well and truly trashed."

Paige blanched. "I'm sorry you had to go through that."

"I feel the same way towards you."

"What Nerissa said to you in the foyer, I have to tell you that I totally agree. My mother died a year ago. Cancer. Her boyfriend—they never married because my mother wanted to keep receiving alimony from my dad—is in jail now for the reasons you'd expect. To her dying day, she insisted that he was framed. The last time I spoke to her, she told me if I wanted to ease her burden during her final days, I'd finally admit that I'd lied about what her boyfriend did to me. And when I refused to recant, she cursed and refused to talk to me again. So, I never got the reconciliation I wanted, but that was mostly on her, not me. But your mother wants to make things right."

Funderburke appeared to swallow his initial reply. "Thank you." Obviously, he wanted to say so much more, but at that moment, he couldn't.

"Seeing you and your mother made me think. I didn't think it was right that there was such a serious rift between you two. It's not natural or right to have that kind of a gulf between a parent and child. I know that from my own experiences. And all of a sudden, I realized that I was responsible for exacerbating the rift between a mother and a daughter, all because I wanted a child of my own so badly, and I wasn't willing to share. You know how this all started? We'd tried a surrogate three times with no success. We'd looked at an adoption agency, but we both work long hours, and for whatever reason, we were way down on the list. Nolan has always wanted his own children, and I couldn't give them to him. One day, I just snapped, and I told him that I didn't want to hold him back anymore, so I left him and let him find someone who could provide him with the family he wanted. I didn't realize how crushed he'd be. I deluded myself into thinking he didn't really love me, and I definitely didn't expect that he'd go on a drunken bender and wind up… and when he told me what had happened and begged me to come back, I suddenly realized that this wasn't exactly what I wanted, but still… Nolan would get a baby of his own, and I could be its mother. I didn't think that Layla would want to stay in the picture, and I resented her for not signing away her maternal rights when Juniper was born. I've been trying to force her out of our lives ever since, and tonight, for the first time, I realized that what I was doing was about me, not Juniper. I want—"

She was interrupted by Layla finally storming out the door. Nolan and Juniper were right behind her. Layla turned to me with cold fury in her eyes. "You faked being my friend. I thought I might actually have a shot at fixing my life, but all the help you offered was just a ploy to investigate me. I never want to see you again."

As she started storming off, I started to say, "I'm sor—"

"Don't apologize." Funderburke interrupted. "You did nothing wrong."

"Nothing wrong?" Layla whirled around and directed her rage towards him. "She must have told your mother about my throwing the bottle at the tavern. How else would she have known about it?"

"If you'd bothered to ask me before leveling false accusations, you'd know that my mother has about a dozen private detectives on her payroll. One of them was probably in the bar that night and reported to her," Funderburke retorted.

Layla was temporarily blindsided by his answer, but she had enough rage left in her to rally. "She still betrayed me."

"She's been an amazing friend to you, and you should be a damned sight more appreciative." Funderburke wasn't yelling at her, but his voice was booming with moral outrage. "Where the hell do you get off saying she betrayed you? The reason why we started looking into your life is because Juniper came to us scared half to death. And you know why? Because of you. Your daughter is frightened of you. That's because she believed that you had murdered Erika, that you'd deliberately poisoned her so you wouldn't have to deal with her addiction anymore. Do you understand? That three-year-old girl is scared out of her wits because she thought that her mother had taken her aunt's life, and if she upset you, she was afraid that she'd be next. Think about that a moment. That child is frightened for her life because she didn't believe she could trust you. You created a situation where a tiny child couldn't feel safe around her own mother. So what did Nerissa do? Did she say, that's not my problem, leave me alone? No. Did she say, that little kid is probably suffering from an overactive imagination, I'm going to brush aside her concerns without any proper inquiry or questioning? No, she didn't do that either. Nerissa's taken dozens of hours out of her very busy schedule in order to look into this matter, because she doesn't believe that a child should be afraid of her mother, and the way to address that situation is not to leap to the airy conclusion that everything is all right and there's no need for hysterics. No, she worked with me to assess the situation thoroughly and honestly, because the safety and mental health of a student is *that* important to her. And, along the way, she grew to like you and saw a lot of good in you, including virtues that you've overlooked in yourself lately. She thought that you could recover your ambition and drive and find a level of happiness that you'd abandoned all hope of ever finding again. Nerissa stepped up to help you, as well as Juniper. She's made room in her already full-to-bursting life to look out for two people that she didn't even know a couple of weeks ago. You are entirely in the wrong when you accuse her of feigning friendship, and if you had any shred of decency, you would fling yourself upon the ground and polish Nerissa's boots with what's left of your hair in order to thank her for all she's done. Nerissa has been the most amazing friend you could ever have dreamed of, and your angry accusation is a total disgrace and a vile slander. So don't you dare treat her actions like some duplicitous betrayal of you? The real betrayal is when you, yes, you, attempted to convince your daughter that she was delusional. How can you live with yourself, knowing that ever since Erika's funeral, Juniper's been unable to sleep, wracked with nightmares where you're shoving a handful of pills down your sister's throat?"

Here, Funderburke stopped his monologue, not because he was out of indignation, but because, at some point, even the most stalwart pair of lungs needs to take a few deep breaths. And his hurricane of invective appeared to have blown away every atom of Layla's wrath. She now looked extremely discombobulated, and I had the sense that if Funderburke had gone on for just thirty more seconds, Layla's legs would be buckling beneath her. As it was, she sagged but remained upright. "I didn't..." she stammered. "I didn't kill Layla."

At that moment, I was basking in an indescribable warm glow in appreciation of Funderburke's impassioned defense of me. I am perfectly capable of defending myself, but *hot damn*, it's wonderful to have a boyfriend who won't stand for any disrespect towards me and can express his disapproval so eloquently. I had started to apologize because I thought that I had hurt Layla, but after hearing Funderburke's words, suddenly, I didn't feel guilty anymore, and I would have retracted that apology if I'd wanted to attack Layla. But that wasn't my goal. I also sensed that now was the time to try to break through the last of Layla's defenses after Funderburke had brought forth the full force of his emotional battering ram. "I don't think you deliberately poisoned her, Layla, but I also don't think that your story about coming home and going up to your room without checking on Erika was entirely true, was it?"

Layla froze. Her mouth stayed open in a perfect circle, and I saw the first signs of tears forming in her eyes.

I stepped forward and put a hand on her shoulder. "You did go downstairs to see Erika, didn't you?"

"Yes." The word was faint, but we all heard it. It was a broken little howl, lasting for seven seconds.

"And when you went downstairs, was she lying on the floor, either unconscious or dead?"

"Yes." She was no louder or faster speaking this time.

"She had already taken a massive overdose when you found her?"

"I guess so." Now, her voice was growing stronger.

"And once you found her, what did you do?"

"I ran upstairs and got some Narcan and brought it down to the basement."

"So, did you give it to her?"

"I started to, but I didn't."

"Why not?"

At this point, her knees started to give way out from under her, and Funderburke and I grabbed her arms and helped her over to a short wall separating the parking area from a cluster of trees, half of which were now completely devoid of leaves. "I thought it might be too late. I thought she was finally gone. And I realized I didn't want to bring her back. I just kept thinking about how I'd lost my college education because I tried to help her, and how we couldn't keep anything nice in the house anymore, and she'd stolen my jacket and my hair and…I just couldn't take it anymore. My grandfather didn't have to die when he did. He put off retirement to keep paying for her therapy and rehab, and it didn't work, and it broke his heart. Grandma can't keep working forever, but she'd wear herself into the grave taking another job scrubbing out bathroom toilets if we needed more money to support her. I was going to lose Juniper, and I just looked down at her still body, and I thought to myself, *she ruined our lives*. I know I'm not supposed to blame her; I know she had a disease, but she was crushing us. She'd taken and taken, and there was nothing left, and finally, I just told myself that I couldn't take it anymore. It had to end. I couldn't live in an empty house anymore, because she'd take anything that wasn't nailed down and sell it for pills. I know I should have at least tried to help, but I couldn't! I couldn't squeeze that little bottle. I just walked upstairs and went to my room, because I was afraid that if I brought her back, I'd just be subjecting myself and Grandma to who knows how much longer of constant hell. I didn't poison her. I just didn't try to save her." Tears flowed fast and heavily. "Can't you understand? I thought it was self-defense. I couldn't take it anymore. I just had to stop her from hurting me anymore..." The tears doubled in quantity. "I let her die. I let her die. Oh my God, I let my sister die."

None of them knew what to say or how to respond, and she slumped against Funderburke's suit jacket, soaking it with her tears and pressing her running nose against it. Funderburke met my eyes, and I gave him the universally recognized nod that girlfriends give their boyfriends to let him know that it's perfectly all right for him to put his arms around another woman, as this is a case when a distressed person needs comforting. There was a faint expression of disgust on his face as he hugged her, and I figured that he was relieved that not only was I wearing his coat, thereby saving it from Layla's deluge, but it was also lucky that his suits were machine-washable.

Soon afterwards, around the time when it became clear that Funderburke was getting tired of being used as Layla's handkerchief, Juniper and Nolan stepped out of the building, tentatively approaching Layla before Juniper slipped her hand into her mother's. After a moment, Layla became aware of her daughter's action and let go of Funderburke, pressing Layla against her. There was no lessening of her crying.

A familiar minivan driving by slowed and turned into the parking lot. Mom and Dad stepped out, and inside the dimly illuminated vehicle, I could see my siblings surrounded by boxes and canisters. The family had made a mid-week Costco run to replenish our supplies. I hurried up to them and explained the situation.

Mom and Dad introduced themselves to Paige and Nolan, and Mom asked, "Would you like to come to our house for dinner tonight?" After the usual dissembling about not wanting to impose, Mom insisted, saying, "I think you have a lot to discuss, and I think that a friendly meal at a neutral place will be a lot more conducive to working out a plan than at these offices."

So Paige and Nolan got our address, and Layla and Juniper rode with Funderburke and me on the way home. Funderburke looked down at his stained jacket with disgust, and he folded it up and set it on the back seat next to Juniper. I handed his walking coat back to him, and he slipped it back on with palpable gratitude right before opening the passenger door for me.

We drove back to my house in near silence. Layla was still crying, and she used up the entirety of the box of tissues Funderburke kept in his car. Juniper was crying too, but much more lightly than Layla—only a single tear at a time as opposed to Layla's steady stream. Mother and daughter held each other's hands for the entire ride.

Twenty-two minutes later, we were back. Juniper played with my siblings while Funderburke helped Dad unpack the groceries. Mom helped her grandmother put the finishing touches on dinner. Fortunately, there's always enough on the table to feed the whole neighborhood. We could take in five unplanned guests (Celeste would be joining us after her shift at the bookstore ended at seven), and the only concern was having room for all the chairs around the table. Toby was in her room doing her homework, Mom's younger sister Rally was watching the younger set of triplets, Mom's brother Ted was napping, Dad's grandfather was in his room arguing with a roundtable of journalists on television, and I was in the living room with Layla, Paige, and Nolan as they had the friendliest conversation they'd ever had.

"Why have you changed your mind?" Layla asked.

Paige raised and lowered her shoulders, "What I saw tonight made me realize that I wasn't thinking about what Juniper needed, just what I wanted. And I realized that being a mother was about more than having my way. I thought that I could be the mother I wanted to be by forcing you out of the picture, and I suddenly realized that trying to alienate Juniper's affections from you didn't make me a good parent. Just the opposite."

Layla nodded, and I sensed that she was coming to grips with the new

162

reality that she would have to start reconsidering her long-held dislike of Paige. "How about you?" she said to Nolan. "Where do you stand on this?"

"I told you, I just want to make things right for all the mistakes I made. Seducing and impregnating you, cheating on Paige—"

"Will you stop?" Paige interrupted. "We've been over this a million times. You didn't cheat on me. I told you our marriage was over. I take full responsibility for driving you away. You were a free man that night. "

"No, I wasn't. Not in my heart. And I still—"

Now, it was Layla's turn to cut him off mid-sentence. "Also, as I recall, I was the one who did the seducing that night. All you wanted to do was drink another quart of whiskey and cry."

Nolan sunk back as if he was hoping that the sofa would swallow him whole. "I'm still ashamed of how I acted."

"Do you regret bringing Juniper into the world?" I asked.

He looked at me as if my question was a slap in the face. "No. Definitely not. She and Paige are the best thing that's ever happened to me."

"Glad to hear it. Now I'm going to tell you something I usually tell teenage girls. Every minute you spend flagellating yourself for your actions is an opportunity you miss to show your child how loved she is. Are you Catholic?"

He looked a little shocked by that question. "Uh, no. I'm not really anything."

"Well, if you were, I'd tell you to go to confession and move forward. As it stands now, the same principles are in play. Acknowledge what you did wrong, repent, make it right, and don't let the mistake poison your life. Just don't do it again, and focus on being the best person, husband, and father you can possibly be. Have you ever looked at Juniper and thought about your own guilt?" He didn't need to answer. "I'll take that as a "yes." Well, I can guarantee you that Juniper's seen you looking at her like that, and she hasn't been sure how to respond to it. She just has the feeling that she's a source of shame for you."

We kept talking, and by the time dinner was being brought out to the table, the discussion of how much time Juniper would spend in each household was downright cordial. At five past seven, Celeste rang the bell, and I let her inside the house.

"Grandma, I have to tell you something." Layla told Celeste the whole story, adding details she hadn't included earlier.

Celeste's face was impassive. "I know."

"Yes! You've known from the beginning, but how?"

"Because I know you, and I could tell at once you were lying when you told me and the paramedics what happened. You tugged at your ear, your eyes darted around, your posture slumped... And I saw the mud. As soon as I came home, I saw your damaged shoes, and I saw little spots of mud across my floor, going to the basement door and finally fading away halfway down the steps. I knew you'd gone downstairs. Also, you left the wrapping for the Narcan on the butcher block, next to the scissors, not to mention the tattered jeans you couldn't be bothered to throw into the garbage or down the laundry chute. Obviously, you opened one."

"Why didn't you confront me about it? Why didn't you kick me out of the house or something like that?"

"Because I'd already lost one of my granddaughters, and I wasn't prepared to lose the other one." The stern expression on Celeste's face slowly began to waver, until finally the two women fell into each other's arms, and both were soon in need of tissues.

We avoided talking about custody issues or Erika's death during dinner (turkey fricassee, buttered egg noodles, mesclun greens salad, peas, popovers, and assorted reheated leftovers from the past two nights). Mrs. Stutschewsky joined us as usual, but we forgot that Mom's aunt and uncle were also coming over that night. Dad and Funderburke had to set up a little table for the kids to make room for everybody, but the night was a success. Celeste left early because she had to pick up her medication before the pharmacy closed, and Layla, Paige, and Nolan agreed to meet that weekend to make further plans. Paige promised that in the morning, she'd call Ms. Lilith and tell her that her services would no longer be needed.

Funderburke drove Layla home, and I joined them because I wanted to discuss Layla's college application. As we approached the Dolak house, we saw an ambulance parked two houses down the street. After parking in the

Dolaks' driveway, the three of us walked over to see what was happening there. A young woman was being carried out on a stretcher with a respirator on her face.

"That's Jane Doe," Funderburke said.

"That's Izzy. Isabella Botner," Layla explained. "She's one of Erika's friends."

"And a fellow addict," he added.

"Well, yes."

One of the paramedics was speaking to a frantic-looking couple. "It's lucky you found her when you did, Mr. and Mrs. Botner. Administering the Narcan and calling us saved her life."

"Then she'll be all right?" Mr. Botner asked.

"Hopefully, she will be, but you can never tell with a fentanyl overdose."

Funderburke and I stared at each other and said more with our expressions than we possibly could have with words.

Chapter Nine—No Longer Jane Doe

A
s we watched the woman we now knew was Izzy Botner being gently placed inside the ambulance, we noticed that the middle-aged couple speaking to the paramedics was now pointing in our direction. After squinting in the darkness, it became clear that the pair, presumably Izzy's parents, were drawing the paramedics' attention towards Layla.

A somber-faced paramedic with a brown ponytail walked up to us. "Are you Layla Dolak?"

Layla identified herself, and the paramedic showed no interest in finding out who Funderburke and I were. "You're Erika Dolak's sister?"

"Yes."

"Will you please go into your home and wait a little bit? The police will want a word with you. Please relax," she added in response to Layla's tensing posture. "I don't think you're in trouble, but you may be a useful witness."

"Will Miss Botner be okay?" Funderburke asked.

"It's touch and go. I can't say more. Excuse me."

Funderburke and I walked over to the Botners, introduced ourselves, and asked if there was anything we could do to help them. They politely declined and left for the hospital to join their daughter.

Instead of returning to our respective homes, the two of us followed Layla into her house. I was surprised by how much more homelike the place had become since I last visited. Pictures and photographs had been hung on the walls, more knickknacks dotted the shelves, and the place had taken on a bit more personality.

166

Celeste greeted us. "Is something going on down the street? I heard sirens."

We explained the situation, and Celeste shook her head. "I hope that she pulls through. I'm rather fond of Izzy. I prayed this wouldn't happen, but I'm not surprised."

"She told me that she and Erika went to meetings together," Funderburke commented.

"Yes. They were good friends, starting in high school when Erika moved in with us full-time."

"When exactly was that?" Funderburke asked.

"Erika lived with her mother on and off until she turned fourteen. Even before that, there were times when she stayed with us for a few weeks or months at a stretch." There was a sudden stiffening in Celeste's manner, and I wanted to ask more questions, but I had the sense that Celeste had raised her drawbridge. She wasn't going to allow any more discussion of the family history at the moment.

She offered us raspberry herbal tea, and we both accepted a cup after bringing a tray to the living room. The pleasant fragrance had a relaxing effect on me. I sipped it plain, liked it, and decided it would be even better with milk, so I poured the better part of the little pitcher into my cup. There wasn't more than a few drops left for Funderburke, and he firmly refused to let Celeste fetch him more, so he went to the kitchen and added milk himself. He must have used his trip to the kitchen to pour out some of the tea, because it looked to me as if his cup contained mostly, perhaps entirely, milk. We allowed Celeste to ask us questions about our work, how we met, and our interests. Half an hour passed, reasonably pleasantly, and then the police arrived.

Funderburke had met one of them throughout one of his investigations before his employment at Cuthbertson, and they greeted each other warmly. Their visit lasted less than five minutes. Izzy lived in the garage apartment of her parents' home. Her mother walked out to say "good night," found her unconscious, and had behaved in a very different manner from Layla. Mrs. Botner had sprinted back to the house, screamed at her husband to call 911, and returned with a little bottle of Narcan. One squirt had rejuvenated

Izzy, though Izzy had immediately become violently ill all over her mother's shoes.

"Take a look at this." The detective who knew Funderburke held out a slip of paper in a clear plastic envelope. The note read:

Izzy—

I always share with you. Enjoy. But if you don't want them, give them back to me.

—Erika

"We found it in an envelope, along with two loose capsules filled with powder. Any idea what that means?" the detective asked.

Layla nodded. "Erika and Izzy have been best friends since high school. They started using it together. Erika went to rehab three times, and it never worked. Izzy went four times, stayed clean for about six months or so after each visit, and then relapsed. They went to NA meetings together. Izzy tried to make the program work for her, but Erika just went for the free coffee and donuts."

She saw the detectives raise their eyebrows. "I suppose you think I'm being harsh, but Erika told me once that she didn't care if she ever got sober again or not. And I believed her. She was content to spend the rest of her life getting high." The bitterness in her tone was obvious. "But Izzy was different. She tried to kick her addiction. It was just too powerful for her sometimes. Izzy would make a tremendous effort to stay clean for a month or so, and then the cravings would become too much for her, and she'd relapse, just for a day or two, and then she'd pull together every bit of strength she had and try to get back on the wagon. Erika told me once that Izzy'd gotten burned in the past by buying cheap from dealers who sold tainted products and left her sick. Erika prided herself on looking out for her friend. Izzy knew ahead of time when the siren call of opiates was getting too strong for her, and she'd tell Erika, who'd get a one or two-day supply for her." Layla's face soured. "Erika looked out for Izzy much more than she did for me."

"I beg your pardon?"

"Nothing, sorry, it's been a long day," Layla hurriedly dissembled.

"So you think that your late sister gave some of these pills to Miss Botner?"

168

one of the detectives asked.

"That note seems to confirm it, doesn't it?" Layla replied.

It's not dated, I thought to myself but didn't say.

Celeste entered the conversation. "I spoke to Izzy at the funeral. She said that she'd been on the verge of a relapse, and then right before she was going to start taking some more pills, her mother knocked on her door with the news that Erika had passed away." For a fleeting second, I wondered if Celeste might be trying to protect her Layla somehow, but I studied her face, and so no trace of deceit.

"This was a little over a week ago?"

"That's correct."

"So Erika scored some capsules, left some for her friend, went home, and overdosed. Her death kept Izzy sober for a little while longer, but eventually, she relapsed," the taller of the two detectives theorized. "Sad."

"Were the capsules filled with pure fentanyl?" Celeste asked. "That's what they said Erika took."

"We'll need to run some tests. Do you know where she got them?"

Celeste shook her head. "No idea. I tried hard to limit my knowledge of that aspect of her life." Layla similarly denied knowing who Erika's dealer was, and a minute later, the policeman thanked them for their time and left. We followed them.

As we pulled into my driveway, I told Funderburke, "I suppose that's how they'll catch Erika's real killer. Whoever sold her the fentanyl is responsible for her death."

"Maybe…"

I was surprised by Funderburke's tone. "Don't you think they'll find the dealer?"

"Dealers don't give away their product for free unless it's a "first taste" to get people hooked. They don't give out little cards and stamp them every time a customer makes a purchase. Twelve stamps, and you get a free dime bag. Doesn't work that way."

"I know that, Funderburke."

"So, how did Erika pay for the pills? Where'd she get the money?"

I thought about that for a moment. "Stole something, I suppose."

"Nothing left to sell at her house. And I checked the police blotters. No one reported a break-in at their cars or homes in the general neighborhood for three days before her death. Of course, she could've gone elsewhere or stole something that didn't get noticed or reported, anything's possible."

"Or she could have turned to prostitution."

"True. But aside from the logistics of buying the pills, the question remains, why was she the only person reported to have overdosed from them? As I told you, there should have been dozens of unfortunate people who fell ill or died from pure fentanyl. For over a week, there was only one. Now there are two, and apparently, they both took pills from the same batch, and the delay was due to the second victim trying to fight her addiction. Normally, the users would take the pills quite soon after buying them. But there's been nothing."

"Wait. You're not saying that now you think that Layla deliberately killed Erika after all?" I have to admit that I felt indignant, having thought we'd settled the matter, and I'd been waiting for him to admit that he was wrong to have suspected her for so long.

"I don't know, but I need to do more digging tomorrow."

He slipped into his thoughts, and we said nothing more until he dropped me off at home, and we kissed goodnight. It was late, but I hadn't gotten my workout that day yet. Toby had gotten some knots in her hair, so after I helped her brush them out and double-checked her math homework, I changed into my exercise clothes and put an hour in on the elliptical machine. I had a ton of pent-up energy and needed to vent it. After showering, reviewing my notes for the next day's classes, answering emails, and skimming through a few articles, I got three-quarters of a page of my dissertation written before realizing that it was one-fifteen and I had better sleep.

The next morning, I downed double my usual ration of iced coffee and milk and selected a port-wine velvet top and a pair of amber suede slacks to wear that day. For the first three hours of the day, there were no emergencies, and then I got a call telling me that Fiona's grandmother, who had Alzheimer's, had escaped from her nursing home. The establishment was just a mile from Cuthbertson, so Funderburke joined the search. Fiona's grandmother had a tracking device on her ankle, but it wasn't giving off a signal for some reason. After checking the security cameras, Funderburke and the nursing home's chief of security realized that she probably hadn't left the grounds after all, and they found her hiding behind some boxes of paper towels in a rarely-visited storage room in the back of the basement.

As I was finishing my lunch, Funderburke sat next to me. "You're clear the rest of the afternoon, aren't you?"

"I've got assembly and study hall to proctor after that. The last period of the day's free, though."

"You can skip assembly—the alderman who's lecturing is a pompous bore. I already asked your grandmother to cover study hall for you. We're going to do a little more investigating."

So I pulled on my gingerbread lambskin café racer jacket, and we were heading back towards the East Side soon. "If I remember correctly, they're at Celeste's eye appointment now," I informed him. "They won't be back until four or so."

"I don't want to see them now," he answered. "We need to speak to Mrs. Böhm. I told you, I'm still bugged by her saying that she saw Layla walking home that afternoon."

"I know she made notes, but I wonder if there's some way she mixed up the date or the time. Or maybe she just mistook Layla for someone else."

"Anything's possible, I suppose. But she seemed pretty sharp when I saw her."

"How old is she?"

"Eighty-something, but her brain's in good condition. She had some pretty intelligent comments about why one actress of dubious talents managed to win an Oscar the other year, and she also cracked a few jokes. She said her knees aren't in the best shape, and her cataracts are acting up–"

"Cataracts? Any defense attorney would jump on that to discredit her."

"I know, I know. And there's a reason why her television is so large. But she's a likable woman, and she seemed pretty sure of what she saw."

I've got octogenarian and nonagenarian relatives whose mental acumen put half of my students to shame. I did not doubt that Funderburke was right about her cognitive abilities, but I was pretty sure this was a simple case of misidentification.

We talked about the trouble I was having smoothing out the narrative in my dissertation, and twenty minutes later, we were parked in front of Mrs. Böhm's house. After ringing her doorbell, we heard her call out, "I'll be there in a minute!" It took her three before she opened the door. She was leaning on a walker, and from how she squinted at us, it was obvious her eyesight wasn't great, but I could tell from the spark in her eyes that she had plenty of intelligence.

"Oh! You're Funderburke, aren't you? You're that very handsome young man who chatted with me the other day."

Funderburke turned to me with a grin that said, *her eyesight can't be that bad*.

Mrs. Böhm welcomed us in and encouraged us to help ourselves to a bowl of hard candy between our chairs. We both took peppermints and as we unwrapped them, she said, "It's so good to see you again, Layla. It's been years since we last had a chat."

We turned towards each other and stared into each other's eyes for a moment. "This is my girlfriend, Nerissa Kaiming," Funderburke finally explained.

"Oh, sorry, dear. You look so much like Layla."

I looked around. This was a neighborhood where the houses had varied styles and qualities. On this block alone, a quarter of the houses appeared composed of sloppily painted cardboard. About half of the houses were modest, not fancy but functional. The Dolaks' house fit into this category. The remaining quarter of the houses were large older homes with beautiful exteriors. Mrs. Böhm's house was one of the nicest on the block, and the Botner house wasn't far behind in quality. I complimented her on her home, and she waved away the remark.

"It is a lovely house, but it's got too many memories. My husband was a real rotter. It was lots of fun at first, but I won't scandalize you of all the nasty little surprises I walked in on over the years. Anyway, it's much too much house for little old me. Five bedrooms, five bathrooms... I haven't been down the basement in years. I've forgotten how many rooms are down there. You should see the stained glass windows in the kitchen. They're lovely."

We took a quick trip to the kitchen and admired the windows. When Funderburke and I returned, Mrs. Böhm said, "I'm going to put it up for sale in a month or two. My eldest daughter's built a nice little granny apartment on the side of her house. I'll be able to watch my shows and not worry about falling with no one finding me for days."

"How much are you asking for the house?" I asked.

"Why? Are you interested?"

"I am." I explained how I'd like to use the house, and Mrs. Böhm seemed interested in my plans.

Twenty minutes passed as we sat and chatted. By two o'clock, we excused herself, as it was now time for Mrs. Böhm's favorite talk show. The moment the door shut behind us, we turned towards each other.

"You were right. She must have mistook someone else for Layla," Funderburke said.

"Yes, but don't you see? She thought I was Layla. With her cataracts, she couldn't see all the details of her face. She saw a tall, slender woman with long, dark hair, and a brown leather jacket."

In a fraction of a second, Funderburke was on the same page I was. "But that's not what Layla looks like anymore. In the last few years, her appearance has changed a lot. She's... not slim anymore, and her hair's very short. And she didn't even have her leather jacket at that time. Erika had sold it, and you bought it. But if she thought that you were Layla..."

"Then the woman she saw entering the house must have looked like Layla as she did three or four years ago. What about Stella, the girl who lives in their garage? Could that have been her?"

"Stella has medium-length red hair, and she's barely five foot two. I don't think she owns a brown leather jacket—of course, that's the least important part of the identification—but I saw a black puffer and a purple fleece

173

hanging on the hooks in her little apartment. Nothing else. It's unlikely she'd be mistaken for Layla, even at a distance by someone with poor eyesight."

"So a woman matching Layla's description stopped by the house. Maybe she was a political canvasser or a religious proselytizer or something like that. It was just a coincidence."

"Maybe." Funderburke started jogging across the street towards the Botner house. I hurried behind him. We had a much shorter wait there. Mrs. Botner answered the door in seconds after our ring.

"Yes? Wait, didn't I meet you two last night?"

"You did. How is your daughter doing?"

"Izzy's going to pull through, thank you for asking. I just got back from the hospital. I need a shower and a nap, and then I'm going back to spend the rest of the evening with her. Is there something I can do for you?"

"Yes." Funderburke took a breath, and I could tell that he was calculating what tone to take with her. "I know this is a very personal subject, and you're going through a terrible time right now, and I don't want to add to it. But you're a mother, and I know that you understand that other mothers might be facing a threat to their children as we speak. We're trying to prevent other families from losing loved ones due to incredibly powerful drugs. We don't want to get Izzy in any more trouble, but we do want the people pushing pure fentanyl to get their comeuppance. Based on the note, Erika Dolak gave your daughter the pills and then took the rest of the capsules herself and died."

"Yes, that's correct." Mrs. Botner looked sympathetic to us, and I mentally congratulated Funderburke for striking just the right tone.

"On the day she died, Erika was seen leaving her house and heading towards yours. She was carrying a red plastic grocery bag. I think that she brought something to Izzy. Do you remember if Izzy was at home that afternoon?"

"I remember that day very clearly. I've worried about the two of them for years, and I spent the evening worrying that Izzy would be next and chastising myself for being so relieved because that day, it was Erika and not Izzy. No, Izzy was not at home that afternoon. Right after her meeting, I

174

took her around town while I ran some errands. I didn't want to leave her alone. You'll laugh at me, but I had a premonition something terrible would happen."

"Mrs. Botner, I can assure you that neither of us is laughing. Did Erika have a key to your house? Or do you have a key hidden somewhere she could have found it?"

"No and no."

"Is there a place on your property where she could have hidden something?"

"Like the pills? I suppose she just slipped them through the milk chute. You know, a little door on the side of the garage apartment. In the old days, the grocery stores left deliveries in there."

"Well, yes, the pills, but it strikes me that there was something else. After all, she could have tucked that envelope with the note and the pills in her pocket. She didn't need to carry a grocery bag with her and leave it there. Is there a place she could have hidden it?"

"I suppose. Would you like a look inside her apartment?"

We accepted her offer with obvious gratitude. The room was very sparsely furnished, and though I didn't speak my thoughts, I was sure that this was by design to provide Izzy with very few items to sell. It took three minutes for us to search the apartment, and we found no red plastic bag or anything notable.

Mrs. Botner locked the door and left to shower, but she granted us permission to keep looking. I turned over a large plastic flowerpot and found nothing but dead leaves. There was nothing else inside the milk chute, either. By the time I'd looked at those places, Funderburke had made his way to the other side of the garage."

"See anything?" I called out to him.

"Not yet... Wait a minute! Come here."

I hurried over to him and found him tugging at a small stone bench. "Take a look. The seat of this bench lifts up. It's hollow, and inside..." A red plastic grocery bag was folded up inside a little hollow on the bench. I snatched it up while Funderburke lowered the seat back into place.

"What's the prize in the Cracker Jack Box?" he asked.

"It's a diary. And a folder of... it looks like medical records." The diary was bound in laminated aqua cardboard, but the pages were protected with a cheap little lock holding the covers together with a strap.

I pulled a bobby pin from my hair. It didn't take any special skill to pick the lock. I simply slid the pin in and turned it as easily as I would have a proper key. "This is Erika's old diary," I informed him. "The first entry is from a decade ago. Erika must've been about twelve then." Some people might accuse me of violating the sacred confidentiality of a diary, but I contend that since Erika was dead, there was nothing preventing me from trying to figure out why she'd hidden a bag full of her memories and health history in the bench.

I handed Funderburke the medical file, and we made our way back around the garage and studied everything on the patio, where the light was better. The diary was mostly her thoughts about her classmates, crushes, and the various trials of pre-adolescence.

"Holy cow," Funderburke muttered.

"What?"

"These medical records document her treatment for at least four different STDs. And here...this last one was about dilation and curettage when she was fourteen—it looks like there was a miscarriage leading to significant internal bleeding—leading to a hysterectomy."

A sickening chill settled in my stomach. "Damn. Wait a minute..." I flipped through the diary faster. "She's thirteen or fourteen at this point, but she doesn't mention any relationship with boys. She mentions crushes, and she wonders what it might be like to... Here, she's writing about the first kiss she had with a guy in her English class, but it's clear it didn't go any further than that. *I cut my lip on his braces, and I told the school nurse I tripped and bit it. I don't think she believed me, but I don't think she suspected what really happened.* This sounds like fairly clean adolescent stuff. Hold it... Listen to this. *I blacked out again. I don't know what happened. Mom made me a snack, and the next thing I knew the room started spinning and everything was black. Hours later, I was lying on my bed, and Mom was holding my hand, stroking my head, and saying everything was all right. She said we'd just gotten back from the hospital. They diagnosed me with uphillapsy*—She must mean "epilepsy."

"Makes sense."

I kept turning pages. "She went on some medication, but every now and then she had another blackout. Luckily, her mother was always there when she fell ill."

"I'm not sure how lucky that was..." Funderburke muttered. "These hospital records are all from the Las Vegas area. This must be when they lived in Nevada, shortly before Erika moved in with her grandparents and Layla."

"You know, I've been wondering about that," I said. "Why did Shelby keep custody of Erika and not her elder daughter, Layla? Why did Shelby give up custody around the time Erika entered high school?"

"We both met Shelby at that hospital," Funderburke replied. "She didn't display much affection or warmth towards Layla. I wonder why? Think she picked up on the same guilt that Celeste and Juniper did?"

The icy knot in my stomach grew tighter. "I think it could be worse than that. Tell me if I'm putting two and two together and getting five."

"All right, I will. Go on, please."

"Part of the reason you stayed suspicious of Layla is because Mrs. Böhm believed she'd seen her coming back home around noon."

"Right."

"But as we just learned, Mrs. Böhm's eyesight isn't that great. She didn't actually see Layla. She saw someone roughly Layla's height, thin, with long, dark hair, possibly wearing a brown leather jacket like the one Layla used to wear all the time. Well, there's only one person we've met recently with a connection to the Dolak family who fits that description."

"Shelby. She's a little shorter than Layla, but she wears heels. I think she dyes her hair to get rid of the gray, but it's nearly the same color as Layla's. She had it pinned up when we saw her, but it was probably at least shoulder-length."

"Plus the mahogany aviator jacket. With the family resemblance, it's not surprising that Mrs. Böhm could've mistaken her for her daughter."

"If that's what happened. We don't even have any evidence that Shelby was in Milwaukee the day Layla died."

"True. Not yet, at least."

Funderburke shoved the file back into the bag. "Can we go to your house now? I need to use a computer there."

When we let ourselves into the house, Mom approached us with a baby in each arm and another one napping in the playpen. "Are you two playing hooky today?"

"If only," I whispered so as not to disturb the triplets. "I think we're onto something regarding what really happened to Erika."

Once inside my study nook, we logged into my computer, and Funderburke started his online investigative skills. "Did Layla say that her mother worked in marketing?"

"I think so."

"I can't find any records of her employment…. But wait a minute…."

"What?"

"About six years ago, Shelby Wiersma was sentenced to five years in prison in Nevada for theft, assaulting an officer, and some other crimes. That's when Erika went to live with her grandparents. She only served sixteen months, but she's been in and out on minor theft charges since then."

"Seriously?"

Funderburke kept searching. "I need to do more checking, but I'm pretty sure Shelby isn't in town for a business trip. I don't think she's held a steady job other than cocktail waitress."

"With those clothes? I suppose she could've bought them at thrift shops like I do, but you can't get a manicure like she had on the cheap." My phone rang. "Hello?" I turned to Funderburke. "It's Fiona. Her grandmother's missing again, and we need to get back to Cuthbertson."

We drove back, but a minute before we turned onto the campus, I received another text telling me Fiona's grandmother had been found, this time in the pantry of one of the small kitchens serving residents who needed round-the-clock care. Once we walked into the school, however, we saw a distraught Celeste and a calmer Layla talking to Dad.

"What's up?"

"She took Juniper!" Celeste shouted.

"It's nothing.   Mom just picked Juniper up for some grandma-granddaughter time," Layla replied. "I don't know why she didn't check with us first, though."

"That doesn't quite tally," Dad said. "Your mother took Juniper out of school early, saying there was a family emergency and they had to go to the hospital. Her great-grandmother was ill. But clearly that wasn't so."

Celeste whirled around towards us. "You need to find Juniper now!"

Chapter Ten—The Costanza Defense

Layla didn't appear to be worried. "Grandma, you're overreacting. Mom's in town, and she wanted to spend a little time with Juniper."

"And she didn't bother to tell you what she planned to do?" Funderburke asked.

"I...guess it just slipped her mind." A little confidence evaporated from Layla's face and tone.

"Has she ever done anything like this before?" I asked. "Since Juniper's birth, has she ever made a point of spending one-on-one time with her granddaughter?"

More uncertainty seeped into Layla. "No. She's been traveling a lot on business. She's been living in London for most of the last few years on business, and she hasn't had many opportunities to make it to Milwaukee."

Funderburke stared into Celeste's eyes. "I think you know the truth. Am I right?"

I had never seen Celeste look so deflated. "Yes."

"Should we tell her, or will you?"

Celeste staggered over to a bench against the wall and lowered herself down upon it. "Please. I can't."

"What are you two talking about?" Layla stamped her foot with impatience.

Taking her by the elbow, I led her to the bench and sat her down next to her grandmother, and I took the space on her other side. "You need to prepare yourself for some unsettling news. Your mother is not a marketing consultant. She has not been spending most of the last few years in London or wherever for her job."

From the blank expression in Layla's eyes, it was obvious that this was completely fresh news to her. "Wait, why would she lie to me about that? Where has she been lately, if not England?"

I felt the words choke in my throat, and I turned to Funderburke, silently asking him to answer for me. I'm pretty sure that the two of us have some sort of mental wavelength linking us together, because he gave me a nod and provided the information that I couldn't. "Your mother has been in prison on and off for most of the last six years. Two cases of blackmail, assaulting an officer, and multiple theft charges, mostly for offenses in Nevada, New Jersey, and California."

Layla opened and closed her mouth silently, like a goldfish. "You're kidding me."

"I can assure you that I'm not. Your mother's been lying to you for most of her life. Unless I miss my guess, she's also an addict, but whereas your father is an alcoholic and your sister took opiates, your mother's a gambling addict."

"I don't believe it."

"There's a reason why she's currently staying at the Potawatomi Hotel here in Milwaukee. Because it's attached to a casino. We know she's spent a lot of time in Las Vegas and Atlantic City. Also, her key chain fob is a poker chip."

"That doesn't mean—"

"Oh, stop!" Celeste snapped. "He's right. You need to accept that and stop wasting time. Juniper may be in danger!"

"What? From Mom? She'd never hurt Juniper."

"Do you have any idea where she might have taken her?" I asked.

"Tunk-Trunk!" Dad said. When we all looked at him with arched eyebrows, he explained, "Funderburke, you put a tracker—"

"Yes!" Funderburke whipped out his phone and tapped with flying fingers. "Just like Fiona's grandmother, technology will tell us exactly where she is. It looks like she's heading south on the freeway now. C'mon." He helped Celeste to her feet, and I did the same to Layla.

"Wait a second!" Dad halted us. "What kind of car does Shelby drive? What's her license plate number?"

After helpless expressions from Layla and Celeste, Funderburke said, "Since she's visiting in town, it's almost certainly a rental. We don't know, and even if we knew the company, it's unlikely that they'd give us the information we need, and even if they did, it'd take a while."

"All right," Dad replied, "I'll go down to the security offices and see if the cameras caught Shelby with Juniper. The problem is that with all the kids getting picked up, things are crowded. Just in case I can't see Juniper clearly, do you have a picture of Shelby? I've never met her, so I don't know what she looks like."

Layla had ceased being calm. "I don't have any photos on my cheap flip phone! There are paper photographs at home, but they're all years old, from when I was a kid!"

"She looks like Layla, only twenty years older, much thinner, and with longer hair, unless she has it pinned up. She may be wearing a brown leather aviator jacket, but we don't know," I informed Dad.

"The teacher who signed them out may know what she was wearing. She shouldn't have let them leave if Shelby wasn't on the list, but if Juniper said she was her grandmother, she probably just waved them through at the desk." Dad hurried off, and we rushed to Funderburke's car. I called one of our friends on the police force, explained the situation, and mirrored Funderburke's phone to our friend's, hoping that they could catch up with Shelby first. After promising I'd provide a description of the car as soon as I had it, I described Funderburke's vehicle and asked them if they could possibly put out an announcement saying that Funderburke wasn't to be stopped for speeding. Our friend said she'd see what she could do.

The instant I ended the call, Layla screamed, "Just what is going on here? Why did my Mom take Juniper without asking?"

"We told you… Your mother has a gambling problem. She needs money. I believe she has boom and bust streaks," I explained. "Not long ago, she must have had a winning streak, and she bought expensive clothes and treated herself at the beauty parlor. But of course, it didn't last, and I suspect that she's deeply in debt right now."

"But what is she doing with Juniper? Is she trying to steal her allowance?"

"We visited your neighbors this afternoon. We believe that Erika hid her old diary and some medical records at the Botners' house." Funderburke picked up the red plastic bag that was sitting between us and passed it back over his shoulder. "The diary was written during her pre-and early teens when she was living with her mother. She mentions a series of blackouts that were attributed to epilepsy. Not long before she came to live with you in Milwaukee, she was treated for various venereal diseases and a miscarriage, which led to a hysterectomy. There is an implication that her mother may have slipped her some sort of medication that caused the end of her pregnancy. I should point out that while Erika was pretty frank about her thoughts, feelings, and experiences, she didn't mention anything about sex in the diary. Also, the medical records don't appear to be from major hospitals, but instead from a small clinic, and I'm not sure how reputable it is. But even seedy, barely licensed medical establishments may potentially send copies of records if the patient requests them, which is what Erika must've done. She must have remembered the clinic's name even after all these years."

"Why didn't she tell me any of this?" Layla asked.

"You two were never close, partly because you didn't really grow up together," Celeste replied. "And when she moved in with us, you were busy with your own life and school, and then you were off to college...and when you came back, you were resentful, and she was high all the time..."

"Did you know any of this?" I asked Celeste, trying not to allow any accusatory tone to enter my words.

"Erika never spoke to me about those topics." Celeste spoke with such emotion that I was sure she was telling the truth. "Not directly, at any rate. She made the stray comment here and there, hinting that there was a problem, perhaps something traumatic. I just didn't know what. One time, when I took her to a routine doctor's appointment, she insisted that I stay in the waiting room. I figured that she wanted her privacy, so I respected it. But then, as we were leaving, I saw the look on the doctor's face, and I knew that there was something terribly wrong, but Erika hurried me away, and I never got the chance to ask any questions. Though I suppose the doctor wouldn't have spoken to me anyway." She ran a hand over her forehead and groaned. "My working theory was that something unthinkable happened to her while she was on a date with some boy. But now I wonder…"

"What?" Layla was shaking.

Funderburke took his eyes off the road for a fraction of a second in order to make eye contact with me. We'd discussed our thoughts on this matter on the way up to Cuthbertson twenty minutes earlier. "We have a theory," I informed her, "but we don't want to talk about it right now. It could be that our minds have gone to a very dark place, and you'd never forgive us for thinking what we did if we told you what we guessed, and it turns out we're way off base."

Layla produced an unintelligible syllable and then stopped. Perhaps she decided she didn't want to know what we feared had happened to Erika and might happen again to Juniper. As her breath grew shallower, I started to wonder if she'd come up with her own theory and if she'd wandered along the same disturbing lines that we had.

"I think you've suspected something for a long time," Funderburke told Celeste.

"I have never liked or trusted her. But I never had anything solid. If I had, I would have sent her to prison without a second thought."

"But you've never trusted her." Funderburke pressed.

"That's because…" Celeste hesitated, then pressed forward. "She's been extorting money from me for years. And from my husband before he died. Years ago, my son… got very drunk and did something that wasn't illegal, but it was so embarrassing that his daughters would never be able to hold their heads up in public again. Shelby had videographic proof, and when she was out of prison—yes, I knew about that and never said anything—she'd ask for little presents of cash to keep them from being made public. She didn't care about the fallout to her daughters, and we should have told her to fry in hell, but we decided a couple of hundred dollars a few times a year or so was a small price to pay for our granddaughters to avoid humiliation. Please don't ask for any more details."

We didn't. We traveled in silence for another minute, and then Dad called

184

my phone. "I just went through the security footage with Calum,[1] and right away, we noticed Juniper walking out with a woman who resembled Layla. We got a good look at the car and the license plate, and I just relayed that information to the police." He provided the details to me as well.

"How soon do you think it'll take for them to catch up with her?" Layla asked.

"They have her location, provided the tracking device isn't malfunctioning," Funderburke noted. "I wouldn't be surprised if they already have her in their sights. If they're being shrewd—and I suspect they are—they're trailing her in an unmarked car, and they're just following her quietly, waiting to see where she leads them."

"What does it matter where they're going?" Layla sounded frantic. "Why not just pull her over as soon as they spot her?"

"It's not where that matters, but who they're meeting," Funderburke replied.

I think Layla understood, because she sagged backwards in her seat. Celeste folded her hands together and started saying one Hail Mary after another, and thinking she had the right idea, I quietly joined her. Midway through my eleventh prayer, my phone rang, and it was the policewoman friend we'd called earlier. "We've got them. The girl's unconscious, probably drugged, so an ambulance is on its way. We're at the Green Moraine Motel." It was four minutes south of us, and Funderburke made it there in record time. Six blocks from the motel, a police car darted out of a speed trap and signaled for us to pull over, but Funderburke ignored the sirens and continued on to the motel. When we pulled into the parking lot and jumped out, the police car was right behind us. The officer looked pretty miffed at us, but two plainclothes officers hurried over to us, and after a few short words from us explaining the situation, they informed the traffic officer that Funderburke's swift driving was justified under the circumstances.

The plainclothesmen ushered the four of us across the lot to where one police officer was taking Juniper's pulse, as the little girl was lying on the back seat of Shelby's car. Layla and Celeste rushed over to her and were assured that her pulse was strong, but she'd probably be unconscious for a few more hours. Paramedics would be arriving soon to care for Juniper. Meanwhile, another policeman watched over Shelby, who was handcuffed and seated in the back of a squad car. She was yammering at the officer, claiming that she'd make sure he was fired, and when she was through with him, he'd never even get a job as a security guard. The officer looked bored, as if he received a hundred comparable threats a day, and no one had managed to lay a finger on his badge and gun yet.

"Layla! Layla!" Shelby shouted when she caught sight of her daughter. "Thank goodness you're here. Tell them this is all a huge misunderstanding. Explain how I told you that I was going to pick Juniper up from school. Tell them!"

"If you were picking her up from school, why are you several miles south of their home?" Funderburke asked.

Layla was holding her daughter's hand, and from fifteen yards away, she stared at her mother as if she'd never seen the woman before in her life. "What did you do to her?"

"Nothing! I wanted to take her to this really great frozen custard stand on the South Side, and on our way there, she just collapsed, so I was going to take her to the hospital!"

"Did you give her anything this afternoon?" I asked.

"Of course not!"

"She didn't eat anything in your presence?"

"No!"

I pointed to some brown smudges on Juniper's chin. "Then why are there traces of chocolate around her mouth?"

My third question produced no answer, so I asked another one, not expecting a response. "If her blood and stomach contents are analyzed, will the authorities find a dose of some medication that induces unconsciousness?"

"Don't say another word!" A voice called out from behind the car. Funderburke and I followed it, and we noticed a man in double denim handcuffed and seated on the edge of a wall. I couldn't place him for a moment, but I knew I'd seen his face before. I little reflecting, and I realized that I'd seen him on the news. He was a minor but vocal political figure, usually photographed wearing an expensive suit—far nicer than what he was wearing at the moment.

One of the officers held up a plastic evidence bag containing a white envelope filled with cash. "When we arrived, we saw him handing it to her."

"My lawyers are going to annihilate you," the political figure growled.

"Do you ever get tired of having people threaten to destroy your career?" Funderburke asked.

The officer shrugged. "It happens so often; it's all pretty much white noise now."

The next several minutes grew increasingly hectic as the paramedics arrived and began treating Juniper. After confirming that she was in no serious danger, they placed her in an ambulance, and Layla and Celeste rode with her to the hospital. The officers gently but firmly informed us that they did not wish us to continue to ask questions and suggested that as the matter was now under control, and since they had our contact information, it would be best if we left the matter to them and headed home. I'd wanted to confront Shelby about my theory that Brice had given her child support, but she'd gambled it away and then denied he'd sent anything and that her claims that she didn't have any money to spend on her daughter's rehab were bogus—she'd was just out of funds after a run of bad luck. I wasn't given the chance, so we decided to leave like the officers requested.

Before we could make it to Funderburke's car, however, a Mercedes pulled into the motel parking lot, and two men in immaculate dark gray suits stepped out and headed straight for the political figure. From their comments, it seemed like they were fixers for the figure's party, though I wasn't sure how they knew that their man was in trouble. Normally, an arrested person has to wait for a bit before making a phone call.

I voiced my thoughts to Funderburke, and he pointed towards the plate glass windows of the motel's main office. "See that pair of eyes peeping out from between those Venetian blinds?"

Whipping my head around, I managed a quick glimpse of the face staring at us before the opening in the blinds snapped shut. "I'll bet he comes here pretty often," Funderburke continued. "He probably gives the desk clerk a few hundred bucks every so often and tells him to call a certain number if the police ever raid the place. I suppose he's earned his money today."

The two fixers started browbeating the officers, who were responding with admirable calm. Funderburke fished his phone out of his pocket and flipped through his contacts. "Who are you calling?" I asked.

"Our old pal Cole Huebsch at the FBI. I had coffee with him last month, and he mentioned that he's been working on some human trafficking cases. If I get him involved right now, it'll add another headache for these fixers."

"There's a real chance that they'll get this guy off the hook, isn't there?"

"Not if I have anything to say about it." Apparently, Cole picked up the phone because Funderburke turned his attention to his conversation. After a couple of minutes, one of the fixers turned towards us, and with a clenched jaw and fire in his eye, he came charging towards us. Funderburke kept his face impassive, and when the fixer was about eight feet away, he set his phone to speaker and turned it towards the man. "I'm on the phone with Agent Cole Huebsch of the FBI. He'd be delighted to speak to you. Would you care to introduce yourself?"

The fixer snarled like an angry dog, and my recording a video of him with my phone didn't improve his mood one little bit. My turning the camera towards the handcuffed political figure only served to make him even more furious.

"Give me that phone!" he snapped.

"I think you know better than to lay a finger on a woman with policemen a few yards behind you and an FBI agent listening to every word you say," I informed him.

The fixer took a step towards me, and Funderburke crossed in front of him. The fixer made a fist, and with eerie calmness, Funderburke told him, "Please unclench your fist immediately." The two of them locked eyes for thirty full seconds, until the silence was broken by the sound of Cole's voice on the phone, checking to see if Funderburke was still there. Funderburke returned to his call but never broke eye contact, and the fixer stood still, his face growing redder with each passing moment.

One of the officers crossed over to us. "I think you two should head out.

We'll be in touch." I thanked him, and the two of us returned to Funderburke's car, making sure not to rush.

Shortly after we pulled out of the parking lot, my phone rang with a call from Dad.

"Hello?"

"Nerissa, I just heard from the Botner family. They're looking for you and Funderburke. They didn't have your number, but they knew you worked at Cuthbertson, so they called the school, and eventually, they reached me. Izzy is awake, and she wants to speak to you. They didn't go into details, but they said that Izzy wanted to show you a video that Erika made."

After providing us with the name of the hospital and Izzy's room number, Dad asked us if Juniper was all right, and I filled him in on the details.

"Those fixers aren't following you, are they?"

"No, Dad, they stayed at the motel to look after their client."

"There could be someone else working with them."

"We're clear. I always check to see if someone's coming after me, even when I'm just going to the grocery store," Funderburke spoke up so as to be heard over the phone.

Dad continued to do what fathers do and worried about me and Funderburke a little more, and by the time we reached the hospital, I was starting to feel uneasy myself. Dad suggested that I forward the video of the fixers and the handcuffed politician to him and some of our acquaintances in the press, as releasing the story might serve as a form of protection, and thinking that was a fine idea, I did so. Afterwards, I reassured Dad with ersatz confidence, shook off my nerves, and hurried to Izzy's room with Funderburke. We found her propped up in bed, her mother holding her left hand, her father clutching her right. She looked terrible and utterly exhausted, but she was alive.

After the briefest possible greeting, Mrs. Botner told us, "She's very tired, and she needs her rest."

"I just have to show them this video." Izzy's voice was so faint it could barely be heard over the humming of the machines. Her father handed her a smartphone, she tapped it a few times, and then passed it to me. "A couple of weeks before she died, Erika borrowed my phone, asked me to leave the room, filmed herself talking, and made me promise not to look at it unless something happened to her."

"Why didn't you show the video to the authorities right after she died?" Funderburke asked.

"I just forgot. My memory's pretty shaky, especially after I've been..." Her voice trailed away, and her head sank back into the pillow as her eyelids drooped.

"She's been dozing off and waking up a few minutes later ever since she first regained consciousness," Mr. Botner explained.

We settled down in a pair of chairs in the corner and hit play for the video.

I'd only seen Erika's picture a couple of times in pictures at the Dolak house. Those photographs were from four to twenty years old, depicting her as a happy, rosy-cheeked child, a bright-eyed ten-year-old, and a sullen-looking adolescent on Christmas Day. Now, I was seeing her for the first time at the age she was right before she died, and if I hadn't known that she was twenty-two, I would have sworn that she was at least forty-five. Her hair was sparse, and bits of her scalp were visible here and there. Her face was dotted with little scars and scabs, probably the result of the constant scratching due to the dry skin and itchiness that affect many opioid addicts. There was an unsettling corpselike shade to her skin, and her lips were decorated with a faint indigo hue. For the first ten seconds of the video, Erika said nothing, and her breathing appeared to take an enormous effort.

Finally, she began to speak with a raspy voice that sounded like an old, heavily scratched record. "Hello. My name is Erika Dolak. I'm making this video because I think that something awful happened to me several years ago. But I'm not sure. Around the time I was twelve years old, I started having blackouts. I'd be feeling fine, and then the next thing I knew, I'd be in my bed or on the couch, and my mother would be standing over me. At first I believed her when she told me that I'd had some sort of spell, but after it happened a few times, I noticed a pattern. These blackouts never happened at school or when I was hanging out with my friends, only when I was alone with my mother.

Not only that but every time this happened, Mom had given me a little treat beforehand, like a small piece of brownie or caramel. After I woke up, I'd often find myself hurting or even bleeding in... personal places. This happened seven or eight times over several months.

Soon after I figured out the pattern, I skipped school, and a friend went with me to a local clinic, and I found out that I had multiple STDs. And that I was pregnant."

As Funderburke and I watched, I realized that I was squeezing his arm with all my strength. He didn't seem to mind, though I could tell how angry he was getting by the tightening of his jaw.

"I got a bunch of antibiotics, and I was told to make up my mind what to do about the baby. That afternoon, I went straight to my mother and told her about my condition and that I didn't know how it happened. Part of me knew what was going on, but I suppose I was in denial, because I didn't want to believe it.

Mom hugged me and told me everything would be all right. Soon afterwards, she left the apartment, saying she had to run a quick errand, and a little over an hour later, she returned with a chocolate-covered cherry. I noticed there was this unsettling look on her face, so I declined. She got really angry, and she shoved it in my mouth and held her hand over my lips until I chewed it up and swallowed it. There was a nasty medicinal taste in it, and I knew that something was wrong;

Not long afterwards, I got these terrible cramps, and...I don't want to talk about it. I was given painkillers after the surgery, and I took them like they were prescribed, but I still had pains, so I started taking extra, and... I don't have to spell it out, do I?

You're probably wondering why I never told anybody about it. Well, I just couldn't. The thought of other people knowing about what happened made me feel sick. But I knew I couldn't live with my mother anymore, so I talked to my grandparents, who were happy to take me in. They gave me many chances to tell them what was wrong, but I never did. Don't ask me why, but I didn't want them to know.

A while ago, I cut off all of my sister's hair to get money for more pills. I knew I was crossing a terrible line, but I couldn't stop myself. I didn't even try. When I attend the NA meetings, I usually sit there and let other people talk. But a couple of weeks ago, some guy I don't know was saying how he'd hurt the people closest to him, and he had to do something that was totally right in order to live with himself again. I don't know why, but that touched a chord in me, so I dug out my old diary, and then I got the idea to get my old medical records, and now I think I'm finally ready to confront my mother. I'm not sure what's going to happen, but I know I have to do something. I don't think my sister will ever forgive me, and my grandmother will wonder why I never told her before after she gave me a million chances. I don't have any answers for them if they ask why I've done what I've done and haven't done what I haven't. All I know is that I'm finally ready to do something. And I don't know what's going to happen next."

The video ended here, and we sat in silence for a moment before Funderburke started tapping the phone. "I'm sending this to me, to you, to your parents, to the police, and to the FBI."

Mrs. Botner politely asked us to leave, and we returned the phone and left the hospital in silence.

We spent most of the next five hours talking to the authorities and explaining the situation to Nolan and Paige. It wasn't until nine o'clock that we all gathered at my house for a late dinner of sandwiches, as none of us had very much of an appetite. Juniper was out of the hospital and doing fine, and she was playing in another room with Toby. Rally was sitting upstairs near the kids' bedrooms, making sure that they couldn't hear what was going on in the dining room. Both sets of triplets were supposed to be tucked in their cribs or beds, sleeping, but Rally caught Bernard crouched on the floor, with a drinking glass in his hand pressed to his ear, trying to hear what was going on below him. Rally took away the glass and placed him back in bed.

My parents, some other family members, Layla, Celeste, Paige, and Nolan sat around the dining room table, and we answered their many questions. Funderburke transferred Erika's video to Dad's laptop. We thought we'd only have to play it once, but Layla and Celeste kept asking to see it over

192

and over again. By the seventh time, I was fidgeting, because it wasn't any easier to endure with repeat viewings, but I could tell that the Dolaks really needed to see and hear Erika talking about what had happened to her. Dad brought a box of tissues over to them, and steadily, a bowl that had recently held fruit salad was now being filled to the brim with used tissues. Paige slipped her arms around Layla and hugged her gently, and Layla collapsed on her shoulder as she sobbed quietly.

After fifteen minutes of replaying the video, I was getting a little fidgety. Normally, the family laundry is my major job around the house, and I'd planned to take care of a couple of loads tonight, but the day's events had thrown off my schedule, and with a lot of events and appointments coming up, I wasn't sure when I'd have another opportunity to provide my family with clean clothes.

I fidgeted with the cuff of my jacket, until finally I excused myself and hurried down the basement. I needed a distraction from Erika's video, so I filled the three washing machines with clothes and towels—two loads of colors, one of whites—and started them running, relieved by the fact they'd all be dry by the time I went to bed, though I'd have to make time over the next couple of days to get everything folded and distributed to the proper owners.

When I returned, I didn't see Funderburke. Mom and Dad were in the kitchen, with Mom arranging assorted cookies on a platter and Dad brewing a pot of tea and another of coffee. Shortly after they returned with the beverages and dessert, Funderburke followed them, tucking his phone back into his coat pocket as he entered the room. I think I've mentioned before that one of Funderburke's little idiosyncrasies is that he often keeps his beloved coat on even when he's inside. I think it's kind of a security blanket thing, but he'd never use that phrase to describe it, even if he is a big fan of *Peanuts*. As I was still wearing my jacket, I was in no place to judge, though I kept it on for the purpose of keeping my carefully selected outfit together for as long as possible.

Funderburke waited for the video to finish again, handed Celeste and Layla another tissue each, and then gently shut the laptop. "I was just on the phone with some of my friends. Our favorite political figure has hired himself a couple of law firms and a P.R. firm, and he's clammed up."

"What about Shelby?" Celeste asked.

"She's got a public defender, and she's trying to work out a deal. She's arguing that she's deeply in debt due to some massive gambling losses to some terribly dangerous men, and now she's saying that she simply had to raise the money, otherwise her life was in danger."

I made no effort to hide my indignance. "She's claiming she was hawking her granddaughter in self-defense?"

Funderburke snorted. "No. She's using the Costanza Defense."

"The what?" Nolan asked.

"You know the show *Seinfeld*? In one episode, George Costanza has an affair at his workplace with a member of the cleaning staff. When his boss confronts him, he says,'Was that wrong? Should I not have done that? I tell you, I gotta plead ignorance on this thing, because if anyone had said anything to me at all when I first started here that sort of thing is frowned upon…you know, 'cause I've worked in a lot of offices, and I tell you, people do that all the time.' This has become known in legal circles as "The Costanza Defense.'"

"She's arguing that she didn't think what she was doing was wrong?" Celeste called Shelby, a word that I didn't know that women of her generation even knew existed.

"More or less. She claims she had no idea the politico had any nefarious intent, and there must be some mistake, Juniper wasn't drugged, she just took a very heavy nap. No one believes her, of course, but they're offering a deal if she tells them everything she knows about the men she's… done business with over the years."

"And they'll let her off with a slap on the wrist?" Celeste rose out of her chair.

"As one victim's dead and the other was rescued before any harm came to her, that's the working plan. However, after I spoke with them, there'll be a nasty surprise waiting for her after she signs the papers."

"What do you mean?" Layla asked.

"They're searching for evidence now, but if Nerissa and I are right, they'll find proof that Shelby bought or had access to pure fentanyl."

"Wait..." Nolan looked confused. "You think Shelby gave Erika the drugs that killed her?"

"We think that Shelby deliberately poisoned Erika," I informed him. "Erika was digging into her own past, and she was either going to expose her mother or she was going to blackmail her. Either way, Shelby made a secret trip to Milwaukee to confront her daughter, and she brought along a bottle of capsules filled with fentanyl. She didn't know that Erika would share with her best friend."

Everybody was very quiet for a minute. "My mother killed Erika to save herself." Layla made a statement rather than asking a question.

"Maybe more than that," Funderburke responded. "I've suggested to the authorities that they look into whether Shelby took an insurance policy out on Erika. Of course, I wasn't telling them anything they hadn't already thought of."

"Insurance policies pay out on an overdose?" Celeste asked.

"Depends on the specific policy, but in many cases, yes. And they'll be taking a closer look at your son's recent "accident" as well. If there's a policy out on him, then I'd bet a week's salary that she might have given him a little push in front of that car."

The Dolaks both gasped. After Funderburke's theory had sunk in for a minute, I asked, "How is he doing, by the way?"

Taking a moment to calm herself, Celeste said, "He'll live. But he might need to have at least one leg amputated."

This wasn't even close to being one of the more upbeat dinners we've ever had. Mom broke up the evening, saying that it was time all of the kids were in bed. Nolan and Paige agreed, and they retrieved Juniper to take her home. Turning to the Dolaks, Paige said, "How about you two come to dinner at our house tomorrow night? We'll talk more about everything then." Still sobbing, Layla agreed.

We'd picked up the Dolaks from the hospital, so we had to take them home. Funderburke could have chauffeured them himself, but I felt like I should go with them.

As I walked towards the door, Dad stopped me and wrapped me up in a bear hug. "Thanks," I told him. "What brought on that?"

"Tonight just made me very grateful that I adopted you," he informed me.

I hugged him back twice as hard before joining Funderburke and the Dolaks in the car. As I buckled my seatbelt, Layla told me, "I'm not going back to college."

"Don't be foolish," Celeste told her granddaughter.

"I don't deserve it. I'm a terrible mother. I'm an awful person. I let Erika die; I was so mad at her I didn't bother to think that she might be going through something—"

"That's enough, dammit!" Celeste snapped. "I'm beating myself up for not catching all of the warning signs or convincing her to confide in me, but I'm not going to destroy myself in a misguided attempt at punishment."

"Be honest with me. Did you have any idea what was going on?" Layla asked.

"I knew your mother was a gambler, but I had no idea how far she'd go. I guessed something evil had happened to Erika, but my worst guess was that one of her mother's boyfriends, or one of Erika's boyfriends, or maybe one of her teachers…" Celeste dabbed at her eyes. "I never dreamt how bad it was. I had no idea that Juniper was in danger."

"So what do you want me to do?"

Celeste stared into Layla's eyes. "I think we both need healing. I think our souls are injured."

"That's your answer for everything, isn't it? Go back to church."

"Do you have a better idea?"

Layla didn't have a response to her grandmother's question, but she looked stubborn. "I'd like to talk to somebody. An expert. But I don't know what I'd say."

"My uncle, Francis, lives five minutes from here," Funderburke told them. "He's a priest, and he's a great listener. He's usually up pretty late. Would you like me to take you to the rectory?"

Layla made a quiet excuse, and Celeste shouted her down with a "Yes."

After phoning his uncle to make sure he was in and awake, Funderburke drove us to St. Crispin and Crispinian's On-the-Lake, and after we led them into his uncle's office, the two of us wandered into the main church.

"Do you think they'll be okay?" Funderburke asked.

I shrugged. "Not for a very long time. But I realized long ago that the only way your life can get irreparably ruined is if you give up hope of things ever getting better."

[1] Calum is Cuthbertson's head of security.

Epilogue—A Year of Healing

Layla started loving Erika again that night. She wasn't ready to share everything she said to Father Francis with us, but I figured she was entitled to some privacy until she was ready to talk about it.

When Layla did start talking about Erika again, it came in fits and starts. When I sat in on a friendly discussion about co-parenting between Layla, Paige, and Nolan the next day, I was relieved that my presence wasn't needed. During the drive home, Layla mostly sat in silence, responding to my gentle prompts with one-word answers until she finally blurted out, "If I'd only known, I could've done more to help her." A couple days later, when I spoke to her as she picked up Juniper from school, she mumbled, "Maybe seeing Mom in jail would've provided the morale boost she needed to stay clean." It took months before I could coax her into a full conversation about her feelings. Until then, she vented her feelings a sentence at a time. From the expression in her eyes, it was clear that she no longer viewed Erika as a succubus who had drained all joy and light from her life but as the little sister she hadn't been able to save.

Celeste was far more vocal. Her conversation was peppered with constant denunciations of Shelby, the waterfall of venom nearly but not entirely disguising her self-recriminations. Now, she was determined to do everything in her power to pull up her surviving granddaughter and her son, who would indeed be losing a leg due to his injuries and would need several months to recover, during which time Celeste and Layla could care for him at home, with the help of a retired nurse who lived down the street and was willing to look after him for a modest fee while the women were at school or work. During this long recovery period, Celeste could keep her son away from liquor. The hospital staff had their hands full as Brice agonized his way through alcohol withdrawal, as in between fits of violent illness, he would unsuccessfully try to charm the nurses into smuggling in booze for him and growing increasingly emotional when his passes proved unsuccessful. The doctors warned Celeste that he'd have a steep uphill battle staying sober, and she nodded grimly, informing them that he wouldn't be fighting alone.

Based on personal observation and Layla's occasional griping, Celeste had decided to adjust her grandparenting tactics and adopted a policy of constant, persistent pressure. At meals, she would make comments like, "Will you have some lemon with your fish? The vitamin C will help keep you sharp when you're applying to go back to college." Layla explained to me that two weeks earlier, she would have snapped at her grandmother for nagging, but now she grudgingly conceded that a little pressure—Mom called it "tiger grandmothering"—was just what she needed to dig herself out of her rut.

So, after four days of Celeste dropping hints like a crop duster strews pesticides, Layla phoned me and asked me to help her with applications for both college and the basketball coaching job. We brainstormed for an hour on what to say in her letters and why she wanted admittance and employment. I think the results were reasonably impressive.

The interview for the coaching gig came first. After a week, the powers that be at Cuthbertson called her in for an interview. Realizing that her one formal article of clothing, the black funeral dress, wasn't the best option, I took her to one of my favorite thrift shops, and after a little rummaging, found a full-length cranberry wrap sweater dress balled up on the floor after it fell off the hanger on an overstuffed rack. It was the nicest item the shop had in her size, and the price tag asked for ten bucks, but after pointing out the little dust bunnies that decorated it, I was able to talk the proprietor down to five. A cycle in the washing machine, and it was as good as new. Layla and I rehearsed for the interview, and eventually, we hit upon the right notes as she elaborated on her love of the sport. Between the practicing and the new outfit, she must have made a good impression, because she was hired right away.

The good news kept coming, as soon afterwards her acceptance letter for UWM arrived, and the two of us looked over the course catalog together, finally deciding that based on her previous credits and interests not only could she get a major in Community Engagement and Education, but a minor in biological sciences as well. She could earn her degree by next Christmas with a full course load over the spring, summer, and fall terms. I brought up the possibility of graduate study, and she shut me down hard and fast, saying she could only handle so much at the moment, and frankly, looking too far down the road was giving her an upset stomach. So I backed off, figuring this was a conversation for another time.

Basketball practice began in early November. After getting up at seven for classes and then having four courses in rapid succession, Layla was a bit bedraggled by the time her first meeting with the middle school girls started at three-thirty. She had just enough fuel in the tank to handle the initial practice with a cup of iced coffee with a splash of milk from my giant thermos. When you're just starting to work with kids whose ages are just barely in the double digits, and it's been over a decade since you were that age yourself, you can be blindsided by just how energetic young people that age can be. Certainly, Layla had trouble keeping up with them, at least at first. After five minutes of running around with them around the Middle School basketball court, she was panting and sweating hard.

But she bonded with the girls pretty fast, and it's amazing how much her rediscovered love of the game rejuvenated her. Starting school again was exciting for Layla, but returning to the basketball court restored the light to her soul. If that sounds a bit overdramatic, it's not. It's accurate. By the end of the first week, when I drove her home after practice, she looked like she'd been squeezed through the wringer, but her eyes were shining, and she couldn't stop talking about their upcoming first game.

The physical changes were a bit subtler than the emotional ones, at least at first. Running around with preteens for two hours a day, five days a week, coupled with no longer relying on the deep fryer at Grobel's Tavern for lunch and dinner, was starting to have an effect. By the start of December, she informed me with disbelief in her eyes that she was down nine pounds.

At this point, she announced that if her girls were to be properly coached, she'd need to get back into training. Some mornings, she'd join me and Mom on our morning runs, and sometimes, when afternoon meetings and other extracurricular responsibilities delayed our early evening workouts, Layla joined me, Funderburke, and my parents in the Cuthbertson weight room.

By New Year's, another nine pounds had melted off, and the changes continued at a steady rate over the rest of the winter. The two of us made monthly trips to the thrift stores for replacement clothes in smaller sizes, as the cheaply made items she'd grown out of over the course of the preceding years were all too worn out to renter her wardrobe again.

As the end of March approached, she secured the newly opened assistant coach job for the varsity girls' soccer team, and I was thoroughly pleased with how well the two of us worked together. By this point, Layla was over forty pounds down, and when the two of us led the girls on three-mile warm-up runs through the cross-country course, she could complete the trek and only be mildly out of breath by the end.

Her new exercise regimen continued through the spring, and as summer started, she joined Mom and me on our morning runs at least five days a week, and Funderburke accepted her occasional presence on our workout dates. As a result of all the physical activity, on an unseasonably cool late August afternoon, Layla sorted through the freshly washed old clothes from high school she'd recently retrieved from storage in the attic and donned a faded pair of black jeans she hadn't been able to wear in six years, pairing them with her favorite green sweater and the jacket I'd returned to her ten months earlier, which finally fit her again. The weakest part of her wardrobe was the most recent pair of dollar store sneakers, which had about five more miles worth of running left before they disintegrated.

As I waited patiently, Layla looked herself up and down in the hall mirror, tugging at her jacket, turning back and forth, examining her newly slim body, and running her fingers through her hair, which, after months of being left alone, had recently been trimmed and reshaped to make for more elegant continued growth. The length of her hair was about two weeks away from touching her shoulders. As she'd predicted, it had exceeded the average rate of half a foot of new length per year, growing at three-quarters of an inch per month. In another year and a half, perhaps a little more, it would reach the former glory of the days before Erika picked up the scissors.

We were celebrating, as a new grant had made me hire her as my assistant for running the Bialowsky Fund. She would only be working part-time until January when she'd have earned her undergraduate degree after a year of hard work, but as her wardrobe needed replenishing, we figured that now was the time to shop for new work clothes. I'd managed to wrangle her a few hundred dollars as a bonus for starting her new job, and all of it was allocated to refreshing her wardrobe.

We'd started the previous night by checking some of the better resale websites out there, and in the course of an hour, we found a handful of new or nearly new items being sold by women who'd either grown bored with them or grown out of them before having a chance to wear them in public. Layla found a couple of blouses, a nice black and white houndstooth blazer, and a brown pantsuit that I disliked, but at four dollars brand new, it was too good a deal to pass up, although I couldn't stop wondering why it was being let go at that price. I found an opal-blue silk skirtsuit, a gold satin button-down top, a jade velvet pullover, a scarlet leather blazer, and a new pair of snakeskin-print trousers, each less than ten dollars.

The next day, we journeyed from thrift shop to resale store, searching for bargains in our sizes. It soon became clear that Layla's style tastes were quite different from mine, though that's certainly not meant as a criticism, just an observation. Personally, I felt that Layla incorporated way more pink into her wardrobe than I ever would, such as the pantsuit that appeared to have been dyed in Pepto-Bismol. I also winced a bit at the full-length teddy bear coat that appeared to be designed for people who are into Snuffleupagus cosplay, but my personal feelings are that if someone likes something, that person should wear it. I don't criticize people's style choices to their faces, and I certainly don't care for it when people mock my clothes. Besides, Layla looked so happy, finding items and admiring herself in the mirror as she tried them on, that I didn't want to say anything that might spoil her fun.

Shoes, at least, should be bought new, and she finally bought a couple of proper pairs of sneakers for twenty-five dollars each at the outlet mall. They would last for years, provided the students didn't tread on her toes too often during practices. At a little shop in an obscure corner of the Lower East Side, we found her a few pairs of dress shoes that I was jealous I couldn't wear with my sensitive feet.

That evening, as we unpacked her new wardrobe, I caught her sighing, and I saw a touch of the old helpless despair creeping back into her eyes.

"What's wrong?"

She pushed a lock of hair out of her face and, without looking at me, said, "I'm thinking about Erika."

"What about her?"

"For years, I resented her. I felt she was holding me back from living the life I wanted to lead, though I realize now I was blocking my own path just as much as she was. And now, I have the life I dreamed about having a year ago. Everything's great with Juniper. I'll have my undergraduate degree in one more semester. I've got a job I love where I feel I'm making a difference, and my waist is a size I never believed it'd ever be again. But just being thin and having better hair doesn't make me happy, plus I keep wondering if I'm a worthy role model for the girls. And I can't stop thinking about how if I'd just sprayed that Narcan into Erika's nostril, none of this would ever have happened."

"We'll never know for sure, but you know there's a strong probability it wouldn't have helped her, given the dose she'd had and the time since she took it."

"I know that, but my conscience doesn't."

"Is the guilt so bad you feel like sabotaging your own life again?"

"No. The guilt comes and goes." Layla toyed with a little silver St. Jude medal she was wearing around her neck. Celeste had bought it in honor of the patron saint of lost causes that Christmas, and she'd insisted that Layla start wearing it. As part of her campaign to drag her granddaughter back into the Church, kicking and screaming if necessary, Celeste had started waking Layla every Sunday morning, throwing the sheets and covers aside and refusing to leave until Layla joined her for Mass. At first, Layla's participation had been extremely reluctant, but as the weeks passed and Layla conversed more with Funderburke's uncle, she found herself attending far more voluntarily. By summer, she'd retitled her status to "relapsed Catholic," and Celeste beamed with satisfaction when she heard Layla's self-declaration.

"I just feel like I don't deserve this second chance," Layla added.

"Well, whether you deserve it or not is irrelevant," I told her. "The plain, simple fact is that you've got it. You spent the last few years wishing for a better life, and here it is, wrapped up with a shiny bow. A lot of people don't get that, and it's not going to do anybody any good if you waste it."

"I know. I just feel like there's a bill for all of this good fortune that'll have to be paid somewhere down the line."

"Everybody on earth racks up an account throughout their lives that has to be settled at one point or another. Maybe we can square our debts, maybe not. Very few people make it to the end with credits on their ledgers. Look. You're still haunted by that afternoon you did nothing to help Erika, right? You still feel like you did something wrong?"

Layla opened her mouth, but said nothing. Eventually, she simply nodded.

"Well, then you have a responsibility to do as much that's right that you can."

"For how long?"

I shrugged. "Not to put too much on you, but for as long as possible."

And she did. We discovered that Layla had a real talent for finding grants and writing applications. Within weeks of filing her first proposals, we were getting checks from all sorts of organizations, allowing the Bialowsky Fund to take in more teen mothers. The school administration was starting to get a little fidgety at the increased number of Bialowsky Fund attendees, and some parents were saying that they didn't want Cuthbertson turned into a school for wayward girls, but for the time being, our work continued apace. A fifteen-year-old and her daughter were the only survivors of a family annihilation. She had a real gift for music. A young woman of eighteen, with a ten-month son and an eidetic memory, who'd been sold to traffickers by her parents when they lost their jobs and had barely been able to escape alive. A seventeen-year-old with twins, who never knew her own father and whose mother had one day emptied her savings account—all seven hundred dollars of it—packed two suitcases full of clothes and left without a word. This last girl dreamed of being a surgeon, but didn't know how she'd manage it. I had no idea if a scholarship to Cuthbertson Hall was going to make all of their dreams come true, but darn it, I was going to try.

Just shy of one year after Layla's death, it was time for the official opening of Bialowsky House, the new name I'd used to christen Mrs. Böhm's home after we'd bought it from her and refurnished it to house seven girls who either had no parents or none who were worthy of the name, as well as their little children. It was a bit crowded, but all of the residents seemed pleased with it.

As it was right across the street from the Dolak home, Celeste and Layla had both taken an additional job as housemothers, paid for by the Fund. They proved popular with the girls, especially when Celeste cooked for them.

On a beautiful Friday afternoon, just as the trees were reaching peak autumn color, we held a party to celebrate Bialowsky House being up and running. A few donors made an appearance, such as the Tokays, as did a bunch of Cuthbertson teachers, but most of the attendees were either the Fund girls, their relatives (those that had them), the Dolaks, or members of my family. The girls gave brief speeches about their lives and their studies and hopes, and I milled around, thanking all the guests for their support.

Izzy and her parents were there. The Botners had made a substantial donation. Izzy was just about a week away from making it to a full year of sobriety and had managed to hold down a clerical job for the past six months.

Everybody had distinguished themselves well with the potluck, and the girls were all wearing the Nerissa Loophole version of their uniforms, as were I and Layla, though Layla was looking a bit self-conscious in her new clothes that the girls had insisted she start wearing, as she was "one of them" and needed to look the part. I had found the outfit cheap online and bought it for her as a present for starting her new job, as well as a volume of the complete short stories of Flannery O'Connor to jump-start her recreational reading. As we chatted while clearing some empty platters and refreshing them with fresh appetizers, she told me, "I was talking with Nolan and Paige last night about Christmas."

"And?"

"They suggested we all have an early holiday at our house on the 22nd, and then Nolan and Paige offered, as their gift to us, to pay for tickets for me and Grandma to fly to Florida for them for a week to stay with Nolan's grandmother. We could all take Juniper to the various attractions down there. She'd enjoy that."

"That sounds like a great plan to me."

Layla smiled. By my calculations, she was smiling approximately twenty times as often as she did a year earlier. "I'm looking forward to it. I haven't had a trip outside of Wisconsin since I was forced out of college."

One of the kids knocked over a cup of juice, and I rushed away in order to grab a few paper towels. Once I'd cleaned up everything, the girls were calling upon Layla to make a speech.

"I don't have much to say," she told us all. "I just feel like I should make it clear that if you want to do anything in life or do any good in the world, you must never give up, not on yourself or on anybody you care about, not even when you think you'd be freer if you cut off all emotional contact. I guess that's all I have to say."

The party continued for a while, but it petered out as most of the guests left to enjoy their weekend plans.

With so many hands on deck, it was easy to clean up the house, only a matter of fifteen minutes or so. As I packed up some leftovers to take home, I saw Funderburke and Dad out on the back porch, looking somber. Neither of them cared much for parties, but judging by the looks on their faces, they were overdoing their discomfort. I stepped out to confront them and saw that Bernard was off to the side, playing on a little plastic jungle gym we'd installed for the kids. "Why are you two so glum?" I asked.

"I got some news earlier today, and I didn't want to spoil the party,"

Funderburke replied.

"What's up?"

"Shelby will be released from prison in a couple of weeks," Funderburke explained.

"What? How is this possible?" I'd known that Shelby wasn't going to be in prison for life, but I thought that she'd at least be behind bars for several years. She hadn't been charged for Erika's murder, as the authorities hadn't been able to prove that she had provided her daughter with the fentanyl. A security camera from a gas station across the street had caught Brice getting hit by the car, but the footage was ambiguous as to whether Shelby had pushed him or if she'd tried to pull him back after he'd stumbled forward into traffic. As there was no conclusive evidence regarding what she'd done to Erika, she was only convicted of what she'd almost done to Juniper. The politician we'd seen that afternoon had disappeared after being released on bail after his initial arrest, and there'd been no news about him since.

"She's made a deal with some authorities in order to testify about the men connected to her... *dealings* involving Erika years ago. Apparently, some very wealthy and prominent men and their wives or ex-wives are now the focus of some criminal investigations, and she's willing to testify in exchange for her freedom. Some of it is covered by the statute of limitations, but she's got a little black book that she's ready to parlay into freedom, and the authorities will use it somehow to take down some scumballs."

"And nothing we say will put her back in prison?" I asked.

"Apparently, it's a done deal. We weren't supposed to know about it, but Cole Huebsch found out through his colleagues and passed on the information to me."

I sank down on the railing surrounding the patio. "How am I going to break this to Layla and Celeste?"

"With us right beside you providing support," Dad told me. "Like always."

I hadn't thought that I'd be able to smile for a while, but I did. Before I could respond, Toby stepped outside. "Can we head home soon? I want to finish my book report before the math meet tomorrow morning."

"Sure," I nodded, "but let's just take another minute to enjoy the evening

207

before we go." I know that part of it was delaying the inevitable discussion with the Dolaks, but it was a gorgeous moment. The sun was just beginning its descent below the thick canopy of vibrantly colored trees, and as the breeze increased, the branches all swayed, and the light caught the leaves, and they glowed like a crackling fire. Toby stepped forward, and I put my arms around her and held her in front of me as we appreciated the sight. Bernard ran up to us and hugged my left leg, and as the sun dipped lower, the wind grew chillier. A genuine and involuntary shiver ran through my body, and Funderburke slipped out of his coat and draped it around me, adjusting it so as not to block Bernard's view and then standing on my right and sliding his left arm around my shoulders. I clasped his right hand in my own and put my hand back into position as I pressed Toby against me. I could feel her flinch, but she allowed her head to lean back on my chest. Turning, I gave a little nod to Dad, who stepped forward and held out his hand after I outstretched my left hand towards him. I gripped his hand as tightly as I could manage, sighing and smiling.

In a few minutes, we'd return to the controlled chaos of our daily lives—grading papers, fielding calls from frantic parents, changing diapers, doing laundry, cleaning up messes, preparing lectures, and looking out for kids in crisis. This constant busyness was an integral part of the lives we'd chosen, and I had no complaints. But for a brief moment, as the sky turned fluorescent shades of watermelon and apricot, the sound of the rustling leaves drowned out the noise of street traffic, and as the wind tousled my hair, I basked in the presence of my loved ones, and I luxuriated in a powerful feeling of gratitude for all the wonderful blessings of my life.

A Note from the Author

The reference to the FBI agent Cole Huebsch in Chapter Ten is a "shoutout cameo" to my fellow Level Best Books author from Southeastern Wisconsin, Kevin Kluesner, the author of the Cole Huesbsch novels.

Acknowledgements

Special thanks to the Dames of Detection: Verena Rose, Harriette Sackler, and Shawn Reilly Simmons of Level Best Books for their belief in this book.As always, none of this would be possible without my parents Drs. Carlyle and Patricia Chan. I also need to thank all of my friends and teachers from the University School of Milwaukee.

About the Author

Chris Chan is a writer, educator and historian. He works as a researcher and "International Goodwill Ambassador" for Agatha Christie Ltd. His true crime articles, reviews, and short fiction have appeared in *The Strand, The Wisconsin Magazine of History, Mystery Weekly, Gilbert!*, Nerd HQ, Akashic Books' *Mondays are Murder* webseries, *The Baker Street Journal, The MX Book of New Sherlock Holmes Stories, Masthead: The Best New England Crime Stories, Sherlock Holmes Mystery Magazine*, and multiple Belanger Books anthologies. He is the creator of the Funderburke and Kaiming mysteries, a series featuring private investigators who work for a school and help students during times of crisis. The Funderburke short story "The Six-Year-Old Serial Killer" was nominated for a Derringer Award. His first book, *Sherlock & Irene: The Secret Truth Behind "A Scandal in Bohemia,"* was published in 2020 by MX Publishing, and he is also the author of the comedic novels *Sherlock's Secretary* and its sequel *Nessie's Nemesis*. His book *Murder Most Grotesque: The Comedic Crime Fiction of Joyce Porter* (Level Best Books) was nominated for the 2022 Agatha Award for Best Non-Fiction. *Murder Most Grotesque, Sherlock's Secretary*, and his anthology *Of Course He Pushed Him & Other Sherlock Holmes Stories: The Complete Collection* were all nominated for Silver Falchion Awards.

SOCIAL MEDIA HANDLES:
  Twitter: @GKCfan

Instagram: https://www.instagram.com/chan3589/
Facebook: https://www.facebook.com/chris.chan.7374

AUTHOR WEBSITE:

https://chrischancrimeandcriticism.blogspot.com

Also by Chris Chan

Full-Length Novels

Sherlock's Secretary, published by MX Publishing (November 2021)

Ghosting My Friend, published by Level Best Books (March 2023)

Nessie's Nemesis, published by MX Publishing (September 2023)

Full-Length Non-Fiction Books

Sherlock & Irene: The Secret Truth Behind "A Scandal in Bohemia," published by MX Publishing (August 2020)

Murder Most Grotesque: The Comedic Crime Fiction of Joyce Porter, published by Level Best Books (September 2021)

Anthologies

Of Course He Pushed Him and Other Sherlock Holmes Stories: The Complete Collection (June 2022– Volume One published separately in September 2022, Volume Two published separately in November 2022)

Additionally, numerous short stories, nonfiction articles, and book reviews.

www.ingramcontent.com/pod-product-compliance
Lightning Source LLC
Chambersburg PA
CBHW050202120726
47903CB00002B/733